# RIDE THE

# MOON

## AN ANTHOLOGY

# RIDE THE MOON

## MOON

### AN ANTHOLOGY

### EDITED BY

### M. L. D. CURELAS

TYCHE BOOKS LTD.

**Ride the Moon: An Anthology**

Published by Tyche Books Ltd.
www.TycheBooks.com

Copyright © 2012 by Tyche Books Ltd.
All stories are copyrighted to their respective authors, and used here with their permission. Some works have been previously published, published in other editions or previously performed.

ISBN: 978-0-9878248-0-6

Printed in the United States, United Kingdom and Australia
First Printing: 2012

Cover Art by Malcolm McClinton
Cover Layout by Lucia Starkey
Interior Layout by Tina Moreau
Editorial by M. L. D. Curelas

# CONTENTS

# THE SECONDARY 4 CLASS OF PRETTYGOOD PARK HIGH SCHOOL

By Claude Lalumière

A few minutes before 6 a.m., on the first day of spring 1982, the entire secondary 4 class of Prettygood Park High School gathered at the foot of the Montreal moonbridge, a few blocks west of the Jacques-Cartier Bridge, which at dawn was already bringing the South Shore suburban traffic into the city.

The nearly one hundred students chattered among themselves. Punks, preppies, stoners, freaks, geeks, jocks, brainiacs, squares, loners... all those arbitrary divisions melted away in the anticipation of the journey to come. Mr. Saint-Michael, the math teacher and field-trip coordinator, wended his way through the crowd of teenagers, all of them equipped with camping gear, and took attendance.

Stopping next to a long-haired boy dressed in frayed white jeans, a black T-shirt emblazoned with a blood-red anarchist symbol, a too-large beige business jacket, and mud-encrusted sneakers, the teacher exclaimed, "Mr. Fort!" Mr. Saint-Michael always addressed the students with a formality that was equal parts respect and irony. "How good of you to grace us with your presence today!" The bite was taken out of the sarcastic rebuke

1

by the conspiratorial wink the teacher exchanged with his favourite student.

It was true that Luke Fort was notorious for skipping class. But he also achieved the highest grades in school and had a knack for charming his teachers, who all let him get away with showing up in class sporadically, as long as he was careful not to miss exams or deadlines for handing in assignments. The charm that made him breeze through the academic part of school life did not, alas, work on his peers. Luke wasn't exactly friendless, but he wasn't exactly popular, either.

After Mr. Saint-Michael had walked on, Montague Farmer hissed into Luke's ear, "So, Tofu." Luke hated that nickname; he wished no-one had ever noticed that he didn't eat meat. Luke didn't even like tofu. "Do you suck him off, or does he prefer to fuck you in the ass?"

Luke tried to ignore the taunt, but he couldn't help turning to sneer at Montague. Although he behaved like a jock, Montague was a short, mousy, shifty twerp, a used-car salesman in a rat's body. And yet, he got invited to all the parties and was dating Blair Jonas, who was right at that moment holding Montague's hand and pointedly avoiding Luke's gaze. Blair was a full six inches taller than Montague and much too pretty to be seen at his arm. At least, that's what Luke thought.

Luke had had a crush on Blair since the previous year, when he'd tutored her in math. They had sat close together; she exuded a peach scent that ensorcelled him. She'd found out about the vegetarianism when she stayed for dinner at his house once. He'd always been careful to keep that detail about himself private. The next day, she'd starting calling him Tofu at school, and the nickname stuck. For some reason beyond Luke's control, his crush had stuck, too.

Luke's train of thought was interrupted by a loud, wince-inducing sound of metal grating against metal: the guardian was opening the moonbridge portal.

Every day he could manage it, just before breakfast and just before dinner, Luke jogged the eight kilometres from his house to the moonbridge, so he could witness this moment—the opening of the portal—and see the guardian. The moonbridge

2

was on a six-hour schedule: open from 6 a.m. to noon, and then again from 6 p.m. to midnight. Most days, the guardian looked more or less the same to Luke: a ten-foot marble giant dressed like a Roman legionary. The most spectacular aspect Luke had ever witnessed was that of a gargantuan thousand-armed snake whose colours changed every time the guardian moved in the slightest. No two people saw exactly the same thing when they looked at the guardian, and on film or video the guardian appeared as a blur. It was the same with moonbridge guardians all over the world.

Today, the guardian appeared to Luke as a winged woman hovering a few feet above the ground. It had long, flowing white hair, wore a dress of white mist, and held a silver caduceus in each hand.

Luke felt a tap on his shoulder. It was his friend Benjamin House, the only one in school who didn't call him Tofu. Benjamin was the secondary 4 class's other teacher's pet. His grades matched Luke's, but Benjamin was a hard worker and assiduous, obedient student with a clean, conservative look, unlike Luke, who ignored most rules and who dressed with clueless randomness, as if fashion of any kind were an utterly alien concept. For the last three years, the teachers and other students had been trying to foster rivalry between the two boys, but, despite their differences, the two enjoyed a relaxed camaraderie, oblivious to everyone's expectations. "Luke, is it true we all see something different?" Benjamin's face had lost all its colour.

"Are you okay, Ben?"

"Tell me what you're seeing, buddy. Tell me you're not seeing what I'm seeing."

Luke told his friend about the winged woman. "What do you see?"

Benjamin stammered something incoherent, but then managed to collect himself sufficiently to say, "I can't tell you. I don't ... It's too ... Holy! I don't know if I can go through with this." Ben was shaking, now.

"Not go through...? You mean not take the Moon trip? But, Ben, you have to. You might never get another chance. It's so

3

rare to be allowed through by the guardians ever again. This is our time."

Absolutely still, Ben stared at the guardian. He whispered, "It's changing."

Luke said, "Changing? I've never seen the guardian actually change. It never looks exactly the same from one time to the next, but to see a transformation..." Luke, for whom the guardian still appeared as flying woman with wings, became wrapped up in his long-nurtured obsession with the moonbridge and didn't notice his friend's increasing terror.

And then Ben screamed, which silenced everyone, even the Gaul twins, who never seemed to stop muttering to each other. Ben's scream was a horrible thing, a high-pitched screech that froze Luke's heart.

Luke reached out to clasp Benjamin's shoulder. "Ben..." But the instant his fingers brushed the other boy, Ben sped away. Within a few seconds, he was gone from sight.

Mr. Saint-Michael's face betrayed consternation and a tangible tension started buzzing through the assembly, but the teacher lost no time steering the situation back on course. In his loud, theatrical voice, Mr. Saint-Michael addressed the gathering: "We can't let Mr. House's personal drama interfere with this momentous day, which is a once-in-a-lifetime event for you all. Mr. House will just have to live with his own decision."

Luke, who had been looking forward to this day for his entire life, hung back while the other students started to walk up to the guardian, who scrutinized each student before letting them through and onto the bridge.

Once the procession acquired a momentum of its own, Mr. Saint-Michael walked over to Luke. The teacher spoke in a low, calm voice: "Luke," hearing the teacher use his given name imbued the moment with a fragile intimacy, "you're not seriously thinking of not going? I know Benjamin is your good friend, but this is too important. Mr. House would not want you to stay behind on his account. It would only increase his distress for him to know that he had caused you to not undertake this journey."

"Don't worry, Mr. Saint-Michael. I'm worried about Ben, but there's no way I'm not travelling to the Moon this morning. Still, I wish he'd come back. I think I'm dithering because I want to see if he'll return. I want him come."

"There's almost no-one left. You should get in line, Mr. Fort."

"Yes, sir. Are you coming, too? Sometimes, the guardian lets people go through again."

"No. I undertook the journey when I was your age. This is for young people, Mr. Fort. It wouldn't be right for me to risk interfering. Besides, there's no guarantee the guardian would let me through, so why even entertain the notion?" For a moment, Mr. Saint-Michael appeared lost in a daydream, but he abruptly snapped out of it. "Enough of that. Go now, Mr. Fort. Go!"

Luke nodded at the teacher and walked toward the bridge. Before stepping up to the guardian's post, he scanned the horizon one final time, hoping to see his friend, but Benjamin had not returned.

Luke now stood facing the guardian. From this close, Luke experienced a disconcerting, overlapping double vision: the guardian as a winged woman hovering a few feet in the air but also—at the same time and occupying the same space—as a giant mechanical construct made up of gears and hydraulics whose full geometry defied the limits of his perception. Luke tried to concentrate on that second image, convinced that it was the guardian's true mien, convinced that seeing the guardian for what it really was would grant him an understanding heretofore denied him. But before another moment had elapsed, the guardian's appearance solidified into that of the winged woman, who motioned for the boy to step onto the moonbridge.

Even standing a few steps from the ornately decorated metal portal, Luke could not see anything but darkness beyond its threshold. He took a moment to examine the carvings. He ran his fingers on a likeness of a strange bulbous creature with no eyes and three limbs. The metal felt unlike anything he had ever touched. He took another step and climbed onto the moonbridge itself.

Into the distance, Luke noticed small shapes moving along the moonbridge. But there weren't enough of his classmates to account for all the moving shapes. Who else was on the bridge?

The scaffolding of the moonbridge was part metal, part grey stone, part gigantic wooden vine—or was it of one material that somehow took on aspects of all these things? Leaves of muted reds, browns, and greens grew from "metal", "stone", and "wood"—or whatever the moondbridge materials were—confusing Luke's notions of living and nonliving. Grabbing hold of a support beam, Luke was reminded of the texture of the portal doorway.

The sky was a subtly iridescent indigo blue that, mixed with the faint golden glow of the stars, suffused everything with a subtle green tint. Planets, stars, and other celestial bodies appeared much closer than they did from the surface of the Earth, yet also more otherworldly and bizarre than Luke had previously imagined.

As with the guardian when Luke had stood right next to it, Luke mistrusted the evidence of his eyesight. The entire universe, and everything in it, shimmered, as if unable to hold on to any specific form. Even the moonbridge itself seemed subtly different every time Luke focused on it.

In the sky—above, below, and all around him—Luke could detect movement between the various celestial bodies. There was an irregularity to path taken by the flying objects that suggested biological rather than mechanical locomotion.

In the far distance, the bridge reached the Moon, haloed in undulating shades of grey, blue, and green. Luke marched forward, toward that destination he had dreamed of for so long.


Swallowing his last handful of trail mix, Luke looked back toward the destination he had come from. He could no longer detect the source of the bridge. Forward, the Moon now loomed much larger than it had when he had set off on his journey. But of the Earth, there was no sign. Nor had he yet encountered anyone, although a few times he'd heard the leaves rustle as if someone were moving through the strange rock-metal-vegetation the bridge was constructed of. It could not have been the wind, because there was only the slightest of breezes, nothing strong enough to cause such commotion. Despite himself, despite his desire for this entire journey to be a wondrous adventure, Luke was growing scared at the thought of who or what might be hiding from his sight in this alien environment, and the longer he stayed on the bridge the more the fright settled into his bones.

He thought he had packed sufficient provisions for the journey—enough to last him three or four days. He wasn't sure how long he'd been travelling, because his watch had stopped working the moment he had crossed the portal and there was no day-and-night cycle on the moonbridge—only an unchanging jade-blue crepuscule. It felt as though he had been walking nonstop for close to a week, but he had not yet slept and up to this point had been only mildly tired. Looking at the Moon, though, which, in spite of its larger size, still looked unattainably far, Luke was seized by despair at the notion that he might never make it there. And with that despair came a deep exhaustion that made him want to lie down on the floor of the bridge, which was of the same rock-metal-vegetation as the rest of the structure.

Just as Luke was getting ready to succumb, he heard and saw the leaves move behind him, to either side, and atop. He now fully gave in to the fear that had been gnawing at him and mindlessly ran forward toward the distant Moon.

When his aching legs and burning lungs brought Luke back to self-awareness, he stopped running. He unstrapped his knapsack, which contained all his camping gear, bent over, hands on his thighs, and panted coarsely.

The boy took stock of his situation. There was no doubt that the Moon was now much closer, but how close he could still not determine. What little encouragement his progress might have inspired was mitigated by his physical condition: his stomach growled in hunger; his eyelids rebelled against staying open; his throat was raw from dehydration; his legs ached from overexertion. He could not imagine how he could ever make it across the bridge to the Moon. He knew for certain that he could not turn back; he would not survive the duration of the return journey.

He yearned to sleep, but he dared not. He thought he might never wake, that he would fall prey to some fatal violation. Feeling as though there were no other option open to him, Luke strapped on his knapsack and trekked onward toward the Moon and the shimmer of its faintly reassuring blue-green-grey aura.

A few hundred metres back, Luke had entered a particularly lush section of the moonbridge. Fruit of strange shapes and unfamiliar colours hung from the bridge's vinelike framework. Luke was wary of eating the alien substances, lest they be poisonous. But he had not eaten in what now seemed like weeks of nonstop walking and sleeplessness, and his resistance wavered. He approached one fruit that was shaped somewhat like a small rodent and smelled it. It had no aroma. He smelled other fruits of other shapes and disquieting colours, but none of them exuded a detectable odour.

Hunger got the better of caution, and Luke ripped off a fruit that looked like a tumescent saxophone and ravenously bit into it, before he could second-guess himself.

The thing tasted like chalk and was very dry at first bite. In his mouth, though, it dissolved into a thin, watery substance that immediately refreshed him. He devoured the whole thing and afterward felt sated and restored—euphoric, even. He grabbed an empty plastic bag from his knapsack and filled it with the bland bridgefruit.

Luke contemplated the Moon, which now loomed larger than anything he'd ever seen. He strutted toward his destination with a new bounce in his step.

The lushness of the bridge increased as the Moon neared. Soon, Luke was engulfed within the stone-metal-plant material of the moonbridge, unable to see either sky or Moon. Unable, in fact, to see anything. He scraped and scratched his hands and face repeatedly as he moved forward within the dark tunnel of the moonbridge. Whenever panic threatened to overwhelm him, Luke ate some bridgefruit; while it didn't completely reassure him, the taste was calming him enough for him to continue his journey with a modicum of levelheadedness.

At one point, Luke thought he'd hit a dead end, but, after eating more bridgefruit to stave off despair, he palmed the walls of the tunnel until he found a narrow opening at a tilt from the direction he'd come from. The tunnel remained thus—mazelike, confining, difficult—for several turns, during which the boy further lacerated his already ill-treated flesh on the thorny walls of his surroundings.

After a dozen turns, though, the tunnel opened up. At first, elated at the turquoise demi-light of the sky and the open space, Luke failed to notice that the Moon no longer loomed ahead. In the distance, he noticed pitched tents and the sound of conversations reached him. It was only then that Luke realized that he had reached the Moon.

He headed toward the camp, toward his classmates from the secondary 4 class of Prettygood Park High School.

As soon as Luke reached the periphery of the camp, conversation stopped. No-one greeted him, and his classmates either avoided his gaze or looked at him in icy silence. He was used to this kind of treatment, but it nevertheless stung that none of them was able to move beyond that pettiness, so far from everything any of them knew.

Still feeling unsettled from the bridge crossing, Luke pitched his tent near the others, not wanting to be isolated. Regardless of what the others thought of him.

Inside his tent, exhaustion overwhelmed Luke and he promptly fell asleep, before he could unroll his sleeping bag.


Sometime later, Luke awoke to an eerily seductive cooing. The sound was unmistakably feminine, yet unlike anything he had ever heard before. From the outside, someone unzipped the flap of his tent, and to his surprise Blair Jonas slipped inside, without a shred of clothes on, her skin glowing with the same colours as the Moon.

A pungent loamy smell invaded the tent. Blair smiled at him with a mixture of the predatory and the submissive, not saying a word but cooing that strange sound that had roused him from sleep. Her eyes were now black instead of their usual light brown, and as she drew closer to him he realized that the rich odour emanated from her. There was not a trace of that peach scent he associated with his fantasies of her.

She brushed her lips against his lacerated cheeks. There was not a mark on her flesh, though. She was perfect.

Blair fumbled to remove Luke's clothes, growing more impatient, almost angry, and the cooing abated, which left Luke with a stark sense of loss. The boy shed his clothes, and the girl relaxed, resuming her soothing coo.

She kissed him, and Luke lost himself in a brew of new sensations, unsure of the details of what transpired between them. The blissful state segued into sleep, and when Luke awoke the girl was gone.

Shaken, elated, confused, smitten … Luke dressed and stepped outside, eager to find Blair, to hold her, to kiss her again. But Luke was immediately surrounded by a pack of his male classmates—naked, crouching like monkeys and snarling at him, their eyes wild, violent. They blocked his every attempt at moving away. Even more shocking to Luke was that his friend Ben was among the pack. Ben had made it to the Moon after all, but why had he joined the others against him? Luke whispered, "Ben?" but his friend bared his teeth at him. Beyond, Luke could see that all the other boys were naked, too, roving the camp grounds on all fours, like wild beasts.

Soon, Montague Farmer, in the same feral state as the others, approached the pack that surrounded Luke. They deferred to Montague. Unlike the others, who were no smaller or larger than they'd been on Earth, Montague had grown to nearly double his usual height and girth. Montague was now in all ways the alpha he'd arrogantly strutted around as back home.

Where were all the girls?, Luke wondered, as he avoided Montague's hateful glare. Scanning the horizon, a mass of pinkness caught his gaze. On a rocky shelf overlooking the camp, the girls had gathered, naked, their various limbs lazily entwined. They looked down at the scattered wild boys with amused superiority. Blair was among them, but her skin no longer shone with the hues of the Moon.

Montague growled, seizing Luke's attention.

The two boys stared at each other. Luke was terrified of the violence that was threatening to erupt at any moment, but he refused to let his fear show; he didn't flinch even a smidgen from Montague's glare. While the two boys were locked in that stalemate, all the other feral boys gathered around them in concentric circles.

From afar, the congregation of girls laughed mockingly. Montague cringed at the derision and shrank back to normal size. He cowered away and the feral pack scattered. The girls laughed even louder.

Luke spent the next several hours wandering around, examining the strange vegetation that grew on lunar soil. The other boys still ran around naked and feral, but they stopped harassing him. Luke yearned to seek out Blair, but the gathering of girls intimidated him too much, and he kept to himself until he grew tired enough to slink back into his tent. Sleep never did come and, although he pined for her in silence, neither did Blair.

Luke stepped outside frustrated and disappointed. He heard snoring from the nearby tents; no-one else was out and about. Everyone was sleeping. Luke gathered his gear, and, having had enough, set off for the moonbridge.

He barely noticed the trek back, although it did seem to take quite a long time, but he no longer cared.

The next day at school, Luke didn't feel like speaking to Blair or Benjamin or anyone else. He considered talking to Mr. Saint-Michael about his experiences on the Moon, but the teacher's affected mannerisms now struck Luke as smug and ridiculous. Mr. Saint-Michael was the same as ever, though, Luke knew. It was himself who had changed and not his former mentor.

Luke kept to himself until school gave out for summer. Blair never gave him another look. Benjamin tried to hang out with him, but Luke avoided him.

For his next year, his graduating year, Luke transferred to another school. It was thirty years before he saw anyone from Prettygood Park High School again.

A few minutes before midnight, on the first day of autumn 2012, Luke sat at a hotel bar near Bloor and Spadina, not paying attention to anyone around him; he was in town for the Toronto International Film Festival. None of the films he'd seen that day were any good. Before going up to his room, he'd decided to order a hot toddy to soothe himself to sleep. The guy to his right blurted out, "Luke? Luke Fort?"

"Yeah," Luke said absent-mindedly. He turned, but then was shocked to recognize his old friend Benjamin House, albeit somewhat balder and greyer.

They shook hands, exchanged pleasantries, gabbed about cinema, and talked about their recent divorces. Luke grew bored with that conversation, though. Remembering the last time he'd spoken to Ben, he said, "Hey, sorry to change the subject, but that Moon trip, back in high school—that was too weird and creepy. What the hell happened to you up there, man?"

Ben looked puzzled. "What do you mean? It was the most boring thing ever. The portal jumped us instantly from Montreal to the Moon. Then, there was nothing up there but dusty rocks. No-one spoke to anybody. We just sat around the fire, bored out of our skulls. I thought the thing was supposed to be the adventure of a lifetime. Anyway. I tried to find you; I hoped you'd be proud that I'd made it after all, but where were you?" Resentment crept into Ben's voice. "You weren't with any of the others. I know you went up. I saw you go through the portal from where I was hiding, trying to muster my courage to confront that nightmare guardian."

Luke hesitated, then said, "That's what you remember?"

Ben nodded and took another sip of his drink, obviously trying to find a way to end the encounter graciously.

In his mind, Luke tried to reconcile Ben's story with his memories, but gave up and downed the rest of his hot toddy. "Listen, Benjamin, it was great to see you again, but I've got to be at a press conference at eight tomorrow morning. Here's my card. Stay in touch, okay? We shouldn't let another thirty years go by." Luke tried but failed to keep the insincerity from his voice.

Ben's tone was curt and dismissive: "Absolutely, Tofu. Good night."

But Luke didn't leave. He sat there, unmoving and silent. Through the tall tinted windows, the Moon had captured his gaze and refused to let go of his imagination.

# THE BURIED MOON

By Marie Bilodeau

Rachel woke up, her gasp filling the cave. She reached out, but Max was no longer beside her. Darkness filled the cave; night had fallen.

She grabbed her pants and jumped up, hopping into the first pant leg and negotiating the second with a single hand as she grabbed her shirt and slipped it over her head. She scraped her arm trying to get both boots on at once and she hurled insults at the rock.

"You trying to kill yourself?" Max asked as he strode in with an armful of scraggly birch logs.

"Damn it, Max. Why didn't you wake me?"

"You're pretty when you sleep?"

"It's the new moon. I should be with Jenny!"

"Seriously? She's twelve. Is she that scared of the dark? She can take care of herself."

"Not tonight she can't," she mumbled as she pulled her flashlight from her pack and pushed aside the bushes that covered the cave, a hideaway from the eyes and tongues of her minute village.

Max stumbled behind her, her urgency kindling his speed.

She tripped over a root and forced herself to go slower. She wouldn't be of any use to Jenny if she cracked her head open in the thick forest.

14

She pushed branches and let them swing back, too harried to warn Max, who mumbled behind her. Still, he kept up. The flashlight beam bounced ineffectively before them. Rachel barely remembered to use it to ensure her own path was clear, resulting in her tumbling and falling several times. She pushed on, not brushing the dirt from her jeans or worrying about her scraped knee.

"Would you slow down?" Max cried after her. She answered by going faster, until she had reached her destination. Max stopped short behind her, out of breath.

Jutting out of the ground like a crooked stump, her small house stood silent in the dark landscape of the moonless night, lit by the faraway street light—the only one her village boasted.

She walked through the backyard and through her small garden, knocking some of the precious tomatoes that, once canned, would feed them through the harsh winter months.

Rachel didn't slow, nor did she tell Max to be careful where he stepped. Surviving the winter months hardly seemed to matter, now.

She cracked open the back door. It was unlocked. Jenny always locked it.

She bit her lower lip and stepped in, wishing she had more than a flashlight to fight with. Max followed close, whether to protect her or to be protected by her, she wasn't sure. He was a nice enough lover and had been great company for the two months since he had arrived in her village on a research project, but they'd never had the opportunity to discuss latent fighting abilities.

Hearing his ragged breath behind her, his frame leaner than hers and his arms as thin as sapling branches, she somehow doubted he was an expert boxer in disguise.

"Where's the light switch?" Max whispered beside her, his warm breath making her jump.

"We don't have any. House too old."

"Jenny?" Rachel called out tentatively. The creak of floorboards under her feet was her only answer. She took a deep breath and rounded the corner, toward their living room that doubled as a shared bedroom. She flashed the beam of light around madly, to illuminate every corner in case something lay in waiting. No flash of eyes greeted the beam. She let her breath out, which turned into a hiss as she took in the state of the room. Their beds were turned aside, and their shared winter blanket, knitted by their grandmother before she had passed and left them all alone, had been ripped.

Rachel knelt beside it and took it in her hands, the wool coarse and thick. She brought it to her cheek and burrowed her face into the scratchy fabric to hide her tears. A hint of vanilla and cinnamon still clung to it, the same as her grandmother's favourite perfume, even though she had been gone for almost five years and the blanket had often been beaten in the river since.

She had promised her grandmother she would always watch over Jenny. That she would never leave her on the dark nights, the moonless nights and that, some day, she would find a way to leave the land of their ancestors, to a safer place.

Far away.

"Should I call the police?" Max asked, his voice thin.

Rachel pulled her face from the blanket, but still rested her cheek on it. "We don't have a phone," she answered numbly.

She thought of Jenny, trapped and screaming... "And what would they do? Seriously? Would they come over here and save her? They wouldn't! They don't even know how!"

"What do you mean? They're the police! It's their job to stop thugs who steal little girls!"

He paused and narrowed his eyes. "Wait. You know who did this, don't you?"

She made a conscious effort to stop biting her lower lip before she pierced her skin with her teeth. Gently, she folded the blanket and laid it on Jenny's bed, cozied up next to hers.

"Rachel? I know you probably think of me as more than useless, studying lichen and all while you're just trying to survive, but..." he paused and looked down. "I really want to help you. And Jenny." He looked back up. "Won't you please trust me?"

Rachel gave him a thin smile. "Are you good with any weapons?"

16

To his credit, he pondered the question. "I took fencing in undergrad for a year. … are we going to beat someone up?"

She shrugged. "Depends. Do you think you can use those moves with a shovel? It's the best I've got."

He nodded, though she could see the uncertainty in his eyes. She grabbed a shovel for him, a rake for herself. Poor weapons, but still the best they had.

He held the shovel awkwardly. "So, um, where are we going?"

"To the edge of town. The bogs. They'll take her there."

"Who? Why would any one take her there?"

She didn't look at him as she answered. "Frightened people, Max." People bargaining for safe passage in the bogs. She handed him Jenny's flashlight. Batteries were their one big expense. Light was their lifeline. Her throat closed.

Jenny was out there, somewhere, without any light.

Without any hope.


Jenny cried, but her cries were muffled by the waters. The bogs were thick with dirt and years of slime, and they all slid down her throat as she screamed. She pushed and kicked, her legs heavy under the silt, her nightgown riding up, her struggles cut short by the bogles' tentacles wrapping around her thin waist and pulling her down, pinning her arms.

One large kick and she was up for a moment. For just a moment, and even in the darkness she could see the crawlers all around her, with the legs of centipedes, the tail and pincers of a scorpion and the round body of a spider. Three crawlers moved in, stinging her face and neck.

She felt her body grow cold and numb, and the bogles drew her down and she closed her eyes and mouth against the murky waters. All that she could hear was the sound of rock shifting over her.


The bogs were not far from town, though part of them had been covered by road and houses. They were still there. Rachel could smell them despite the concrete and oil stains.

She stopped near a house, put her hand on Max's chest to stop him short. Wide eyes met hers. "I shouldn't bring you with me. You shouldn't come."

He looked towards the bogs, starting just past the next yard. All of the lights in the houses were out, even though they had power and it wasn't that late. Rachel suddenly understood who had bargained for their safety.

"You gave me a shovel," Max snapped. "It seems to me you need my help if you felt the need to give me a shovel."

She looked up at Max as though seeing him for the first time. He'd strolled into town two months ago, studying lichen in the forest nearby. She liked that about him. He didn't study bogs, so never smelled of them.

She'd seen him as a way out, for her and her sister. A scientist had a future. She had just a few months to win his heart, to ensure that when his research was over and he left town, he would take them with her. Away from all of this.

"I can't let you do this." She shook her head at the protest forming on his lips.

"Um, shovel?"

"It's too dangerous, Max. You have no idea what you're up against."

He shrugged. "People who took a little girl. I don't do heroics, Rachel, but that's not right." He paused. "But, the more I know what to expect, the better off we'll all be."

She bit her lower lip again before looking up to meet his eyes. "You wouldn't believe me. No one ever does."

"Well, I believed you enough to grab a shovel and follow you."

Rachel was surprised to find she could still laugh. She resumed walking towards the bog, slowly, mostly so she could look at the ground before her and not his eyes.

"Generations ago, the moon strolled down to see what dark creatures lurked in the bogs. The night was dark, the creatures attacked, and she was captured. Villagers saved her." She paused. He said nothing.

"She would come down every month, after that, and wander. Once, she came back her, and met a young man. She fell in love.

Bore his children." She took a deep breath. "We're her descendants. Of the moon. There's nothing special about us, except the creatures of the bog, still intent on claiming revenge, still try to capture us. That's why we hide every dark moon. They can't leave the bogs themselves, but always send someone to find us. Someone terrified."

Max piped up. "What do these people expect will happen? By bringing Jenny to the bogs?"

"They think their loved ones will be safer, that children and pets will stop getting swallowed by the bogs."

"I swear, religions and myths should all fall into history. What a useless time waster," he huffed, and Rachel winced. She knew he wouldn't believe her, but it still hurt to have him cast aside generations of fear as though they were fuelled only by make-believe.

She couldn't bring him along. He would be dead before he realized that darkness held more monsters than they could fight.

She gave him a wry smile. "I've been using you," she said, louder than she'd meant to. He flinched a bit, and her pulse quickened.

"I thought you could get me and Jenny out of this town. So I've been trying to win you."

Her face was flushed, but she forced herself to keep looking at him.

"I'm sorry. I thought you should know if you're about to go in there to help me. It's dangerous."

He shrugged again. "Rachel, you're honestly great fun, but I can't say I haven't been using you, too. I mean, you're great on a cavern floor." It was her turn to flinch. "But, that being said, I can't pretend I don't care about you and your sister. You're at least good friends, though don't expect a marriage proposal by the time my research is over next month."

She lowered her head. She needed to focus on the here and now, and that was Jenny.

"Fine," she said curtly before continuing to walk towards the bog.

"You've been reading too many fairy tales, Rachel. Been stuck in a small place with small ideas for too long." He grew silent as he followed her, crouching as she crouched.

The flashlight shook slightly in her hand as it struck the edge of the bog. Hundreds of yellow eyes peered at her before scuttling out of the beam.

"What was that?" Max was suddenly closer to her.

"Turn on your flashlight. Stay close. Use that shovel on anything with red or yellow eyes."

Her beam illuminated patched of bog at a time, revealing nothing else. Max's soon joined hers. She cocked her head, listening closely.

She had seen the creatures that lurked here only once when, a foolish child, she had disobeyed her grandmother and wandered here. She shuddered, remembering the fear as they'd dragged her down… her grandmother had found her quickly enough, fighting against the creatures, pulling her up and holding her close.

The moon had not come to save her. She'd asked her grandmother why the moon had not come. She had looked up to her grandmother as the light painted every crease of her face, especially the hard bend of her mouth. She had never known her grandmother not to smile. "Because the moon has better things to do than worry about her disobedient descendants." Rachel had never spoken of the night again, but she had always understood that staying away from the bog was imperative, especially on moonless nights, when the creatures stirred and dared breach into their world.

Rachel took a breath and stepped onto the small path that led into the depths of the bogs. The ground sucked down her feet and she almost lost a runner a couple of times. The sucking noises behind her indicated that Max still followed her. She wanted to scream at him to run away, to hide, remembering the clutch of the bogles.

Her breath came in short spasms and her grip on the rake became sleek with sweat.

"Jenny?" she whispered. The bogs were still, so still it made her skin crawl. No reed rustled, no bug scampered on the water, no frog called in the night. The air smothered her lungs with humidity, despite the chill of the night air.

She couldn't even see any bogles or crawlers.

"Jenny!" she cried this time, a sob breaking the name. Was it too late? Was she already down below?

"Maybe she's not here," Max said, looking around with his flashlight at the still bog.

"No," Rachel said numbly. "She's here. They've taken her below." She heard a rustling to the left. The skittering of thousands of small feet to the right. The rise of water behind her. The creatures were listening. They were waiting.

"I know you're here!" She turned around and screamed, her voice swallowed by the encroaching darkness. "I know you're here!" She screamed again, and pivoted to catch a glimpse of the entire bog.

Max gasped and shifted closer to her, his eyes like full moons as he met hers. "Something touched my ankle," he whispered.

"You're lucky if that's all they do," Rachel kicked at the murky water near her, slipping and landing in the muck. Pinpricks exploded on her legs and back, and she rolled around, bringing up her arms to cover her face.

This time, Max screamed. She struck out, kicking and hurling insults, slapping the air around her. She hit nothing, the crawlers too fast for mere human speed. Tentacles wrapped around her leg.

"Give her back!" She kicked out and connected with the bogle, but others lifted their murky arms from the depths and wrapped around her legs, tugging her down. Max grabbed hold of her armpits and tried to pull her up. She screamed in pain, feeling as though she was being pulled in two.

"Let go, Max!" She hit him, trying to make him let go of her shirt as he tightened his grip. He lost his footing and fell partly under her, but he didn't lose his grip on her shirt. "Let go!" She managed to hit him square in the nose and he let go for a moment, long enough for the bogles to pull her down. Max's fingers slipped through hers as he made a final effort to grab her.

Water rose up into her mouth and nose, plugged her ears and blinded her with grit. She screamed an airless scream, looked up to where she thought she saw the light of Max's flashlight and realized that hers had slipped from her grasp.

Her only weapon against the darkness, and she had lost it.


Max plunged his hands frantically into the thick water, coming up with old sticks and grit. He could touch the bottom of the bog without having to dip his head underwater. Yet he could find no sign of Rachel.

He held the flashlight with his teeth, the beam bobbing uselessly on the still waters. So still even he barely made them move.

"Rachel! Rachel!!"

He stopped and straightened, looking for a sign, any sign, of her. The bog around him was so still it made his skin crawl for want of movement. The reeds stood like silent sentinels over a sheet of old, tired water. The creatures that had attacked them but moments earlier had vanished as quickly as they had appeared.

Had they even been real?

He walked deeper into the water, using the shovel to carefully feel his way forward. He slipped a few times, barely catching himself before being swallowed by the water. He stopped. This was foolish. He could easily slip and drown. But Rachel had been down so long already!

The houses. Nearby. They must have heard their struggles.

"Help! Please help us! My friend is injured!"

No light went on, no indication that anyone was home or, if they were, that they cared about anything but their own safety. He whipped around, thinking he had heard something, but no one was there. What was he supposed to do now? He studied lichen and read books. What use was he in a bog, having just watched his friend being pulled down, her eyes filled with rage and terror as his grip loosened on her...

"Please! Won't someone help me?"

He suddenly noticed movement on his left. Bubbles coming up from the depths. He splashed towards it, his legs weighed down by his wet pants.

He reached the bubbles, his feet kicking a large stone slab, sending him to his knees before it. His ragged breath filled his ears as he tried to see if any of those creatures were nearby. He looked around, but the bogs were silent.

But… he could see. He had dropped his flashlight when he had hit the stone, though he still held the shovel. He had seen the bubbles, he could see the swamp… he looked up, gasped. The moon, which was on its new phase and dark this night, was now full, providing him plenty of light by which to navigate.

And scaring the creatures away?

Lights danced above him. Bog lights. Created by a mix of gasses. That's what was happening. The gasses were making him hallucinate. Bubbles popped near him and he scrambled off the rock.

With his fingers he felt the shape and length of the rock. He located a crack, where the bubbles were escaping. More than a crack. It was a seam. He could trace it with his fingers.

He grabbed the shovel and forced it into the section where the bubbles were seeping out. He pushed down, grunting, hoping the shovel wouldn't break, until he heard the stone shift and topple sideways, its corner surfacing. The stone stayed standing for a few seconds, like a gravestone, before toppling back and vanishing in the dark waters.

Rachel splashed up, holding her sister, both coughing and almost falling straight back into the water.

Max grabbed them and pulled them clear of the water, into the backyard of one of the dark houses. Rachel and Jenny still clung to each other, both covered in muck and some leeches. They needed a bath, a change of clothes.

A change of life.

"Come on," Max said, helping them up. Rachel looked at him with wide eyes, the moonlight shining deep within them, making them look silver. He placed a kiss on her lips, which were warm despite the chill of the night.

"I'm taking you out of here," he said as he broke away.

She gave him another wry smile, but the fear in her eyes tore at his heart.

"How far away?"

He returned the smile and took her hand.

"As far as you want."

He walked them home, keeping them close, grateful that, even though she looked up once and smiled at the full moon, Rachel said nothing to him about it.

# THE DOWSER

By Kevin Cockle

"Why me?" I asked. We sat on a second floor balcony overlooking the floor show at The Batucada. It was noisy, but a glass partition between us and the mob downstairs made it possible to have a conversation.

Ms. Hastings ("Please: call me Diana") sipped her Kir Royale and smiled. "You're the best dowser we know. This job may well require your fearsome talents."

"What—identifying different brands of whiskey in blind taste-tests?" I joked. I hadn't worked the oil patch in years, and every energy company had a dowser on staff, if not officially labelled as such. Decades of experience had taught the oil and gas industry that you didn't rely on geologists and 3D seismic alone. There was something about black gold that didn't fit neatly into stats and charts and formulae, and everybody knew it. But the question remained: why me, and not someone younger, or more importantly, someone already under contract?

"Don't be modest," Diana smiled. "You found the Viking dome outside Turner when everybody else thought Turner was dry. You put Exxon back onside in Saskatchewan, and helped turn tiny, independent Lunaco into a major player over night. There are dowsers, and then there are dowsers, professor Warren. You are among the latter."

"Jack," I said on reflex.

"Excuse me?"

"Just call me Jack. It's a habit, I suppose. Nobody in the oil patch calls me 'professor'."

I watched through the glass as down upon the dance-floor, two half-naked men in Aztec feather skirts grabbed a pretty mulatto girl out of the audience (a plant: it's always some model); watched as they hauled her kicking and screaming up the stairs onto the stage. It wasn't a bad set—sort of like the Vegas idea of Mexico with jade bas-reliefs in pre-Columbian fashion along the front lip of the stage, and all along the back wall. The girl writhed picturesquely—kicking off her expensive pumps; ripping her powder blue power-skirt; popping buttons on her midnight blue blouse. The coke-and-booze fuelled after-work crowd roared: "Human Sacrifice Fridays" at The Batucada was always a big hit. One of the ersatz-Aztecs produced a curved dagger meant to represent a side-winding serpent; rolled his eyes like a horse on meth.

I felt my age at that moment, knew myself to be out of touch. The stockbrokers and petro-lawyers, accountants and admen and models and bankers, and all the assistants who had been invited along for the ride—all of them bellowed in anticipation of the I-Can't-Believe-It's-Not-Slaughter to come.

Diana glanced down at the stage as well, dark eyes shining. She was one of them. Whatever else she was, she belonged here more than I did.

"You like this?" I said, trying not to be judgmental; failing miserably.

She smiled. In fact, she almost always seemed to be smiling a little.

Below, on the stage: impressive sleight-of-hand. A dagger plunging into a girl's chest; a heart yanked out; a geyser of blood; the victim screaming her last. I cringed in spite of myself, because knowing this was fake wasn't good enough. Everyone knew it was a trick: everyone screamed in mindless approval regardless. Sacrifice a suit, and our mortgages get paid; things we can't control at the office work out; all the parts of the machine continue to grind away sans-a-glitch.

You didn't "turn the other cheek" in Calgary—not anymore: this was Coyolxauhqu's town now. Maybe it always had been. Maybe those little white churches on the prairie had always been mere place-holders, waiting for the real juice to come along. Whatever the case, Aztec schtick was big these days—had been for years. I took a jolt of Jack Daniels; felt the ice click against my teeth.

"Brass tacks, " Diana said. "You know the original Athabasca deposit—what we call Site 01 now?" I nodded. The first surface mine conducted by the Great Canadian Oil Sands company had become something of an Albertan legend. It was ancient history now though: the area had long since ceased to be productive.

"It's under reclamation now isn't it?" I said.

"It's actually been reopened," Diana smiled. I was starting to get irritated by that oily smirk—no pun intended.

"Why?"

"A new survey uncovered a promising depression in the limestone—or readings to that effect—so we allowed an operator to go back in."

I frowned: "going back in" on reclaimed land would have been a bit of an issue, at least in theory. Diana Hastings was attached to the Trans North America Environmental Ministry, which although ostensibly a government agency established under NAFTA III, was funded largely by a private energy consortium, so it was difficult to get a read on where her loyalties lay. Taken at face-value however, it looked as though someone from Environment might be on the hook if the geologicals had been wrong, or weak in this instance. Made sense that they'd want their own independent assessment done, although it wouldn't be public...not with a dowser on board. You may as well admit to people you were investigating a murder with a psychic.

"We'd like you to confirm the hydrocarbon feature of course," Diana continued. "There have been conflicting reports on-site. If it's not panning out as anticipated, we need to get out of there. In addition, there may be some...anomalies we'd like your opinion on. Some health concerns have been reported. We actually don't have linked communications at the site, and we're a little fuzzy on these findings. Area residents have been making some noises about noxious odours—the usual sour-gas complaints. And there have been a number of…suicides."

"Suicides? How many?"

"Thirty three." Smile.

Ah: there it was. Thirty three "suicides" was code: they hadn't come up with anything plausible for the media yet.

I felt an old familiar chill creep up my backbone. There are dowsers, and then there are dowsers, and I was indeed one of the latter. A dowser, true enough, but also a professor of classics with knowledge of what an earlier, gentler time might have termed "unspeakable" rites and histories. I had found that the unspeakable had become—if not routine—then perhaps merely "uncomfortable" in this day and age of commonplace atrocity. Massacre was spectacle, after all. As I watched waitresses clean fake blood off the stage downstairs, I began to see why Diana had contacted me in particular.

I had always had a special affinity for and connection to oil, and that had made me useful. But it was my knowledge of the occult that made me valuable, even if nobody ever said so aloud.

I'm no environmentalist, but it seemed as though a good deal of the first-stage exploitation-land of the Athabasca deposit had been recovered, at least to look at it. Driving along the bumpy gravel road, I was bound on both sides by young, but healthy pine trees, and could see no visible evidence of the decades of strip mining that had once decimated the area. There were always concerns about what one couldn't see beneath the ground—the water quality in particular—but despite the geo-political climate of the age, it looked as though companies had followed the letter of the law with respect to reclamation. They need not have—the oil companies owned the regulatory agencies, and the politicians had long ago defaulted to production and defence as the national priorities in an age of ever-increasing scarcity. And yet…the ride was pleasantly arboreal; a rough-hewn jaunt through the country-side with crisp, clean air whistling through the open roof of the jeep, and the occasional bird circling above the trees. The area looked like a government television spot; an advertisement for the good work being done, despite the mounting geo-political pressures.

It looked that way right up until I reached the work-site.

Due to the curvature of the road, I had had no advance visual warning of the site and nearly had to pump the brakes to slow down as I emerged from the trees into a clear-cut staging area at the lip of a fresh pit. I came to a full stop in a cloud of yellow dust, and looked around at the collection of heavy diggers, trucks, sheds, pipes, wire-spools, hoses and other construction paraphernalia. It was the base-camp for the new dig, and it was a miniature ghost-town.

I got out of the jeep, my hiking boots crunching on gravel as I got my bearings. From my breast-pocket, I withdrew my crystal-and-chain and took a quick reading, getting my intuition dialed in. The dowsing pendulum I used was headed by a large purple quartz and had belonged to my grandfather. I've always thought that long family connection was part of the process, somehow. As though the energy of generations had set up a sympathetic resonance in that beautiful stone.

I wandered about the camp at random, letting the crystal guide me. My footsteps made the only perceptible sound in the place: all else was silence. There were signs of habitation—a half-empty thermos; newspapers open on field tables; a pair of extra boots outside one of the trailers—but no sign of life. And no sign of struggle.

I came at last to the lip of the dig, and winced at a sudden shock of pain spreading up from my neck and throbbing through the base of my skull. Pain was the sign: oil was here. Hydrocarbon feature confirmed.

I gasped at the awful majesty of it all.

The crater was some sixty metres deep, cyclopean cliffs sloping down to the limestone floor in graduated grey/yellow walls. A wide earthen-ramp had been engineered along the eastern side of the pit to allow easy access, and the entire site appeared to travel north for some distance, then veer to the east in an L shaped configuration.

I began my descent down the ramp, my temples pulsing.

Making the floor of the pit, I proceeded north, letting my pain draw me on. The silence in the pit was like a weight, like a physical presence. I felt the quiet pushing down on me, giving me the sense of having submerged into a pool of water, rather than having walked down into an open-pit mine.

I was struck suddenly by a thought I'd had on many previous occasions: oil had been the making of me, and in the making of me, I kept coming back to oil. More and more often, as exploration spread into the least accessible areas of the globe, it was the oil industry uncovering some of archaeology's most significant and bizarre finds. Oil industry endowments often financed the very departments with which I had been affiliated, and it was the oil industry that had proven to be the most open-minded towards the resultant—frequently unconventional—scholarship.

It was impossible not to reflect upon these interconnections as I approached the bend in the mine. I was there because of my talent, and my expertise, both of which were predicated upon oil.

I turned the corner to the east, and immediately doubled over, retching my eggs benedict into the dirt.

Pain lanced through my skull and spine: pain the likes of which I had never experienced on any previous dowse.

The extension to the pit was not extensive, running for perhaps only another hundred or so meters to the east, with the bowl of the crater extending up on all sides in a nearly perfect curve.

And in the center of the pit, emerging from the limestone to a height of some sixteen feet, rose an octagonal obelisk of what looked to be polished hematite.

I recognized it almost immediately, both from its shape and general dimensions, as well as by the presence of engraved pictographs which decorated the top half of the stone. I recognized it from writings in Kurtz, and in the dreamlike jail-house poetry of Artemis Jones, and had even seen a passage in Welton's Folkloric Origins concerning it, but more significantly than any of these, I had seen the edifice with my own eyes. Seen it, and photographed those designs, on a hilltop outside the town of Stoianacavar in Hungary!

I staggered forward, mind reeling with disbelief and agony. Pain so sharp as to make me gasp for breath bolted through my nerve endings as I fumbled for my phone. Addressing my pictures, I brought up the Stoianacavar obelisk, isolated on the pictographs, and expanded them. A moment's examination proved to my satisfaction that although both symbolic structures were of the same language, the symbols were not identical on both stones. Somehow, two culturally specific structures had been raised thousands of miles apart, and thousands of years ago, and in the case of the Athabasca deposit, how many untold eons must have passed since the pillar's construction? I stood sixty meters from the surface! And the obelisk had only been unearthed at all, because in some way, by some unknown process, it had presented as being geologically consistent with a hydrocarbon feature.

Almost as if it had known that only such a feature could motivate the Herculean task of digging the pit in the first place.

Almost as if the hydrocarbon sign had been a lure.

I swallowed, tasted the brackish backwash of my own vomit; spit, and wiped my mouth with my right shirtsleeve.

I advanced to the pillar, squinting with the effort of detecting what I thought to be a slight vibration coming from the surface of the stone. As I closed, I felt the vibration more certainly, resonating in the crystal in my breastpocket—could feel the sympathetic harmony against my chest.

I reached a trembling hand to the surface of the stone—so impossibly silver and smooth—contrasted against the muted yellows and greys of the surrounding ground.

My fingertips met with the stone, and confirmed the vibration. I felt it in my feet then, on the top of my head, in my clenched teeth. I felt the stone singing, for I sensed it as a song, and all the world fell away in a sudden directionless acceleration into the infinite.

I saw, I felt, I heard...

A war amongst the heavens; a God-like son slaying his leviathan mother, removing her heart, throwing her head into the sky. Coyolxauhqu she came to be named, her head becoming the moon; her life's blood flowing thick and black into the bowels of the earth. Blood boiling with viscous energy, waiting for discovery; the moon guiding searchers through the millennia via unseen forces and dreams, pulling at psyches even as it pulled on the seas...

An ancient Byzantine galleon spewing Greek fire from a bronze nozzle carved in the likeness of a dragon, the vulnerable wooden decks protected by eldritch sorcery. The original petro-magic, binding petroleum and war...

A young Winston Churchill seated in the library-office of the First Sea Lord, coming to the realization that the British navy must convert to oil-driven dreadnoughts in order to maintain supremacy. It's the decisive step, the hydrocarbon rubicon, the first domino to fall...

Standard Oil rising and combining its various tentacles in trust, seething with life and power, its agents scouring the planet in search of precious reserves. I see them then, the new petro-sorcerers, the inheritors of Byzantium, hidden from history and dreaming of Coyolxauhqu, placing the planet irrevocably upon the hydrocarbon path, gradually invoking the goddess of the moon...

Standard slain by her offspring: Exxon, Chevron, Conoco, Sunoco, Mobil, Amoco even as Coyolxauhqu had given birth to the gods who would vanquish her. Her unseen hand behind everything now; her mind the engine, her blood the fuel...

War. I feel the explosions, hear the roar of the Merlin engine, the Daimler-Benz engine, smell the gasoline and diesel of the tanks and planes, feel the grease amidst the pistons. It is the joy and laughter of Coyolxauhqu; blitzkrieg another of her children...

Black, billowing, pluming smoke: to breathe it is to die...

The fire, and the horror.


I awoke to a strange piping sound, a sound that soon resolved itself into a singing voice.

I lay on my back, at the base of the silver stone where I had fallen. I felt no pain. Day had passed, and through the rim of the crater I observed the whirling immensity of the cosmos, the scattered stars cold and vivid in their indifference.

The singing came closer, and I saw her then—a beautiful, pale-skinned girl with hair as black as crude, whose naked body seemed to glow in the moonlight though I could see no moon above. Her eyes were dark, and long lashed, and her thin, yet sensual lips formed a secret smile as she hummed her sibilant tune.

She knelt beside me, singing softly, and adjusting her notes as though trying to recombine the sounds. In a few moments, the music resolved itself into English, and she spoke: "Thank you, Jack."

I turned my head towards her. I felt no pain, but I was weak, and my limbs tingled, the nerves deadened, and sluggish.

"Who…?" I croaked, my throat thick and dry with sleep.

"You know who," she said. She was right.

With an effort, I struggled to sit up. The girl helped me upright with a small, cool hand at my back. She smiled, and I knew I'd seen that smile before.

"Diana," I mumbled.

"A projection," she purred.

"If I call her on her cell?"

"There will be no answer. I needed to bring you here. I sent a figment of my mind to get you."

I swallowed again, wincing at the constriction in my throat.

"I don't understand."

"Yes you do," she said, going to her haunches, placing her hands in her lap. She looked as earnest as any pupil I'd ever had, her staring, black eyes more intent than menacing. "I've been singing to you your whole life. Calling to you to come find me. You and only you—the others are but shadows compared to your light. I knew that you would find me, and bring me through."

I frowned at that expression, felt the blood drain from my face. All my talents, and all my studies…how much had been my decision, how much her design? Lunaco…had the company

33

been formed knowing that I would find the oil? The Lunaco stock options had financed all my subsequent endeavours; made me what I was to become.

Had I ever truly found oil, or had it always found me?

"Yes," she said, reading the comprehension dawning in my expression.

"What about…what about the men, the miners? Where did they…" I stopped speaking as I looked into her eyes, and sensed her smile in the darkness. She was so close, I could hear her breathing softly through her nose; smell the scent of a tropical rain forest upon her skin. Her eyes were pitiless, unblinking: the eyes of a mamba.

"I'll need some clothes," she said at last. "I want to drive with you to my city."

Calgary, Alberta, she meant. It all made sense then, the changes I'd seen there over the decades.

Coyolxauhqu was alive at last, the moon made flesh, and she was coming to reclaim her throne.


I've written this out of guilt, I suppose.

Shame for my part in things, my ignorance. I've consulted Kurtz; emailed an associate in Britain who owns original leather bound tomes from the Inquisition which might have held some answers, but the fact of the matter is, it's simply too late. The coming of Coyolxauhqu was a century in the making. The time to stop her was in the late nineteenth century, not in the mid twenty first. We are all of us bound to her through our economies, our behaviours, our cars, our jobs, our mortgages. She spent thousands of years learning to correct her past mistakes, and when she came at us, she used our own minds to prepare the ground. We've been taking her sacrament too long. We'd be lost without her now.

She wanted to drive to Calgary so she could feel the wind on her face. She put her feet out through the side window and tuned the radio to classic pop, singing along to Katy Perry and Britney. When we got to town, it was dark, and she made me drive to Riley Park—just up tenth street from The Batucada. She held my hand as we lay on our backs in the middle of the central field and looked up into stars dimmed by the city lights. None of the junkies in the shadows even thought about accosting us. I imagine their drug-induced dreams were more hideous than ever before, on that night.

Lying with her then, our backs chilled by night-dewed grass, I could sense her immensity. The great cosmic dragon crystallized in the shape of a girl; the shape I had given her.

I've wanted for nothing from that moment on. I am the consort of Coyolxauhqu—her unwitting high-priest. The form-bringer. The finder. I rattle around in our mansions, unable to concentrate, unable to sleep.

When she dematerializes into the city, I sometimes hear her in the wind, that piping sound, an ululation you can hear whistling between the buildings downtown during a Chinook. You can catch a whiff of sulphur at the most unexpected times, and wonder if there's been a gas-main break. There'll be an odd light in the sky sometimes, and you'll wonder if there's been another tornado warning. You'll see the full moon shining a shade of blood red, and you'll click your tongue at the air pollution.

She appears in the hallways of our companies; places calls from a hundred head offices; announces directorships and partnerships, and I'll hear her words coming from the mouths of our leaders on the television.

We drift towards war with clockwork inevitability, yet nobody seems too concerned. The talk in the coffee shops and after-work lounges is all of showing strength, of being hard, from people who never used to say such things aloud.

Sometimes she'll call to me, and I will summon her body, and we'll go to The Batucada where she can dance, and snort coke, and drink throughout the night.

And on those nights, I cringe in terror when an unsuspecting girl is pulled out of the audience by men made up to look like Aztec priests. For the sacrifices are no longer staged: the hearts pump, and the blood flows viscous and real, and my Coyolxauhqu exults in the roaring of her chosen people.

# ΠOON DREAM

By Rebecca M. Senese

Ever since she was a little girl, Julia Threswald loved the moon. She used to say she was born during the full moon but that was a bit of a fib. Julia's mother gave birth to her on a late Friday afternoon and although the full moon rose that night, Julia had already made her appearance by that time.

But Julia never let that get in the way of her story, and her fascination with the moon began.

As Julia's father worked as a chemist at drug company, Julia grew up with an appreciation of science (if not much appreciation for drug companies that laid her father off when he was two years shy of retiring). She studied physics and chemistry, anything she thought might get her closer to her dream because as she grew it no longer became just about seeing the moon, she dreamed of visiting it. She imagined herself dressed in a white space suit, taking her first tentative steps on the surface of an alien world.

Magical.

Shortly after Julia graduated with honours, the Big Collapse happened. Governments around the world started defaulting on loans. Economies sputtered and struggled. Unemployment exploded. More and more people grew desperate for work. Resources became strained to the max. No jobs existed and certainly no jobs for a young woman who wanted to work on a moon landing project.

Then the weather worsened with droughts and sand storms. Even God is against us, people started to say. Julia piped up it was time to head into space but a few shouting arguments with friends and near strangers in bars or grocery stores while redeeming food stamps convinced Julia to keep her opinions to herself.

Evangelists took to the airwaves and Internet, proclaiming the end of days. Food shortages became the norm even in the western world as hoarding and lousy weather conspired to worsen conditions. During this time, Julia realized no one was going to hire her to work on a moon landing. No one was interested in space anymore.

If she wanted to go, she was going to have to do it herself.

She started small, and because no one had any money, she took anything, pennies, nickels, the old ereaders or button computers, fashions from ten years ago, anything she could sell. Her friends called her mad, some with affection and others with anger. The angry ones she dumped. The affectionate ones she kept around.

She worked out of her one room apartment, using a ten year old computer she scavenged. After reviewing data from the most recent attempts, she went back to the beginning, to the first moon landing. Reading about the primitive conditions, she realized that was the way to go. Keep it simple. She didn't need sophisticated computers. If they could do it then she could figure out a way to do it now!

And every month during the full moon, she sat on the roof of her tiny four storey walkup and raised a glass to the bright shining orb.

"One day," she promised. "One day we'll meet in person."

Then she met Allan.

He worked in a grocery store, as much job security as anyone could have nowadays. He began to slip her little extras, a few more slices of vat meat, an additional scoop of soya wafers, three bottles of decontaminated water for the price of two. When he asked her out after a month of these little niceties, she said yes. He seemed nice enough.

She told him right away that just because he'd done her favours and given her little extras, he shouldn't be expecting much; she wasn't that kind of girl. Although he was almost a foot taller than her five foot three frame and could easily overpower her, he nodded and made no move even after dinner and an evening sitting on the roof of her tiny walkup. It happened to be a full moon that night. She held her glass against her chest, almost in reverence. Allan noticed her gazing at the moon and spoke the fateful words.

"So you like the moon?" he said.

He spoke with such curiosity she found herself pouring it all out, her love of the moon and dream to visit it. Before she could stop herself, she told him how she'd collected almost five thousand dollars toward her project, not much, but a fortune in these hard times. As his eyes widened at this news, she almost cursed herself for mentioning it out loud. He'd probably try and steal it from her and she'd be back where she started. Well, just let him try, she thought. She'd give him a fight he'd never forget!

"You've done all that to get to the moon?" he said.

"Yes," she said. "So what?"

"You don't think we need to take care of things here?"

She shook her head. "It doesn't matter about taking care of things here. One day the sun will die and take Earth with it. If we stay here, that's the end of us. We've got to get off this planet and the first step is right there."

She pointed at the blazing full moon.

He looked at it and then back at her. "You'll need an engine for your rocket," he said. "I'm pretty good with engines."

She saw the slight smile on his face, not one of scheming to get her money, but open and confident.

"I know a guy who helps out at the junk yard. He has access to lots of metal. He could get us what we want."

"Us?" she said.

The smile sputtered on his face like a faltering engine. "Well, I mean, I could help you. If you wanted. If you don't have any help. But if you don't need help..."

His wide shoulders drooped. His head dropped down, turning away from her. He set his own wine glass on the scratched metal roof. His hands wiped on his pants as he leaned forward, getting ready to stand up. He was going to leave, she realized and then thought of what an idiot she'd been. Of course she needed help. She couldn't possibly build a rocket by herself.

"We couldn't get any metal with wear in it," she said. "I'd have to know for sure that it was strong enough. Space worthy."

He'd stopped moving at the sound of her voice. As she finished speaking, his head turned to her.

"And any welds or joins would have to be absolutely perfect. Not a leak. And super strong," she said.

He nodded. "It will take some doing," he said. "It could take time to find all those perfect pieces."

"Yes," she said. "It will probably take years."

His shy smile curled his lips. "I've got time."

They married two months later.

Moving into his small, two room apartment didn't save any money since she kept her old place to work in. Years passed and they struggled through, first just the two of them and then when their daughter Amelia came along. Julia took Amelia to her old apartment every day and talked about the project as she worked. Even the day of the big riot.

At first Julia didn't realize anything was happening. She sat at her desk, engrossed in the current orbital projection charts when the sound drifted up from the street four floors below. Amelia, now five years old, picked up her doll and carried it to the living room window facing the street. The sound grew louder. Amelia turned around to face Julia.

"Momma, where's all the people going?"

"What people's that, honey?"

"Them people."

"Those people." Julia corrected automatically before she looked up to see Amelia pointing out the window. She set down the charts and crossed to the window. One hand drew Amelia closer even before she looked out the window.

People flooded the street for as far as she could see. Now with her attention on them, she heard the yelling and shouting.

Raised fists swung in the air along with sticks or shovels or other implements she couldn't identify.

"Is it a parade, momma?" Amelia said.

Fear tightened Julia's grip on her daughter's shoulder. "I don't think so, honey. We're going to stay here for a while." She turned her daughter away from the window. "Why don't you come play near the desk? Keep momma company."

Amelia shrugged. "Okay." With a final glance at the window, she dragged her doll back toward the desk.

As her daughter sat down on the floor and began to play with her doll, Julia looked out the window at the growing crowd. Already the volume of the noise had increased, even four floors up. Trying to stay casual, Julia crossed to the worn couch and picked up her purse. Several minutes rooting around didn't conjure up the cell phone. She'd been in such a rush this morning, finishing breakfast with Amelia, seeing Allan off to work, she hadn't even grabbed the phone off the charger station. She clenched the purse to her chest, feeling her heart pound against it. Allan. The grocery store was right at ground level. What would this crowd do to her husband?

She bit her lip. She couldn't show her fear in front of Amelia. The child picked up on everything. Normal, Julia would have to act normal. Keep working.

She set the purse back down on the couch. Thank goodness she'd packed food for lunch and snacks. If she delayed long enough, maybe the crowds would disperse by nightfall. She didn't relish the idea of taking her daughter home in the dark but it couldn't be helped. She wouldn't chance the streets with a crowd like that.

Work progressed slowly as the day wore on. The noise outside the window ebbed and flowed. At lunch, Julia proposed a picnic in the living room with a fort made from an old sheet. Amelia giggled as they tried to stop the middle from collapsing. Any time it touched the top of her head she squealed with laughter. Julia tried to laugh along with her but over the sound of her daughter's delight, Julia heard the angry buzz of the crowd outside.

After lunch and the tearing down of the fort, Julia set Amelia down for her nap in the small bedroom off the living room. Tucking the old sheet up to the girl's chin, Julia leaned down and kissed her cheek. The child's eyes drooped even as she fought to stay awake.

"Sleep now, little one," Julia whispered. "Dream of better days. Dream of walking on the moon and among the stars."

When her daughter's breath slowed and deepened, Julia tiptoed out of the room, closing the door until she heard the click from the door jam. She crossed over to the window and looked out. If possible, the crowd was bigger.

Allan, she thought, the fear gnawing at her. If only she had a way of contacting him. The small computer she had here didn't have Internet access, even if it was available in this old building, which it wasn't. It wasn't available in most of the cities these days. The economic depression had stunted everything, even caused them to revert, and it wasn't just the dissolution of space exploration, it was everything.

People had lost the ability to dream or care about anything.

Keep working, she thought. Without a cell phone, she had no way to contact Allan and would only get more worried if she just stood here looking out the window. That wouldn't help Amelia when she woke up. Keep working.

She returned to her desk and sat down in front of the orbital charts and building schematics. Her hands rested on the papers without picking any of them up. She looked at the words and lines without reading them.

What was she doing? What had she been doing for years? What kind of life was this, poring over orbital charts and the fiftieth revision of some rocket schematic? Begging for pennies from people worse off than she? Struggling to follow the dream of a naïve child when she now had one of her own to think about? How fair was she being to Amelia?

Tears burned her eyes. Her fingers tightened on the flimsy pages, crunching them.

Pounding sounded on the door behind her.

Julia jumped up from the desk, clutching the papers to her chest. She ran to the door and looked through the peep hole.

Two men stood outside, dressed in worn pants and shirts. They pounded again, pushing and working at the door lock.

What could she do? Any minute now the pounding would wake Amelia.

"What do you want?" she said.

The pounding stopped. Through the peep hole, she could see the startled looks on the men's faces.

"Who're you?" the first one said. "No one lives here."

"I rent this place, it's mine," she said. "What do you want?"

"We need money for food," he said. "Can you give us some? Or something to sell?"

"I don't have anything, I'm sorry," she said.

He frowned. A moment later his head bent down, blocking her view. She heard more fiddling with the lock.

"Please," she said. "Leave us alone!"

He didn't hear or chose to ignore her. Julia ran back to the living room. The only food left were a few cookies for Amelia's treat after her nap. The only money she had was enough for transit home. There was nothing she could use to defend herself.

The door flew open behind her. She spun to face the two men as they entered. They walked in with heads bowed. An air of apology hung around them.

"I'm sorry, ma'm," the first one said. "Don't give us any trouble."

"Did you ever imagine you'd be doing this?" she said. "When you were little, did you ever picture this?"

He frowned. "No."

"What did you dream of?"

His frown deepened. "I don't know."

"Of course you know, you've just forgotten," she said. "It's such a mess now. We've forgotten about dreams. But you must have had one. What was it?"

His shoulders shifted. "Maybe I did. So what? Why?"

"I used to dream of walking on the moon," she said. Her hands pulled back from her chest, revealing the wrinkled pages. She put them on the desk and smoothed them out.

"I thought we would make it," she said. "We've got all we need to do it. I thought for sure I could walk on the moon. This is

42

the latest projections of the moon's orbit. That's where it'll be on my birthday."

She pointed. The men stepped forward and peered at the paper, at the lines and squiggles, the tiny mathematical notations and calculations. She pushed that paper aside and showed them the latest revision of the rocket.

"I'm trying to build a rocket to get there," she said. "They already did it once with less computer power and technology than we've got. We should be able to do it, right?"

"Who's doing your drawings?" the first man asked. "There are some errors here."

"Are you sure?" she said.

"I used to be an engineer, before I got laid off. Reggie was an electrician." The second man nodded.

"I could use you," Julia said. "You could help me build this rocket."

The men never knew what hit them as Julia started talking again. When Amelia woke from her nap twenty minutes later, she shared her cookies with Momma's new friends who were going to help build the rocket. By nightfall, the crowd thinned out enough for Julia to leave and the two men, Tom and Reggie, escorted her and Amelia home, Amelia draped over Tom's shoulder. With the transit not running, they walked the five miles home. At her doorstep, Julia pressed the money she'd been saving for transit into Tom's hand but not before extracting a promise from him to meet with her in two days to discuss the design of the rocket.

She waved goodbye to the men and picked up her sleepy daughter. Before entering the building, she looked up into the night sky. Tonight the moon was a slender sliver. God's fingernail, her mother used to say.

Today it had brought her another two allies to help her reach her dream and shored her up when she'd begun to doubt.

I'll see you someday, Julia thought.

She never doubted again.

She didn't doubt even when Allan returned later that night with a black eye and torn shirt, telling her how the store had been overrun in the riot then set ablaze. They lost their livelihood that night and moved out of Allan's apartment back into Julia's small flat. As Allan looked for work, any work, Julia took in neighbourhood children and started explaining computers, rockets, trajectories and the difficulties and necessity of getting to the moon.

They called her the Moon Lady.

Work on the project continued.

By the time Amelia was fifteen, the first spells began to affect Julia. Just a minor shortness of breath, she told everyone but Allan insisted she see a doctor. After saying they couldn't afford it, Allan spoke to Tom, who contacted a friend of his brother-in-law who worked in a doctor's office. They slipped Julia in on a cancelled appointment and the doctor waived her fee.

Weakening of the aortal walls causing a loss of blood pressure and less oxygen getting into her system was the diagnosis.

Julia would never walk on the moon.

But she didn't doubt.

Her project would reach the moon, even if she couldn't, she told Amelia as the girl cried over the news.

"Hush now," Julia said, kissing her daughter's tear-stained cheek. "You'll walk for me. Better get those science grades up."

By the time Amelia graduated university, Julia walked with a cane and could only stand for a few minutes at a time, but she stood and gave her daughter a standing ovation as Amelia claimed the dean's award for excellence in science.

Julia Threswald died three weeks later. She did not reach the moon in her lifetime.


"Stop shoving. You, Billy, in the back. Settle down." Mrs. Fisher gave the class her special glare. Even with the helmet, it worked. The children quieted down.

"Everyone have their helmets fastened? Good. We'll be stepping outside now. Make sure you hold onto the main line even with your waist line fastened to it. I don't want any wandering."

"Mrs. Fisher!" Stacey held up her arm, stretching the white space suit.

"What is it now, Stacey?"

"Why is it outside? Why didn't they put it inside with everything else?"

"We'll talk about that outside. Everyone ready? Let's go."

The inner airlock door sealed. Air hissed out, causing the children to chatter with excitement. Mrs. Fisher faced the outer door, stifling the smile on her face. No need for them to see her own excitement. Teachers were supposed to be calm and stable.

The outer door opened and she stepped out onto the moon's empty surface. Here at the far edge of the main station, the settlement maintained the area as close to a natural state as possible. In her helmet, she could hear the children talking all the way as she led them along the dark surface. Dust hung in the meagre atmosphere and small rocks bounded away as the children shuffled along.

After ten minutes, the squat rectangle came into view. Made of grey metallic material, it almost blended into the surface except for the words etched in white. As they drew closer, the children's chatter died off.

Mrs. Fisher reached the rectangle first. Using her gloved hand, she brushed the thin layer of dust from the clear surface of the window cut into the rectangle.

"Is it really her?" Billy spoke with a hushed voice.

"Yes, it is," Mrs. Fisher said. She straightened and faced the group of twenty children standing in a semi-circle around her.

"These are the ashes of Julia Threswald, the woman whose dreams brought us to the moon. Without her determination, we would never have made it this far. She died before she reached the moon but now she rests here forever. And I am proud to be her granddaughter. Yes, what is it now, Stacey?"

Mrs. Fisher watched as the little girl straightened her shoulders. Even with the hormone shots, Stacey still lagged behind the others in her growth.

"Mrs. Fisher, I...I..."

"Yes, Stacey?"

"I want to go to the stars," the girl blurted.

Around her, the children erupted in laughter. Mrs. Fisher watched Stacey's face redden inside her helmet, saw how her shoulders drooped.

"Stop it," Mrs. Fisher said. Her voice carried over the laughter. It stopped except for a few snickers. Another of her glares finished those.

With a sliding step, she moved to stand in front of the girl. She bent down to the girl's eye level, still the shortest in the class.

"Stacey," she said. "I know you'll go to the stars, or my name isn't Julia Threswald Fisher. And when you go, may I come along?"

The girl's slender shoulders straightened.

"Oh yes, Mrs. Fisher, I'd love for you to come along."

Mrs. Fisher smiled even as she felt tears prickling in her eyes.

"Then let's go, shall we?"

# TIDAL TANTRUMS

By C. A. Lang

"It's just that the moon was supposed to be white. The bottle is white, the perfume is white, and even this suit I'm wearing is white. Nobody told me the factories in Blightcross were going to turn the damned thing orange."

Zerj Faulon adjusted his cravat and glared at the water just below the yacht, where the moon shimmered on the waves. A roar swept across the ocean—another flying boat crawling towards the sky, drawing a line of black smoke across the horizon.

Kheman shrugged, made a face, and once again showed that being the boss' chum was the only way to get away with rolling one's eyes at him. "It's more red than orange. Anyway, enough with the perfectionism, friend. These actresses and politicians are already half-cut anyway! They're not going to care about your subtleties."

Perhaps. It should be enough to capitalize on the current astrology fad spreading among the élites. Couple that with the new interest in luxury goods filling the gap left by the death of magic and a catastrophic world war, and moving Faulon Syndic from a military-industrial giant into the shaky realm of cosmetics could very well work.

Kheman nudged him. "Relax. Security's in place."

C. A. Lang

Fuel refinery smog be damned—time to unveil the most sought-after luxury item ever dreamt. "Ladies and gentlemen," Zerj said. The murmur dwindled to clinking glasses and the hum of the yacht's engines. Even these people had to marvel at Zerj's brand new oil-powered ship—most of them had only been able to refit their old steam ships.

*Remember those diction lessons ... don't remind them of where you came from ...* "We read astrological reports to gain the upper hand on our emotions. And more importantly, to understand, and even influence, the emotions of others. What astral body is responsible for this?" A pause. "Yes, the moon. Now, with the aid of the most advanced magic and technical achievements in the cosmetics industry, I bring to you the most desirable fragrance ever created—one imbued with that very property of moonlight."

He paused for effect, and the ladies gasped as planned. Most of the men crossed their arms, or rolled their eyes.

"While I can't tell you exactly how I've done it, I can tell you that the moon's power over emotions is in this perfume. It will, in effect, enable the wearer profound control over a love interest's emotions." His heart skipped at the thought of his massive stockpile of the stuff. When the death of the last magic user spelled the death of magic for good, it would be completely unique.

*You're just a gambler, not a businessman. Ruled by whims and fancies ...*

He checked his crystal-accurate pocket watch, as much for the tide indicator as the time—in just seconds, the moonlight would hit a prism specially designed for this event. He grasped the perfume bottle.

"Ladies and gentlemen, I give you ..." Another look at the time. The faintest sparkle burst in the periphery of his vision. "... the only perfume infused with the spirit of the moon itself."

A bolt of orange light struck the pedestal at Zerj's hands. He lifted the lid. "I call it, Aurojére, the word used by—"

Silence. Slack jaws, wide eyes. He froze at the sight. A ray of moonlight whipped across the room.

Zerj glanced at the pedestal. Then he dropped the lid, where it clattered and rolled across the floor, the only sound in the room, besides a slight ticking noise. A ticking noise emanating from the bundle of wires and tubes sitting where the bottle ought to have been.

"Oh shit."

At that, the crowd erupted.

First instinct: grab and throw it. He stopped himself, hands hovering near the contraption. "Everyone remain calm."

Kheman elbowed through the crowd.

"Don't touch it," he said. "One of the mages says it's got a motion charm on it. Let's evacuate. We might lose this yacht, but—"

"Look at the clock. It would take too long to get everyone into lifeboats." Zerj glanced out the starboard window. "That munitions shipment we filled for that dictator here is within blast distance."

"Zerj, we're—"

Zerj ripped away the cravat's knot. "I need you to keep these people in order." He paused. "Your people saw nothing?"

Kheman shrugged. "Nothing. So—"

"So the thief is still aboard. Got it."

With that, he cantered out of the ballroom, Kheman at his heels.

"Where are you going?"

"There's no way the person who did this could swim back to shore. They have to still be here."

"Are you crazy? They could be long gone."

Zerj reached into his coat and found the pearl handle of his hand-cannon. He skipped three stairs in each bound towards the upper deck.

"I'm going after this person. Go make sure the outside walkways are all covered. If this ship must explode, I want that thief and all this perfume to go with it."

"Zerj?"

"Do it!"

"Right away."

Zerj bolted through the halls. Gripped the hand-cannon tighter. He skidded to a stop at the ship's bridge. He could get the captain to warn the harbour, at least. Just as he raised his fist to the glass, he recoiled at the sight of crewmen lying in puddles of blood.

Shit.

So now what?

Signal them himself? As if he could remember how.

"Mr. Faulon, Sir?"

A ghost-faced young man sprinted to him.

"It's the ship, it's been sabotaged. I tried ... I tried everything. It's heading towards the harbour."

"The controls aren't working?"

"No!"

"Did you try the wireless?"

"I'm no wireless operator, Sir. I just—"

"It's worth a try. Go on, then, hurry."

He could have figured out how to work the wireless. It wasn't physics or even knot-tying. But there was a boil in his gut that said *find that bastard and cut out his tongue. After he disarms the bomb, of course.*

A metallic bang sounded from the deck above. Kheman's security people? A quick look into the water—not even a fishing boat in sight.

How did this thief mean to escape?

Zerj rounded the bow, hesitated.

He caught a flash of movement—a figure gripped the railing. A cloak whipped in the breeze. The ship pitched and tossed Zerj against the gunwale.

"Stop." He lowered his hand-cannon.

The intruder faced him. One of the ship's lanterns swivelled, flashed across the intruder's face—a white mask, pure as bones bleached in the desert sun.

"Who sent you?"

The intruder remained silent.

Zerj swallowed hard. "Kheman? I found the thief!"

Silence. The intruder unsheathed a sword, whose blade burst into flame upon touching the air. Zerj fired. The intruder flew back, slammed against the railing. Zerj stowed the weapon and hurried to the body, nostrils burning from the hand-cannon smoke.

At least it had looked like a corpse—it jumped to its feet and threw Zerj to the deck. The two grappled, but Zerj's hands slipped. Frictionless armour?

"At least tell me which one of those bastards thought he was good enough to steal my god-damned perfume!"

But instead of slicing him, the intruder tossed him to the deck, hopped onto the railing, faced the ocean below.

*Big mistake, friend.* Zerj flashed a sardonic grin. "Give back the perfume, and disarm the bomb, and maybe we can work something out."

The intruder glanced back at him.

"Where are you going to go? There's no boat within leagues of this yacht, besides my own arms freighter over there. You can't swim to shore. Not with these currents!" He came closer. Soon he approached striking distance, but the intruder remained calm. "I'm a fair man, whatever your employer has told you."

The intruder stood. Balanced on the railing with the steadiness of a sparrow. And with a deliberation that mocked Zerj, buttoned a satchel at his hip.

"Don't!"

The intruder leaped from the railing. Without hesitation, Zerj tossed his coat to the deck and jumped. He sailed towards the water, directly behind his target. The only hope lingering behind the heart-thudding and buzzing limbs was one thought: unless this person was insane, they had to have some kind of way out of the water.

He braced for the inevitable splash, but a single breath before the two hit, the water became a flash of blue, then ...

...hard ground. Heavy air—not like factory smoke, but weighed by humidity. Neither of these things Zerj had anticipated when he'd taken that dive from the yacht, yet here he was.

He leaned against a boulder. That damned headache, like he'd drank too much ... the blur, the way the light stabbed his eyes. Only now did he see that the boulder wasn't a rock, but part of a statue the size of his company building.

Light?

Zerj bolted to his feet. The ship must have already blown—

"I wouldn't think of running if I were you." The source of the muffled voice emerged from the surrounding bush. The strange garment it wore—a thin film of diamond-textured fabric—gave this person, this *woman*, the same glimmer as the statues.

Yet she still wore the mask. Where the eyes ought to have been—only an amber burning.

"How long—"

"About two minutes ago." There was a strange depth to her voice, as if it were both inside his head and in the air at once.

"What? But it's daytime."

"Not there." She chuckled. "They told me you were well-educated. I'm beginning to wonder."

She sashayed past a statue—one depicting a lithe female, masked, and with the same cords of hair.

Two minutes ago. That meant there was still time ... if he knew where he was, and could muster a speck of magical know-how. Nobody did anymore, because engines and gunpowder were more profitable, more socially acceptable. And more predictable.

So he reined in the desire to bring out his hand-cannon. For now.

"But how did you know I—"

"Move. The boss didn't expect that I'd bring you back with me. I can't wait to see the joy on their faces when I bring both the perfume and the head of Faulon Syndic."

"Like I said before, I can offer you more than anyone could be paying you right now."

The woman brandished the flame-sword, her footsteps strangely quiet. It could have been a hallucination, for all the noise she didn't make. Maybe she was?

What if the perfume had malfunctioned, what if they'd made a mistake in producing it, and instead of being ravished by feminine magic, he was imagining a female captor who would slice him into pieces?

She led him to a rocky beach. Fog clouded all but the shore.

Before he could ask whether or not she meant him to grow gills and continue into the water, the sound of oars broke the silence. Soon a rowboat pierced the mist. Once it stopped, a woman in knee-length boots hopped into the water and strode towards them.

"Really, I don't have time to wait for your employer's dramatic entry." Behind the sarcasm was the thought of whether or not his yacht had exploded—

"Quiet. Your desperation is obvious. You're not as good as you think at hiding your restless mind."

The woman glared, and a nervous heat crawled up his neck. Cold was not the right word for this person. Precise, active, fiery, logical.

"Mr. Faulon! This is a surprise!" said the other woman. "Leen, you can relax now."

"So that thing does have a name. Do I know you?"

"Know me? Don't insult me even more, you lousy bastard."

He threw his arms in desperation. The woman circled him.

"Parnella Fionketta Vijn Tradellia. Does this name mean nothing to you?"

He shrugged. The woman looked vaguely familiar ...

"Nothing?"

He needed more specifics. Someone from the office. Olive skin, eyes strangely set wide apart, broad forehead. Nice earrings, tailored skirt and jacket. Hair pinned back, glasses. This woman could have been any number of hangers-on linked to the boring high-society crowd in which he found himself.

"Sorry."

"*Duchess* Parnella Fionketta Vijn Tradellia? Does that help?" Ms. Tradellia ceased her pacing and closed in on him. Her breath fluttered against his neck.

He kept still. Something squirmed in his chest.

"A sparkle of recognition. Is it your guilty conscience or your overindulgence clouding your mind?" With a flourish she swept the glasses from her face, then unpinned her hair. Brown locks gushed over her shoulders. A glow in her cheeks, a pained, yet somehow pleased curve at her lips ...

"Shit ... Ella ... Parnella. Of course."

"A sudden change of heart, huh? You're good at those."

"Look, Parnella. This isn't fair. You knew what you were getting into. Nobody who has ever heard of me would think that day could have been taken seriously—"

Parnella bit her lip. Oh, that same look ... "To think I left my private room at the horse races because I saw you mingling with the workers in the pit, obviously alone. At times I want to regret it."

He smirked. "But you don't."

She slapped him. "And you left the workers you so sympathize with in a heartbeat once I invited you to my room, isn't that so?"

"I don't know what you're getting at, but you approached me. All I recall is that you were working with one of my project managers. They all called you 'Ella' for short and as much as you hated it, I figured you were used to it and that's what I assumed you were used to being called. So before you try to pull this bratty nonsense about me being a womanizer, consider that you didn't seem concerned about whether or not I knew your full title or significance in a society that bores me, and the only name you felt like repeating that night sure wasn't your own—"

Slap.

She turned to Leen. "The perfume?"

Leen tossed the bottle to Parnella. She lunged to catch it, and nearly tripped on the rocks.

Parnella clutched it to her chest and said, "Do you have any idea what this is worth, you stupid demon?"

"All the more reason for you to catch it," Leen said.

They discussed compensation, which didn't particularly interest Zerj. Instead, he found himself ferreting through his memory for anyone who might have provided "services" to his company, was mentally unstable, and had the resources to pull off this kind of stunt.

"Now, enough of that. Let's refresh your memory. You contracted out the development of this perfume."

"Agreed."

"To whom?"

"A firm that specializes in blending magic and science. Looking back, yes, it was your firm. But after the initial meetings, I left it with the project manager and moved on. After that, I was more concerned with—"

"Drinking and trying to evade your guilty conscience with some whore from the gutter?"

"Probably. Why?"

Parnella circled behind him, and clapped her hands onto his chest. "I sent you flowers once, you know."

"Maybe I didn't get them."

She whispered, "I know you got them. You just didn't care."

Zerj shrugged.

"Let's say your project manager, terrified that your brilliant idea to delve into the cosmetics industry was going to fail and that he would be on the receiving end of your wrath, did exactly what you told him to: find a source of the moon's power at any cost, and make my firm, which is basically just me, distort it into a consumer product."

"Okay. Now we can talk. Listen, I—"

"Do you know the only way to actually do that?"

"No."

Parnella eased in front of him. "You need to slaughter elves."

"What?"

"I said, 'You need to slaughter elves.' Then you distill their blood with my patented process, and extract the moon's essence. Beautiful, lean creatures they are ..."

Bile rose in his throat.

"Good. You're squirming. And of course they don't take kindly to being bled out of their alleged immortality and left back in their fairyland powerless. Before I was able to enlist Leen here, they destroyed my family's estate. Including its inhabitants. Don't you recall?"

"I don't pay attention to news that isn't political or business-related."

"Of course you don't. Those moon elves are deadly things, Zerj. That's why the only way I could capture them was to enlist the help of this sun demon, you see. Honourable, proud, straightforward sun demons."

She turned her back to him and stepped towards the shore.

Zerj smirked. "I find it hard to believe you'd go to such lengths for a lucrative contract. It's not like you need the money."

"Does a privileged brat learn how to do the impossible? Does a privileged brat fashion a mask from the bones of those bloody moon elves in order to give a sun demon the power to transport themselves from this realm to wherever moonlight falls?" Parnella's voice faltered. "Does a privileged brat not still fall in love with ..."

Zerj's throat tightened. He'd heard that kind of crack in a woman's voice before.

"... with trash like you?"

He stepped towards her. "Listen, Duchess ... I'm sure you're smart. I'm a very busy man, you see. Love isn't exactly something I—"

Parnella's leather gloves squeaked with the clenching of her fists. "Are you that self-absorbed?"

He kept the answer to himself. But that didn't stop her from rushing to him and kicking him in the crotch.

First he reeled, then wondered that it actually didn't hurt as much as it should have. But a handful of heartbeats later, he crumpled to the ground, a sickness climbing his abdomen. He gasped and clawed the rocks.

"It's only fitting that you're the first victim of my handiwork."

In a haze of pain and groaning, Zerj heard the hiss of a perfume spritz. Between breaths, he said, "Oranges, violet, and black pepper ..."

Parnella chuckled. "Those are just the opening notes, dear. The enchanted accord will hit you in a moment." She paced. "And it only works if the wearer truly is attracted to the target. It pains me that for you to learn your lesson, I have to actually continue admiring you!"

A cough. "We don't always control these things ..."

"I did it all because I thought it would win you over! How stupid was I?"

A boot to the face.

"This is what he deserves. He's earned it. All that hard work ... all that hard work inheriting an empire, anyway."

Another boot.

He spat a string of blood and stood. Only now when he looked at Parnella, gone was the shrill harpy in designer clothes. Instead, the bitch who had kicked him was something divine; a bucket of sunshine sparkling in some light issued from far beyond this foggy dimension, with ringlets swaying like fields of rye in the spring breeze, curves greater than the most celebrated goddess statue of antiquity, eyes like royal jewels or oceans or the sky—

Zerj shook his head, turned away from the woman. He reeled from a faltering, a weakness in his chest.

"Of course I'll never be yours, Mr. Faulon. Not now. But you can suffer like I did. Oh, how poetic that you landed here, how perfect."

Those damned scents, clouding his brain like she had injected herself into him, replaced his blood with liquid images, sensations, memories of things that never happened, but oh how great it would be if they had—

"This is why your people will fall one day," Leen said. "The way you use what little magic is left. It's like a toy to you."

"Quiet."

"Then perhaps you should compensate me so that I may leave you to your childish torture."

Something wasn't right, but what? There was the perfume, yes, and this strange place far away from his yacht, then what?

*This is why it's going to sell, you idiot. Think past the fog.*

"I'm getting tired of your pedantry, Leen. I don't know what your people are, or what you do in this realm of moon people and sun demons, but you've outlived your usefulness."

It seemed so wrong—that this perfect woman would threaten anyone. But that's what she was doing. If that's what she wanted, though, who was he to argue?

*Think, idiot.*

Once more, he went with a general mistrust of his upbringing. He jumped in front of Leen, tackled her. There was a boom. Another. Pain bloomed in his shoulder.

Zerj groaned and rolled. Then came the sounds of a scuffle, a short scream, and the sound of bone cracking. Then the eerie sigh of Leen's sword and searing flesh.

"Are you okay?"

Zerj rubbed his eyes. Leen was there, hand outstretched. He paused when he saw the mutilated body staining the rocks.

"I might be, if I can get this wound to stop. I'm a bit of a bleeder, Madam." Then it hit him that this was the thief who had started the whole thing. He went for his hand-cannon. "Sorry, but I tend to hold grudges. Care to explain this?"

"You saved my life. So I owed you the same."

"And my yacht? My employees, all those innocent lives?"

Leen removed the mask. Brown skin, dark eyes, and cheekbones quite like the gigantic statues. But she lacked the pointed ears and long face. "The moon is still out in that part of the world, yes?"

He lowered the weapon, if only slightly. "Is that some kind of cryptic offer?"

Leen sheathed the sword. She then sat cross-legged, back perfectly straight.

"So you go where the moon goes? You can just flick back and forth like that? Genius ... night raids, good tactics. No wonder you've become a hot commodity in these times."

"I'm trying to concentrate, Sir."

He pressed on his wound. "Sorry." Blood now seeped from the fabric of his waistcoat and stained his hand.

And to believe that Leen had nearly killed him, and had killed his crew, all because that stupid woman had told her to, and now she seemed like some eternal feminine goodness.

"Listen, maybe it's just the perfume, but—"

"Shh."

He would have apologized, had the same blue flash not stunned him again.


"Zerj?"

Zerj turned onto his side and vomited.

"We caught the intruder!"

Kheman helped him upright. All round stood the respectable, the rich, the powerful. Most of them were either pale or green. Hairstyles had fallen. Buttons were undone, comportment disintegrated in the face of that ticking menace at the front of the ballroom.

"It's okay," Zerj said. He stood. "Let her go."

"Are you mad?"

Leen surveyed the crowd. "Shall I just kill them all instead of waiting for you to explain?"

Zerj quickly explained the situation. The men released Leen.

"You do know how to disarm the bomb, right?"

Leen approached the pedestal. "There's no time."

The murmurs dropped into a silence, until it rose to a roar. People trampled, rushed around like animals.

Zerj dashed through the throng to join her. "What do you mean there's no time? Just turn it off!"

"I ... I can't." She removed the mask.

"Nonsense. I'll help. What do you need me to do?"

"You're a good man, Mr. Faulon. If the gods ever return, I know they'll be on your side." She met his eyes for several breaths—it must have been enhanced by the perfume's effects, the way it seemed to shore up heavy bulwarks against the precious seconds bleeding into nothing. She then took his head in her hands, kissed him, donned the mask once more and threw herself onto the pedestal.

The flash was so brilliant that it knocked him back, however much he wanted to dive after her again.

When the flash burned away and returned the ballroom to the clutches of moonlight, both the bomb and Leen were gone. He could do nothing more than sit on his knees and stare.

Kheman joined him, rested a hand on his shoulder. "I don't know how you did it this time."

Zerj made no answer.

"Well, I can't wait to hear how you're going to explain this one."

"Kheman, all I know is that this stupid perfume of ours works like a charm."

# WITH THE SUN AND THE MOON IN HIS EYES

By A. Merc Rustad

The sky has not always been dark.

"My lord," I greet Moon in his cell. A simple room: obsidian blocks set with a thousand mirrors. There are no doors. "How do you fare?"

Moon sits in the center of the floor, hands relaxed upon knees, face serene and eyes closed. He will not look at the mirrors. "Better than you shall."

I kneel beside him and trace the line of his smooth, silver jaw. I remember his lips, cool and soft, a caress in the never-darkness. "More empty threats, my lord? Surely, if your lover were to come to your aid, he would have done so." I smile, but Moon does not see. I grip his chin until dark bands spread across his flesh.

He shrugs aside the bruises. "Your time is not ours."

I release his jaw. One day, I will force him to look on me and remember. But not yet. (My weakness will show, not his.) "Sun will not come for you," I tell my once-lover. "He is vain and stands alone in the sky now."

Moon touches a finger against the darkened imprints of my hand upon his chin. His eyes remain closed. "You know nothing," Moon says, lip curled. I used to love that contempt, the hauteur, the pain-laced affection.

I laugh, furious. "Alas, my lord, I know everything."

I step through the mirrors and leave him alone.

The sky once contained three sources of light. Few live who remember that now.

"Sire," says my architect, a slim, dark-eyed man. Gray shivers in his hair and beard, wrinkles sketch his weathered skin. "The workers grow anxious. Crops are failing, and our livestock is withering. How soon before we have light again?"

He was beautiful, once, and still I find him so, a thousand years later. But even I cannot forestall the end.

I look away from his patient gaze. "Soon," I promise. "Soon."

His hands clench at his sides, knuckles paled with strain, but he bows and does not protest. His time is not mine.

Three beings once lived in the sky: brothers, lovers, friends. "We will always be together," they said to each other. "Nothing will come between us."

Sun paces his cell, each step and each turn sharp, taut. The walls are bleached, two mirrors parallel on floor and ceiling, and there are no doors. (My architect built each cell around its occupant.)

He spins, golden radiance flaring mane-like around his face and shoulders. "Release me!"

I lean against the inside walls that burn under his stare. "You have answered none of my questions, my lord. Did I not tell you, your cooperation will result in your freedom from this cage?"

Sun cocks his head and pauses, a rare moment of stillness. "You would make demands? I can incinerate everything you hold dear with a thought!" He stalks across the floor and slams both palms against the wall on either side of my face. Heat curls against my jaw. "You do not know what suffering is."

I incline my chin. "Perhaps." I smile, slowly, and tilt my face up to his. White-hot light flares in his eyes. "But I still hold you here, do I not? Who now controls whom?"

He seizes my throat and slams my body against the floor. Heat sears my skin and knots in my belly. I have never flinched from his touch. I cough and lie still when he drives a knee into my ribs and sharpens each fingertip into razors. Pain means nothing any longer. Has he forgotten?

The first cut slices my shoulder from collarbone to elbow. Heat burns into bone. I arch my spine under his weight. "Stop," I cry, hollow protest.

(I will never tell him how much I missed this.)

"You will free me." Sun's words slide molten into my ear and he rips away the illusion of clothes. His reflection turns the white room into a furnace. His flesh burns against mine. "Or I will destroy you."

(You cannot destroy me twice, Lord Sun.)

I let him have his way. I let him think he has broken my will. I let him believe I am nothing but a mortal lord: he refuses to see who I am.

When he is finished, I call the pieces of myself together and slip through the mirror. Sun screams in rage as I leave him trapped once more. Alone.

When the architect constructed each cell, he asked me, "Shall I build them below the earth?"

"No," I said, and pointed to the tower. Cold stone stretched into the heavens, higher and higher until no eye could see its apex. "Construct two arms from the peak and build them there. In the sky they will never see."

Moon sits unmoving as ever when I step through the mirrors.

"My lord," I say with mock surprise. "I thought you would be freed by now, carried back to the sky in Sun's arms."

"What have you done with him, brother?" Moon asks.

My body tingles with shock. I press a palm against smooth glass so I do not stumble. He remembers? How long has he known?

"An answer for an answer," I tell him.

Moon's lips twitch, a cruel smile. "Beg me."

I backhand him across the cheek. "No."

He laughs, watery silver light bleeding from split skin. He licks away the trickle as it reaches his mouth. "Then you will get nothing."

"Oh, I will." I grip his jaw and wrench his neck back, his face tilted toward mine. He bruises so easily, but he never breaks. (Not as I did.) "Tell me why you betrayed me, or you will never see the sky again."

Moon leans into my hands. "You can beg me better than that, brother."

I twist his neck until bones splinter. He only smiles. Even in this constructed body, a prison itself, I cannot destroy him. Not the way I wish.

He must answer me. I must know why.

But I will never beg again.


I was the stars, once, when the sky was not so dark. I gave the heavens light, faint beside and between the Moon and the Sun.

I never kept them apart.


The architect limps into my chambers. I know his footsteps, though they are slower now, and tired. "Sire."

I turn away from the windows. The sky is still dark.

Blood crusts his beard and stains his wool shirt. I swallow a worried cry and glide to his side, cup his face, search for the wound. I am careful my touch will never harm him. The blood isn't his. I exhale, relieved, and search his eyes. He has never lied to me.

"Riots," he says. "The workers are storming the gates. They demand you bring back the light." Wine sours his breath. When has he ever drunk? "Open the cages, sire."

"I cannot. Not yet." I turn from him and look out, down into the darkness. Spread like wings on either side of my tower are the cells: impenetrable, unbreakable. All I must do is shatter the mirrors inside each, mirrors only I can reach.

And then my brothers would turn upon the world they exiled me into. Sun would scour the air with flame and Moon would untether the seas and drive them onto the land.

It took me these thousand years to build a tower that brushes the heavens, to let Moon and Sun forget I was once with them in their majesty, before I lured them into this world with rumor of a fallen star. I knew my former-lovers well. How could either resist finding a way to brighten the part-empty skies again? They were incomplete with only each other.

(I had been multitude, and they sundered me, and the loneliness swallowed everything. They left me alone.)

The architect touches my shoulder, his voice an aged husk. "The lower floors are barricaded. But most of the knights have turned against you, as well as the alchemists. The doors won't hold forever, sire."

Only he remains at my side.

One lamp glows in the chamber. It has no warmth, like the Sun, nor brilliance, like the Moon.

"How long has it been since I took Sun and Moon from the heavens?" I ask, weary. I feel the passage of days but do not count them any longer. In the dark skies, it is all the same.

"Three months, sire." A sigh rattles in his ribs. "When, if not now?"

"They will know who I am." And then they will take me back. They must. "Soon."

The architect's fingers loosen on my shoulder. I lay my hand over his and hold tight. "Speak your mind."

"I have asked for little in my... lifetime." His forehead rests against the base of my neck, between my shoulder blades. (He was the first to find me after I was cast down. He reminded me so keenly of Sun and Moon, but gentler. Mortal. I could not let him go.) His body trembles. "I am tired. Release me, sire."

I cannot answer.

Sun trails heat patterns along the walls of his cell. His fists leave blackened pocks on stone. "You lie."

"Do I, my lord?" I catch his wrist and a handful of molten hair. I pull him around, our faces a breath—an eternity—apart. "Who but I could keep you here? Who but I could drive you mad? You know who I am. Tell me why you did this." I tug him closer, forcing the words into his mouth with lip and tongue. "Tell me why you betrayed me."

"I will tell you nothing," Sun says, kissing me back. "It will not matter. We will not take you back to the skies." His nails impale my wrists above my head. "Not even if you beg us... brother."

He knows.

The world did not fear when the stars went out. Sun and Moon shone brighter, fiercer, and quelled the whispers upon the land: Why did the stars disappear?

The architect waits patiently in my chamber, silent. He sits against the wall, eyes closed, I still cannot answer him. The dark panic swallows me as it did when I fell.

I do not know my place. Scarcely any light lingers within me. I have been dying for a thousand years, and soon I will go dark unless I return to the skies. Unless Sun and Moon hold me again in the heavens, unless we are three, unless we are not alone.

I let the world run its course. This city, this tower, is all I have built and sustained. Kings have become dust; the world has been conquered, and fallen, and risen to be conquered again. Stars are but a myth on the tongues of mortals.

"I have never wished to say this, sire," the architect whispers. "But I must." His breath mists in the air. "I preserved hope—hope that you would convince them to return with you. That all would be the way it was in my youth."

He is the only one who remembers the stars.

I turn away, but he catches my arm.

"Just as the earth bled you near to death, the earth-born stone will deplete them. I monitor each cell, and I..." His voice crumbles. "Sire, they cannot return to the skies. None of you can reach your home again. Not after so long in this world."

"No," I say. He has never lied to me. "Impossible."

"Our world is ended." Salt crusts his cheeks. "I do not wish to see it. I have seen too much. I beg you, sire, let me go. I cannot bear this everlasting darkness, this cold."

I flee through the mirrors so I do not hear his pleas.


The Sun and the Moon bound the Stars without warning.

"Do not do this!" Stars begged, over and over. "Please, my brothers, do not destroy us!"

Unheeding, Sun and Moon cast the Stars down into the world.

Alone.


"My lord Stars," Moon greets me. "How do you fare?"

I crouch before him. He tilts his head and smiles. I grip his jaw, trembling. "I have killed the sun."

The moon does not believe me.

"And I have killed you," I whisper, furious. Undone. "We three will never touch the sky again."

Moon opens his eyes. The cell is like the heavens, when I still webbed the darkness with points of light. But he does not smile.

When I look at him, I can see truth: his skin is darker, weaker, the radiance in his eyes dimmer. Sun is the same, raging in his cell, growing colder.

In time—and it matters not if it is celestial or mortal—they will both fade, as have I. All the lights in the heavens will go out.

Regret supplants the terrible pain inside me, the bitter knowledge I will never be again with the Sun and the Moon.

I begin to shatter the mirrors, one by one.

"You were becoming too bright," Moon says at last. Glass shimmers, covering the obsidian in a patina of silver. "We feared you would eclipse us both."

I pause, a hand on the final mirror. Laughter seethes in my throat. "I would have snuffed out every part of myself if you asked."

"We knew." Moon cups shattered glass in his palms and lets it trickle through his fingers, glittering with his radiant light. "It was less painful to destroy you than if you had destroyed yourself."

Glass grinds into my feet. I cannot endure this knowledge now that it is mine. I yearn to forget, I who have always remembered. It will hurt less, in the end.

"You are free to go, my lord," I tell Moon. "Unleash Sun and find your way to the skies once more, if you can. Nothing will eclipse your light."

He reaches for me. "Wait, my love—"

I ignore his plea and step through the last mirror. I cannot bear to see the Moon again.


"Build one more thing for me," I ask of my architect.

He looks up from his blood-soaked sleeves.

I point above us. "A mirrored room atop our tower's peak." I shattered the mirrors in Sun's cell. In time, he will burn his way free of stone and find Moon.

The architect stares at me with hollow eyes. "For what purpose, sire? There are no heavenly bodies left."

"I still live," I cry. "Build me a room of mirrors, so what light I have left will reflect over all the land." I kneel before him and grasp his hands in mine. Blood warms my fingers.

He says nothing.

I cannot see him like this: in despair, in pain, as if he is alone.

Trembling, I press my face against his knees. (So be it, my love.) I pull back the traceries of starlight I sewed through his veins so he would live as long as I. "I release you, my friend. Do as you will with what time you have left."

Dying is only the loss of light.

The knife falls soundless to the floor from his grasp. He clasps his wrists, red and slick, and begins laughing. I look up. His forehead rests against mine and his body shakes uncontrollably.

I will not ask him to stay. I have kept him so I will not be alone. No longer will I slowly destroy him. "Please do this last thing for me," I beg.

"Yes," he says, "I will do this for you."

My architect begins to work.


When the mirrored room is finished, I kneel in the center, eyes closed, hands on knees.

Each mirror is angled towards the others and a ring of glass curves outward: it will reflect all the light out into the world. It is all I can give.

The architect clasps my shoulders. I lean my head back into his chest, listening as his heart slows.

And I release what light remains in the stars.

We are not alone.


The sky will always be dark.

For a brief time, the world will not.

# ON THE LABRADOR SHORE, SHE WAITS

By Krista D. Ball

*L'Anse Amour, Newfoundland and Labrador, is the site of North America's oldest burial site. I've always been fascinated by this twelve-year-old child buried face-down on the rocky shore of Labrador. Why was this child buried in that manner? What was the significance of his grave items? Who were these people who once walked those shores?*

**7500 years ago**
**Southern Labrador Shore**

Demaswet hunched her shoulders against the frigid air as she sat motionless upon her red, wooden perch. Her muscles ached from five days of sitting and sleeping upright, but she would not remove herself. She flicked a bitter glance at the full moon and heard Father's laugh.

*Stubborn pride brought this fate upon you, not I.*

The drums kept their steady rhythm. Two holy men, the sons of the tribe's wisewoman, Shanaitwasa, sang in their high, wavering pitch, singing away evil spirits and inviting the Father to bless their offering.

Demaswet watched the holy men symbolically sweep out the last of the evil. The torchlights inside the pit flickered and projected their shadows on the earth walls; the evil darkness could not be kept out of the ceremony. It insisted on remaining.

*That is because the evil is inside you.*

Guilt gnawed at her, yet she remained still. Nawdithi would soon be carried into the sacred space. The circle would be complete.

Soon, it would be over.

The holy men crawled from the pit, the torchlight dancing across their dirty, sweating faces. They remained bowed as they exited, giving honour to her. Heat rose in her cheeks, but the darkness concealed her blush of guilt. She did not want their honour.

The drumming stopped and Demaswet could hear the rhythmic crash of the ocean against the rocky shoreline further beyond. She closed her eyes and listened to its soothing song. She drew strength from the tide, even if Father controlled it.

But, the drums began again. A new song and her heart matched the frenzied beat. The song meant the time had arrived.

*You brought this punishment.*

Demaswet did not argue, though she shot the moon a contemptuous look. Her pride prevented the ice from forming. She was not so arrogant to believe she could directly influence the seasons. Rather, her pride offended Father so greatly that nothing short of this could atone for her error.

Bile rolled in her stomach and Demaswet was thankful for her voluntary fast. Four days without food would be four days extra to help fortify the others. It was the least she could do.

At the arrival of the last moon, Father should have brought the seals, as the last of their winter provisions waned. Yet, the seals and their pups did not come.

The oldest of the elder women sacrificed themselves, hoping that it would stretch the food supplies. But the ice remained treacherously thin. The hunters could not even cross the great expanse to the next land; the winds too cruel to allow boats and the ice too dangerous for crossing.

Infants and elders died, this time from starvation.

*You should have been humble.*

Father sent the dreams soon after. No ice, no seal, no breath soon to be drawn unless his people cleansed themselves. Without forgiveness, they would starve. The caribou were gone. The birds of summer would not return for several more moons. No whales washed upon the shores to feed them and fill their stone lamps.

The young men, still strong and full of life, sought out the hunting caches and returned with the smoked caribou, the dried cod, and the crushed, dried berries. It was not enough.

Demasweet watched as her people gathered the last of their meagre supplies and sat them near the pit. She longed to help, longed to be useful. However, her role was to watch and be honoured.

Honoured! When she was the one who brought this curse upon them! They, her own people!

The wind cut through Demaswet's sealskin clothes. Or, perhaps it was the chill of loss and regret that made the hairs on her arms press against the fur lining.

She had made the decision. In the wise woman's dreams, Father did not point to her. That would never be his way. How could a person learn if they did not make the choice themselves? No, he sent the others one dream and sent her another.

*I am not so cruel. I always provide a choice.*

A bitter laugh escaped Demaswet, though none could hear it over the drums and chants. Some choice. Allow Shanaitwasa to choose and sacrifice a child one by one or offer her own child, knowing Nawdithi's death was what Father demanded.

*You could have let them kill off the young, one by one. All of the boys, then all of the girls. Perhaps starvation would have taken Nawdithi instead of me.*

That was not a choice.

Demaswet knew her sacrifice would save them all. Children were in an endless supply, created by only a few tumbles of glory. Simply do not take the herbs and roots and spend time with a man of her choice and she could have as many children as she pleased. Her tribe, however, was not so easily replaced with a quick delight. If they all died, there would be no more children, there would be no more hope, there would be no more.

Just spirits drifting without anyone to guide or protect.

Father controlled the weather and the ebb and flow of the tides that crashed against their jagged shore. Father controlled the water. He could control the ice and bring the seals. He could save them.

Love was a luxury. Life was a necessity.

Two men and two women moved to create an entrance into the sacred circle, never losing the pitch of their song. Two drummers rose and stepped ahead, cutting into the circle. Her muscles tightened. This was it. She would say good-bye tonight to her favourite child.

*Lose him or lose your tribe. It was always your choice.*

Shanaitwasa walked purposefully into the sacred circle, slamming her staff into the ground with every step, singing her own chant. She turned her weathered, wrinkled face to Demaswet and bowed low.

Even though guilt and regret filled her, Demaswet returned the bow, her eyes closed against the tears that welled in her eyes.

Shanaitwasa walked a slow circle around the burial pit and Demaswet could hear the clang of shells as the wise woman walked past her. Shanaitwasa wore the blessed clothing, the sealskins softened by the teeth of a great wise woman now long passed into the next life. Caribou hide wrapped around the staff, bound by sinew. The teeth of a bear hung around her neck.

Demaswet shivered as Shanaitwasa lit the two wooden pillars inside the pit. Death crept in the shadows, as the singers cried out for compassion from Father.

Nawdithi's sacrifice would always be remembered. Her sacrifice would never be forgotten.

*Your people will live because of him.*

One of the holy men handed Shanaitwasa a perfect square of caribou hide. Demaswet's heart sunk. It was the burial items.

*There is more to life than your own feelings.*

A lesson she'd wished she could have learned at childhood. If only she could learn humility, but her parents, grandparents, and ancestors could not teach her that lesson. Only when faced with the starvation of her people could she finally accept that it had been her selfishness, her pride in having the most beloved son that offended Father so greatly.

The death of Nawdithi was the only way for them to live.

She turned and caught sight of Nawdithi. Crushing pain forced her to gasp for air. Tears stung her eyes, freezing her eyelashes in the cold bite of the wind. Four boys carried the still form of her son. He was a slight boy, only beginning his maturity. A man would have easily carried him, but these boys had escaped the sacrifice to Father. They would escort their friend to death.

Demaswet swallowed down envy for their mothers.

She shot a look of bitter frustration at the glowing moon in the sky.

*You should have punished me, not him.*

*You are being punished.*

The last of their provisions went to Father. Every scrap of dried meat from their smokehouse floor. Every dried berry from their storage pits, no matter how mouldy. Even the last of the whale oil that they'd been drinking instead of burning. All of it; dug up, gathered, and returned for Father. Enough food to feed them through one changing phase of the moon, mere days, and it would be offered in exchange for mercy. Perhaps their sacrifice to him would bring back his favour.

She was sacrificing her child; the tribe was sacrificing their lives. She felt the honour of their gifts to Father, gifts needed because of her failings.

More pyres sparked to life beyond the sacred circle. They would dance. They would chant. They would bury her son alive using the large mound of earth behind the drummers.

*And you will sit there and watch.*

Demaswet set her jaw. She would not let the others see her tears. She was in a place of honour. She would not let them see inside her. She would be strong and give as much honour to her position as her heart allowed.

73

Nawdithi was laid between the pillars of fire. His body was pliant. In the firelight, she could see his confused gaze. He did not understand what was happening to him. Perhaps the herbs made him already see the next world, the ancestors who would welcome him as an innocent calf, sacred and special.

"Demaswet, we honour your sacrifice to provide your son as an offering to the Moon Father, to bring us the ice so that the seals may come," Shanaitwasa said. She turned to Demaswet and inclined her head. "You shall have the honour of preparing your son."

Demaswet gulped, but nodded her acceptance. She pushed herself up from the wooden chair that had been made for her and pulled her fur-collared hood tighter around her face. The two holy men emerged once more from the darkness and slid into the pit. The boys carefully passed Nawdithi's limp body to the men. They placed him on the ground, on his stomach.

Demaswet stared and looked wildly at Shanaitwasa.

"No," she mouthed to the wise woman. Her heart pounded and tears splashed down her cheeks, the wind turning them cold in an instant.

Shanaitwasa continued her chant, not interrupting the cleansing prayers. She did, however, look at Demaswet with a nod and eyes filled with both hard resolve and compassion.

Demaswet wept, unable to hold back the tide. If he was buried face-down, his spirit would never be released. Instead, it would linger, trapped and starving in his burial home, unable to join his people, unable to stand and hunt and fill his hunger.

*Why? Was not my sacrifice enough without this?*

*No.*

Hands shaking, Demaswet held out her hands for the holy men to help her down. She rushed to Nawdithi's side, but took a long, deep breath before kneeling next to his limp form. Nawdithi's glossy eyes stared ahead. Hopefully, he did not realize what was happening.

Perhaps he might even forgive her one day.

*It is your fault. Your pride must be punished.*

Shanaitwasa chanted under her breath, the words barely audible over the howls of the wind, the crashing of ocean, and the songs purifying the sacred circle. She continued to circle the pit, keeping the evil away, calling on Father to bless them.

Both holy men held out hollowed soapstone, filled with red ochre. Demaswet slipped off her caribou mitt and dipped her fingers into the sacred paint. Fish sizzled and popped on top of the wood and rock pillars. Pungent juniper filled the air. Women whispered incantations. Men sang in a high, wavering pitch. Shanaitwasa banished evil spirits.

But it was Demaswet who prepared her son for death.

Tears welled in Demaswet's eyes, but she fought them down with the understanding that she was doing the right thing. Nawdithi was too loved, too well liked. She had let her pride swell and, for that, her people suffered. Nawdithi fell to fever twice over winter and, yet, she nursed him back to life, taking more than their share of food and herbs to heal him. She cried to the spirits, the ancestors, the rocks and trees and anyone who would listen. She would not let him go, even as three others died to the fever. She did not care about them; she cared about Nawdithi.

She would not let him go.

Only now, she would let him go, to languish in the next life unable to hunt or pray or help.

Demaswet rolled her beloved son over on his back to cover his simple clothing and exposed skin, painting him for the ritual to return life through the sacrifice of his. He grunted and moaned a few times, but she shushed him to silence. She was to remain silent and not speak to him, for his spirit was already preparing to depart. The sounds above would drown out her words if she uttered them, but Father would hear and only punish her further.

*Yes, I will.*

After she covered his clothing and face, she stepped back. The men carefully rolled Nawdithi to his front. He struggled now, his face pushed into the ground. Once again, she stroked him with the red ochre and shushed him to compliance. He turned his head and rested it on its side. She covered him, her heart pounding and tears falling freely now.

*Can I at least say good-bye to him? I have done as you asked.*

*I am not without mercy. You may say good-bye.*

Exhausted and drained of any reason to keep drawing breath, Demaswet did not argue. She whispered her thanks. She kissed the red-painted face of her son, the paint brushing on her lips. Nawdithi focused his eyes and they filled with fear and betrayal, before his glance drifted off once more.

Demaswet's breath hitched in her throat. It would not be enough to give up her son. No, she would endure an eternity without him or his forgiveness. He understood her punishment. He understood she had a choice.

*Was it not enough to kill him?*

*No, you needed to suffer to learn. Never again will you make this mistake.*

Demaswet stood and squared her shoulders. She would be strong. She was only one person. Her pain was nothing compared to the pain of her people. There was no rush, and so she lingered at her beloved son's side. Then, Shanaitwasa completed her prayers and entered the pit. She inclined her head to Demaswet.

Demaswet was lifted from the pit and returned to her seat of honour. The chants, prayers, and songs grew louder. The holy men placed a large rock on Nawdithi's back, pinning him to the ground. He let out a cry of pain and fresh tears dripped from Demaswet's eyes.

Shanaitwasa grew a circle of red ochre around Nawdithi, his arms waving and legs flaying. The efforts were fruitless; the stone weighed nearly as much as him. Yet, he struggled. A hunter's spirit lived inside her son.

She forced herself to watch. This was the price of pride, to watch the destruction of a prized possession.

The firelight danced in Nawdithi's eyes and Demaswet could see the fear and comprehension in his expression. The herbs and mushrooms did not do enough to cloud his thinking. He knew he was about to die. He knew it was his mother that caused his death.

His eyes said he knew his mother would not save him. Demaswet stared into her son's eyes, tears falling down her cheeks. She betrayed her beloved son.

"We honour your sacrifice, Nawdithi. In your death, we hope to live. We will forever honour you. We pray to the Father to bring us the ice once more. Without the hunt, we cannot live. We have offended the Great Spirits and now we must sacrifice."

Around Nawdithi's kicking body, they placed the sacred hunting tools. A seal harpoon, with its notched head attached to caribou sinew. The knife her brother made for Nawdithi's first hunting. The bird bone flute that his father made.

Then, Shanaitwasa pulled the bone pendant from around her neck and placed it on the stone on his back. "This has touched my heart since I was a child. Now, it will touch yours for eternity. Never forget us, as we will never forget you."

And with that, several men stepped past the drummers and into the sacred space. They began to return the earth and stones to their rightful resting ground, on top of her son.

Nawdithi's wide eyes frantically searched his surroundings, but the herbs had clouded his mind so much that he could not cry out. The pyres continued to burn, the fish continued to bake. Food and tools to tempt his spirit, since it would be bound under the rock, never to be let free.

As the dirt covered Nawdithi's face, so too did it bury her. She murdered her beloved child because she failed. It did not matter who lived now, since she would soon follow her son into the next life.

## Present Day

Endless, unyielding time passed. Demaswet paced around the rock cairn that held her son, as she had done for countless ages. If he could not hunt nor eat, neither would she. She stood guard against time, pacing and wailing and waiting for the day her son would finally join her and the ancestors.

It was her fault. All of it, square on her shoulders. Time taught her that. She had been such a young mother, so very young. She did not understand how to apologize to Father for a failing in her own character. She had wanted to celebrate life and was too inexperienced to understand how to temper her own pride with selflessness.

If only she had learned that lesson sooner. Father might not have taken Nawdithi. She would not have taken her life to tend him in the next.

Though, Father's opinion seemed to no longer matter. He did not speak to her, no longer taunting her. He'd forgotten about her, leaving her and Nawdithi to linger for eternity. Now, she could only exist for her son.

She put aside her fear and regret and instead drew hope from the strangers around her, apprehension and excitement waging war within Demaswet's soul.

The strangers dug their perfectly square pits on their hands and knees. They used their tiny picks and shovels, and brushed aside the centuries of dirt and rock with hand-held brooms.

Would these strangers release Nawdithi or would they doom his spirit to oblivion?

They dug into the earth.

They dug into her Nawdithi.

They dug and dug and dug. They found the rock on Nawdithi's back. They held up black boxes and flashed lights at him.

Demaswet held a hand to her neck, anticipation rising.

The strangers lifted the rock and gasps filled the air. They cheered, and smiled, and laughed. Demaswet just stared and waited.

Her beloved child stepped from the bones. He climbed from his home for too long, his eyes squinting against the bright summer sun. A light breeze tousled his black hair. Then, he turned to her. Recognition dawned on his face.

And then, he smiled, wide and bright and the barriers around her heart collapsed. Her son! Her son!

"Mother!"

As her son wrapped his arms around her, forgiveness flowed from him to her. He understood. His embrace said what words could never define.

He understood.
He forgave.
He loved.

She laughed, a joyous, sobbing bark of laughter. And her heart swelled with maternal pride.

# THE WHITE MOON

By Theresa Crater

An impish breeze slipped into the garden, ruffled the leaves of the gardenia bushes, then rode the coattails of a certain gentleman who was making his entrance into the glass atrium of the hotel. The slip of wind sighed around a planter and wafted into the conference lobby—unnoticed.

"Welcome to the Hotel Imix," the front staff said, pronouncing the 'x' like an 's'. "It means 'light' in the language of the Maya." He seemed used to explaining this.

The man nodded, not really listening.

The breeze left this gentleman at the front desk and floated down the hall. It shook out the silk of scarves and rattled the necklaces hanging in one of the booths at the Lion-Hearted Women conference. Jacqueline paused and sniffed the air. Jasmine? Cinnamon? Imagined an island lying low in the sea under a moon swelling to full in a Maxfield Parish blue sky.

The breeze flowed back and rolled over the rumps lined outside Starbucks. The people shifted and murmured to themselves, thinking of liaisons or the comforts of rain. For it was raining in Los Angeles, and they'd had thunderstorms followed by brilliant rainbows, none of which had slowed the planes across the street at LAX.

The puff of wind blew down another foyer. It passed Don Carlos, who followed it with his eyes beneath his sculpted Mayan nose, then looked back and turned the page of his newspaper with a rustle. The faint scent of charred wood wafted up for a moment.

The breeze drifted down to the last lobby and wound a figure eight around the ankles of the channeler, who heard a tune he hadn't imagined before, smiled and pushed the button of the freight elevators, avoiding the crowds for now.

The wind squeezed under the door of the storage room and riffled the lids of boxes until it found the right one, where it settled in to wait.

People sat on the floor outside the 11:11:11 Crystal Skull conference, hoping for tickets for the evening's special event— the revelation of the mystery skull. The conference goers ate their meals and dressed for the evening, dabbing rose oil over their wrists or putting diamonds in their ears—or quartz crystals. They all yearned for that intangible something they couldn't put a name to, but knew existed. Somewhere. Perhaps in the words of a speaker. In the eyes of a crystal skull. In that perfect dress draped by the perfect scarf with the exact waft of perfume.

The full moon crowned in the east, just as the sun slipped into the vast Pacific, then pushed up from the folds of the horizon and peeked down onto the city of angels.

No one thought of the moon. Only Don Carlos.

And maybe some of the skulls sitting on their keepers' tables, murmuring amongst themselves, dreaming of their old temples. Remembering how they sat atop a particular pyramid, surrounded by bronzed worshipers. Before they were buried, then uncovered again. When they sat in auction houses. Were bid over by mushroom-pale collectors.

At dinner, Mason and Gail sat in a corner by themselves puzzling over the menu. "There's a Chinese restaurant a few blocks away," she said. "And Thai."

"How do you know?"

"Got a map from the concierge." She ran her eyes down the menu again. "Probably half the price."

"But I have to do a sound check. Be sure my power point will work. We don't have time."

"Maybe an appetizer," she said. They ordered and sat in companionable silence, the silence of twenty years.

His cuffs were frayed, his shirt had a spot on it—already and he hadn't eaten yet. His gaze looked everywhere but at her, skimming the conference attendees, who glanced at him over their shoulders. Put their heads together and whispered. Gail wondered if they had anything else to offer each other. Maybe she should slip out of his talk and go to the Lion-Hearted Women presentation tonight.

'Man as Hunter', the flyer read. 'Honour your mate's need to seek out and conquer'.

Not appealing. Whatever happened to the feminist days? Well, she knew the answer to that. The last decade had been hard on all such ideas.

When they'd first made love, Mason had knelt down and said he would worship the goddess in her. An Arabian moon hung in a cerulean blue sky, Venus just above the tip of the crescent. He told her about the Hoopoe birds in Egypt, where he went every year. How the Queen of Sheba had sent that bird, with its black and white stripped wings, red crest, and long, arching beak—like the moon, he'd said, pointing out the window—to tell Solomon when he could come to her.

"I'll make love to you like Solomon to the Queen." And he had.

The waitress delivered fried eggplants and tuna with artichoke hearts. They ate, occasionally tasting each other's dish. But not like they had. Not in that flirty way where they'd fed each other from their forks, mouths opened in anticipation. They skipped dessert and finished quickly. The waitress brought the check.

He pushed his chair back. "Got to go," he said. "Bring those extra skulls down. You were right. I think we'll sell them all." A concession.

She smiled to acknowledge it. "OK."

The moon pushed up higher from the horizon, her whole body clearing Mother Earth. She hung, huge and orange, in the eastern sky. The drivers on freeways gave her a second look.

Gail wandered up to the room, turned on a movie channel and reclined on the bed. Soon she'd refresh her lipstick, comb her hair, choose a different Egyptian scarf and go down. But not just yet. She flipped the channels, looking for something. Something else.

Downstairs Jacqueline tweaked a blouse in her display, spread the folds of a skirt, then stood back and cocked her head. *Yes, perfect.*

She picked up a terra-cotta pot, its cinched waste circled by a turquoise squash blossom, and stood holding the empty vessel at her hip, remembering him.

They'd both worked for IBM back in the day, she writing code, Sam climbing past the glass ceiling. They'd been young enough to hang out in clusters of friends like grapes. He'd asked her up to his apartment once. Served mushrooms in a cream sauce.

A waxing gibbous moon hung in the dark sky. He told her his career was more important than any relationship. He was putting all that off until he was head of something. A vice president.

She'd left town six months later. Heard he married a woman with two kids. Had a golden retriever. Maybe a picket fence.

"Do you have these in purple?" a woman interrupted Jacqueline's reverie. The customer wore a white evening gown, the skirt flowing around her bare feet, the bodice sequined. Amethyst earrings hung from her ears and her lids were the colour of lilac.

"We might have one more left," Jacqueline said. She put down the jug and bent below the table, rummaging in boxes.

"This conference—" the woman said, "—it's changed my life. I believe in my dreams again. I've found my lion heart."

Jacqueline emerged clutching two scarves, one the colour of violets nodding in the shade, the other deep and dark as an eggplant.

"Oooh." She snatched the violet one and wrapped it around her shoulders. "Perfect."

It did look good. Jacqueline handed the woman her receipt and thought about closing up, going to the other conference to hear him.

A channeler? How had that happened? She wouldn't mind hearing the story.

A breeze billowed the skirts. Jacqueline pulled a cloth from beneath the table and covered her wares, turned her sign over, put her money in her purse.

"To start off the evening program, our Mayan Daykeeper will explain today's date, 11:11:11. Plus, I hear he has special news."

Don Carlos walked to the microphone. "I know that many have written about 11:11:11 as a cosmic portal. The energy of Hunab Ku flows from Galactic Center to us. But this is also an important day to the Maya," Don Carlos announced to the several hundred attendees just now taking their seats, shushing those still bargaining for crystals at the nearby tables. "In the Tzolk'in calendar, there are thirteen tones and twenty day glyphs. The combination gives the day its specific character. Today is One Ix."

Silence finally fell over the audience, but he heard something being dragged across the stage behind the curtain. It billowed out.

"The number one begins a new cycle and represents the One Consciousness." His voice was dry and raspy. Several people reached for their water bottles. "This is also what the skulls represent. Ix is the Jaguar. This is the Shaman, the protector of the Temple. Magic."

There was a smattering of applause. One woman thought she smelled smoke, looked around to see if someone was burning incense or copal.

"But there is more. Tonight is the full moon. And when this full moon corresponds with One Ix, we call it the White Moon. It is the moon of Ixchel, our goddess of fertility. Ixchel mated with the Sun and had four sons in the form of jaguars. The first jaguar priests."

"Wow," a lady in the front row said.

Out in the lobby, an elegant, bronze arm reached from behind a planter and tweaked one of Jacqueline's dusty rose chiffon dresses off the rack. Then a velvet fringed shawl followed, which the tall woman threw over her shoulders. She stepped out from her cover and walked into the Lion-Hearted Women's event.

The women lay on rugs, eyes closed. They wore exotic dresses, harem pants, rayon tops from India, blouses from Bali. All manner of jewellery. Their closed eyelids were a field of spring flowers.

"Breathe in and imagine yourself on a..." the speaker suddenly saw an island in the Caribbean beneath the cool, full moon. She went with it. "The waves are gently running up the beach, bathing the sands..."

The bronze woman sauntered amongst the bodies lolling on rugs, their stomachs rising and falling like the waters out in the bay. The scent of orange blossoms rose from the carpet each time she lifted a foot with gleaming nails, pearlescent like the sand just after the wave has receded.

The Daykeeper in the other auditorium continued, "But she is best loved as the mature goddess of midwifery and medicine. Itzamna is her consort, our Sun God. When she tires of his antics —"

Several people were inexplicably filled with grief. One felt the sting of a slap on her cheek, then cowered as an enormous hand seemed to rise to strike her.

"—she retires to *La Isla de Mujeres* where she brings in new life and heals all. Not just the body, but the soul. But she stays away for years—centuries." A yearning burned in his chest—the heat of the desert sun.

A man in the front row squinted at Don Carlos. Reached for his sunglasses.

Oohs and ahs rose from the audience, especially the women.

"Will she come?" one asked.

"We shall see," Don Carlos said. He turned and walked off the stage. Dust, maybe smoke, rose from the curtain.

A surprised pause was followed by clapping that swelled as the emcee returned to the stage. "We shall see," he repeated, drawing the words out. "It is my honour to introduce to you our foremost expert on crystal skulls who—"

Applause drowned out the rest. Mason bounded to the stage. Boyish charm matched with a sharp intellect, plus a sense of humour. The ladies in the room shifted in their seats, leaned forward, dreamed of catching him later, asking him a question, taking him up to their rooms.

*Let them*, Gail thought. She pulled her peacock wrap around her shoulders and sat back to watch him do what he loved most.

He flipped a switch and images of beautiful crystal skulls filled the screen, light reflecting off internal fractures, splaying rainbows. In the large, clear spaces, visions rose—faces of ancient priestesses, the doorway of a temple, a mother with her child, a space ship.

"Do you see that old man?" someone whispered to the person next to him, pointing at the screen in front.

"Where?"

Gail smiled. Everyone expected to see the same thing, but scrying showed you what your own subconscious needed you to see. Or Mother Nature or the Universe—whatever your name was for that guiding intelligence. At least that's what she thought. Not that anybody was asking.

Mason explained some basic terms, his connection to the two important researchers in the last generation, talked about his days at the museum and how he'd first come across crystal skulls.

The seller had said, "This artefact is held in high esteem, but the villagers—they are starving, señor. We ask only that you authenticate this as genuine. Perhaps your museum would like to buy?"

But the huckster had not been lying. The high-powered microscopes had shown no markings from modern power tools. Only hand-rubbed, gleaming crystal.

"And they talked to me," Mason told her.

"Who?" Gail asked.

"The skulls. Annette—"An old lover. No need for jealousy at their age. "—she took mescaline with the amethyst one. When I asked her what it told her, do you know what she said?"

"What?" she indulged his storytelling.

He imitated her expression, hands spread, eyes wide. "Everything."

On the stage now, he flashed a picture of this same skull. "My friend had visions of our lives as Templars together when she scryed with this skull. It was said these knights worshipped a jewelled skull. Perhaps it was this one."

The audience oohed.

Gail's heart warmed and caught flame again.

Jacqueline walked down to the other conference's auditorium. The moon had climbed the sky and hung, white and somehow shrunken, in the darkening sky. She slipped through the side door and found a seat in the back row. Some guy was finishing up, showing a last slide of a perfectly clear crystal skull. It was beautiful, she had to admit. Then he was finished, the audience shouting their appreciation, and the emcee took the stage. She sat forward in her chair.

"Tonight we have a very special treat for you." A continental accent. She tried to place it. "We will reveal our mystery skull."

Oh, she'd come too early. She shifted in her seat. The other conference would be at it for a good while. She might as well listen.

"And Samuel Keeton will allow the skull to speak through him."

The audience thrilled.

Just in time, then. A woman walked by wearing something from Jacqueline's booth. When had she sold that dusty rose dress? She smiled at the tall, bronze beauty, gave her a thumbs up. The woman looked at her through arresting brown eyes and made a curious gesture with her fingers, as if she were sprinkling something, then floated by. Jacqueline thought of a small island in a blue sea, of sun and waves caressing a beach. Of sleeping in hammocks, Sam next to her, of rest and reconciliation, then rising to a new dawn. Even going their separate ways again. Ports in a storm.

She noticed a couple behind her. The man leaned close and murmured something in a round woman's ear. It was the previous speaker. He took the woman in his arms.

"I love you," he whispered. Their lips met.

*Get a room,* Jacqueline thought, then caught herself. She was selling romance just out in the lobby. The woman who'd bought her dress smiled at the couple from a corner and made that same gesture with her fingers, seeming to spread a blessing.

A thin man with a neat goatee stood blinking in the light on the stage. His smile was tentative. "Hello?" he said into the mike, unsure if it could be trusted.

A rustle from the audience seemed to reassure him. "One of my hobbies is antiquities. I'm a collector. I have pieces from sub-Saharan Africa, Egypt—"

"Egypt," the last speaker whispered to his love.

"The birds," the round woman said.

"Asia and Central America. I came into possession of this odd artefact a few years ago. The dealer said it was a crystal skull and provided me with paperwork as to its provenance. The letter reads that the original owner saw it being excavated from a tomb, but doesn't specify the location. Just the year. In the early 1930s, he paid $3,000 for it. A sizable sum at that time.

"I took it home and as soon as I opened the box, the skull started talking to me." He paused as if waiting for derision, but none came. "I suppose you all are used to this. Well, she hasn't stopped since." This elicited a wave of laughter.

He walked over to a table that had been set up next to the microphone and with a self-conscious flourish—he was not a natural showman, but shy and sincere—he pulled a large, white table napkin off the artefact.

A breeze burst through the room, hitting Jacqueline between the eyes. The couple behind her gave a little squeal as flyers blew up into the air.

"Her name is Celestial Light," the skull owner said. He put his hand over his eyes and squinted out at the audience. "Perhaps one of the Maya can give us her proper name."

Don Carlos murmured something beneath his breath.

The bronze woman stirred, alert. She moved to a corner where she crouched like a cat and settled down to wait.

The emcee came forward. "Samuel Keeton spoke to us this morning, so he does not need an introduction. Now he will tell us the message of the mystery skull."

A spotlight lit the right hand side of the stage where Sam sat on a dais, clothed in white, a Tibetan prayer scarf and wooden beads around his neck. An enormous crystal bowl sat in front of him. But instead of speaking, he picked up the striker and ran it around the rim of the quartz bowl. A deep vibration rose from it and filled the room. He closed his eyes and began to sing. A wordless chant.

The room stilled. Jacqueline closed her own eyes. Lines of energy ran white in her body, loosening the knot in her stomach, opening her neck and head. She flowed up and out of the room to the white moon standing sentinel over the earth. She melded with it.

Jacqueline found herself before a pyramid with steep steps beckoning her up to a flat top. Sam stood there in a pool of moonlight waiting. She stepped into his arms and their lips touched, soft then seeking deeper. He pulled her tight and squeezed her hand.

She remembered.

Thousands had gathered in the temple with its rounded domes, tall crystal spires. Her group moved past splashing fountains and pools open to the sea where dolphins gathered, singing their excitement. The gathering was imminent, the inundation, like the Nile when the Dog Star lit the sky. And these people, these gems, their best and brightest, had volunteered to return to the blue planet that hung beautifully beneath their Brother Sun, but was sorely wounded. To incarnate there and raise the frequency of the planet. To return the Celestial Light.

Jacqueline's group walked through the doors and took their place in line before the great stage, waiting their turn. They hummed together, breaking into complex harmonics, coming back together on one vibrating note.

Their time came. They approached the platform where the great Isis sat on her lapis throne, Xmucane to the Maya, Coatlicue. Oh, she had many names. The towering Cat Mother stood behind, her solar disk glinting as she turned her head back and forth watching, guarding. Jacqueline's group bowed as one. The attendants lifted them to their feet.

"Ah, my darlings," Isis said. Light suffused her face. "On the night of the White Moon, you will reconnect to this place and I will come to you. That night, we will awaken the earth."

Then Jacqueline was back in her body. She opened her eyes. Sam sang on the stage watching her. His eyes gleamed love. She looked around and nodded to the others in their group, strangers until this moment. Then Sam's chant intensified.

A column of light extended from her heart up through the Moon into the center of the galaxy where the Great Dipper, the Great Bear, the Urn of Isis, tipped and down poured a balm that healed all it touched, quickened it back to life. Her consciousness melded with that light and she lost her sense of separateness and time.

When Jacqueline opened her eyes again, the emcee was on stage effusing about the wonders of Sam's chant. "I've never heard you sing before. Did the skull have no words for us?"

Sam laughed, shaking his head. "Instead of words, the skull brought us the One Consciousness where all is known in silence."

A contented sigh rose from behind Jacqueline. The previous speaker and his round love sat entwined, luminous. She remembered them from the temple, the group just ahead of them. It seemed they had fulfilled their mission as well.

The Daykeeper stumbled out the back door, his eyes burning in their sockets. If only he had enough moisture to weep, he would throw himself at her feet, beg her forgiveness, but his yearning had burned away all words. He groped his way to the elevator, pushed the button, hoping it would not ignite with just a brush. The door opened. Then he stood in the middle of the metal cage, away from the wires, waves of heat pulsing through him. The door opened on his floor and he felt her waiting for him. He stumbled down the hall, pushed the door to his room open, leaving a charred palm print on the door.

"Don Carlos," she said, her voice honey, the lapping of waves against a dock. The room smelled of oranges.

He walked toward her, flames leaping up from the carpet where he passed. He tried to speak, but only smoke came from his throat. He fell at her feet.

"Itzamna." She reached down and touched his burning shoulders, her hands cool, promising relief, solace and rain. "It is the appointed time, my love."

He sighed, took a deep whiff of her scent—the orange, yes, but beneath the smell of salt and sweat, of new life. He leaned against the wall, fighting tears. "Does this mean ..."

She moved closer, the sound of wind in trees, of water running up a beach. "Mean what?"

"That you'll...." he fought against his voice breaking, but he did not succeed. "...come home now?"

She reached out and put her bronze fingers beneath his chin. Lifted his head. "Is it safe?"

He looked into her face and saw doubt. Now water filled his eyes and tears spilled. Such a relief. "I'm sorry. I'm so sorry."

She clucked, just as she had to their four sons when they had been infants. "When will you ever learn, my light?"

He let himself be lifted up and led out of the room. They walked out into the garden of the Hotel Imix. A breeze blew through the door and wound around their heels, then bloomed out her dress. They moved quickly, as immortals are wont. He lifted his great Mayan nose and snuffled. The smell of water and brine filled him, plumping up the hallows in his cheeks, moistening his mouth and lungs. He took her hand, his skin cooling.

They reached the beach and walked for a while on the sand, letting the waves run up over their feet, then pull the pain of their years apart back into the Pacific, his loneliness, the parched yearning. They watched the full moon slide down the western sky. Ixchel stopped and he moved to her, their bodies touching all down the front, their toes tickling, their thighs pressing, her breasts once more filling the emptiness of his chest.

"Time to go home," Ixchel whispered. She reached down, took his hand and led him out onto the water. They walked on the reflected light from the White Moon laying like a road across the water. By the time the moon touched the ocean, they stepped onto her body, two small dark shadows blending with the marks from meteor strikes. The White Moon took them to her bosom and sank into the Pacific.

The New Sun pushed his head up through the folds of the eastern horizon and peeked down into the city of angels. A new day dawned.

# SHARA'S PATH

By David L. Craddock

Much like the male she would soon marry, Shara did not meet her bridal robe's acquaintance until a time appointed by someone other than herself. She stood before the entrance to the marriage grove, picking at the robe's neckline that dipped down to her belly, exposing her midriff and the sides of her breasts. Mother had done a fair job, she supposed. The robe's ornamented fabric blended perfectly with her snowy Orbian skin. As she moved, columns of soft light drifting down through the forest's thick canopy caught the jewels woven through her robe.

Behind her, bells rang in the start of another Orba's Eve, ushering in a rising wave of music and merriment. Turning as much as she dared, Shara looked through the wall of trees and pictured the tables piled high with food and decorations—much of which she had helped prepare but would not enjoy until after her new husband had finished with her. Her eyes drifted back to her plunging neckline and the bright white nimbus around her skin intensified. She looked away hastily.

"Calm yourself," her mother said from beside her, facing the marriage grove. "You will lie with your husband soon enough. Such eagerness is unbecoming."

Shara grimaced.

"Don't make noises. They are unbecoming."

Shara pressed her lips together.

"Stop fidgeting."

She stiffened.

"Fix your headdress."

She patted the leaves woven through her braided silver hair.

"Stand straighter," Mother said. "Slouching is unbeco—"

Shara hunched.

Rosy spots bloomed on Mother's cheeks just as two robed and bent forms emerged from the marriage grove. At that, Shara did straighten, looking ahead as the Orbian priests paced around her, hands clasped, their roving blue eyes cold despite their warm smiles.

"Orba has blessed this child with great beauty," one of them said in a warbling voice.

Mother bowed low and muttered something incomprehensible and likely unctuous.

"You have come of age, Shara," the other priest said. "Did you bring the crests?"

Mother bowed again and offered him the four silver-gilded leaves she'd clutched to her chest. Shara stopped short of rolling her eyes. Surely the priests had seen that Mother held the House crests. But Orbians never deviated from tradition or ceremony. If they did, she would be dancing and playing Yule games with her friends rather than pledging her freedom and fortune to a stranger. And wearing significantly more clothing on such a chilly night.

The priests examined the crests, nodded, took hold of Shara's arms, and began to lead her into the trees. At once, panic flooded through her, washing away annoyance. She glanced back at her mother, but her head remained bowed, never once looking up.

They strode through darkness along the forest's soft carpet of berries, twigs, and soggy grass, weaving around trees as they went. Like all Orbians, she could see perfectly in even the deepest blackness, but her legs felt weak so she let them guide her, shivering as cold shoots of grass caressed her bare feet. She looked up, hoping to see a hint of Orba's light peeking through the canopy. Not the faintest sliver broke through. The goddess had assigned her this fate, then abandoned her.

By the time they broke through a strand of trees and entered the adytum, Shara felt a glimmer of her usual fire. She would do this because she must, but she could make the ordeal as unpleasant for her husband-to-be as it would be for her. Shaking free of their grip, she strode ahead of the priests to the stone slab in the center of the grove, forcing them to hurry. Here, Orba waited.

A wide shaft of light ringed the stone—Orba's gaze, the place where the goddess watched from where she swam the night sky. According to legend, the goddess had sent two Orbians to the world where they might spread her word. Here they had fallen, along with the stone, a piece of Orba herself; and here they had married and populated the forest with their offspring.

Shara hoped the fall had hurt.

Opposite her, three Orbian males stood whispering just beyond the light's reach. All three were hairless as was their custom. Two were tall and brawny, but the male on the far right stood a head shorter and less burly—toned, but just so. The other two pointedly avoided looking at their shorter peer. They noticed Shara and fell silent.

"We stand beneath Orba to join Shara of House Sonta with her intended," one priest said. "Praise Orba for guiding you through the forest to us this night."

"Praise Orba," the males intoned, far deeper than was necessary. Shara fought another battle against the impulse to roll her eyes and lost gloriously. Then the second priest spoke to her, and his words doused her tiny flame of rebellion like the coldest water.

"The three standing before you have shown desire to unite your House with their own." He held the crests up to the light. "I offer their sigils to Orba for her blessing and consent."

*But not mine.*

The priest stooped and placed the first leaf, depicting an arrow intersecting with a white orb, on the stone.

"Jeffret of House Standen," the priest announced.

One of the males stepped into the light. She ran her eyes over him once, then averted them as he fixated on her neckline.

"Tolbas of House Moltar," the priest said, placing another leaf, this one decorated with a crowned stag.

Tolbas shouldered beside Jeffret, all signs of camaraderie absent as he threw Jeffret a disdainful glance before turning his attention on Shara. Unbidden, she traced his sculpted form and once again her body emitted a low glow. Dozens of other soft white glows shone through the trees around her. Orbian wives, she knew, their intoxicating luminescence guiding their mates deep into the forest to celebrate the fullness of their cycles, pulling them into a lover's embrace.

Except Shara was not ready for that embrace, ceremony and law be damned. Fighting every instinctual urge within her—she did not even *like* overly muscular males—she tore her gaze from Tolbas's thick arms, caught his eyes, and almost shrank back. Looking ravenous, he appeared ready to devour her where she stood.

The priest set the third leaf, this one showing a neat row of daggers, on the stone. "Ketern of House Wollen."

As Ketern took his place beside them, Jeffret and Tolbas renewed their tenuous alliance. They sneered at Ketern, who stood a head shorter and significantly less chiseled than they. Ignoring them, Ketern stood straighter, adopting a mask of cool confidence as he locked eyes with Shara. Shara glared back, ignoring her persistent and uncooperative aura.

"Orba hangs full in the night sky, her cycle complete," the first priest said.

"You entered here as children," the second said, looking between Shara and her potential mates, "but tonight, your childhood ends and your next phase, your life together, begins."

"May Orba choose wisely," they said together, their tone leaving no margin for error. Orba *would* choose wisely. How could she not?

Everyone watched the crests, waiting. Ignoring her clamoring nerves, Shara inspected her three suitors. Jeffret and Tolbas appeared even paler than usual, all pretense of confidence absent from their visages. In contrast, Ketern beheld his leaf with intensity, practically pinning it to the marriage stone as if willing it to flare up.

And then it did, throwing a flash of Orba's light. One of the priests stepped forward and raised the leaf high. "Ketern of House Wollen, come forward. Shara of House Wollen, come forward."

Shara's head swam. *Shara of House Wollen*. One of the priests pulled her to the stone and linked her fingers through Ketern's. His hand felt cool and clammy.

"May Orba bless your union, Ketern and Shara of House Wollen," the other priest said as he placed Shara's leaf, an elegant bird set against Orba's full roundness, atop Ketern's. Turning, the priests collected the two rejected Orbians and their crests and herded them from the grove. Shara watched them leave, too dazed to look anywhere else.

Clearing his throat, Ketern dropped his hands and looked at her. "Your robe is beautiful," he said, clear voice belying sweaty palms.

"Thank you," she said, wrapping her arms around herself. The wind whispered through the trees, carrying far-off sounds of the party and, slightly closer, the sounds of another couple whose union Orba was in the process of blessing. Shara tried to close her pointy ears and examined the ground. She found grass and creepers and dirt quite fascinating.

Ketern cleared his throat again and raised a hand toward her. She flinched away and his hand retreated.

"I'm sorry," he said quickly. "I was just—"

"I know what you were just," she said, forcing her body to relax. She would have to go through with this. It was expected, and truth be told, might not be so bad if her damned urges could be trusted. She thought back to the way the other two males had stripped her down with their eyes, and the likelihood that, had Orba chosen the gargantuan Tolbas as Shara's mate, the consummation might already have ended. Her mind spun an image: his great form rising from atop her, leaving her plastered to the grass as flat as a leaf.

She permitted herself a silent laugh at the thought, then clapped her hand to her mouth upon realizing that she had laughed aloud. No, she hadn't. Ketern had. Blinking, she looked over at him and saw him swallow a smile.

"What's funny?" she said.

Picking at a blade of grass, he shrugged. "You said, 'I know what you just,' but I don't think you do."

"Don't think I what?"

"Know what I was going to do."

"Oh? You have different urges than other males?"

"My urges are the same, but aren't guided by rote or instinct. Not usually, anyway. I don't know you, Shara. Tonight marks the first time in my life I have seen you, and you me." He sighed. "And yet despite mutual unfamiliarity, I saw the way you looked at me from across the marriage stone, removing my garments with your eyes as if I were some carnal plaything made for your amusement."

Her mouth fell open. "I didn't... You... But I..."

"You glowed, yes?"

"Well, yes, but I couldn't help—"

He looked away and sighed again, deeper this time. "I beg you: do not wrestle me to the dirt and ravage me ."

"I would *never*—"

"Resist your feminine instincts and get to know me for *me*, not as an object made for your consumption."

She collected her thoughts. "Get to know you? How?"

"Why, by talking, of course. Is your thirst for my perfect male form so unquenchable that you can only think of—"

"Perfect?'

"That depends on who you ask," he said airily.

"Who should I ask?"

"Me. I'm the expert, after all."

She found herself smiling uncertainly. "You—you really don't want to...?"

"Eventually," he admitted, then held up his hands in a conciliatory gesture. "Should we come to care for one another in that way. But the fact remains, Orba, in her infinite wisdom from her place high in the sky apart from all our thoughts, feelings, and struggles, has chosen us to be together. Or perhaps I simply polished my crest more. Either way, we are married. We had no say in that, but we have say in other things."

"Such as?"

"Friendship."

"Consummation is expected," she began, then clapped her hands over her mouth again as Ketern let fly a passionate bellow.

"We mustn't have them think we aren't getting along," he said.


From across a copse bedecked in twinkling decorations, Shara meandered through the gathered Orbians, her gaze slipping past Orba's Eve dancers and delicacies until she caught sight of Ketern leaning against a tree at the entrance to the marriage grove. Looking bored, he scanned the crowd, nodded imperceptibly, then ducked inside. Grinning, she waited a few minutes before following.

She could just see him in the darkness far ahead, winding his way past trees as silently as a shadow. All around, hazy white glows flowed behind curtains of vines and brush, mates doubtlessly close behind.

Then Ketern vanished.

She pulled up in surprise then hurried into the grove. Orba watched from above, her light encircling the marriage stone. Shara checked it, looking every which way—except above.

"We were married four weeks ago, my dear," he whispered, soft as a breeze. "Only newlyweds may share this grove, as its name conveys."

Shara spun and gave him a cross look to mask how startled she felt. "I know what it's called."

"Then why...?" His eyes widened. "Unless you wanted to...?"

She shook her head hastily, willing herself to dim her faint glow. "No. Not yet."

He nodded, giving her a teasing smile, yet she could see its falseness. "Interrupting me again, I see," he said smoothly.

"And what were you going to say?" she asked, injecting playfulness into her tone.

"Unless you wanted to devour me with your eyes. Again."

She laughed, then her face grew serious. "I have enjoyed these past weeks, Ketern. I hope you are not growing too impatient with me. I just want to know you more."

"I understand and agree. I didn't mean to pressure you. It's been good to have a friend." His face grew troubled. She knew him well enough to know why.

"How goes your training?" she asked, knowing the answer. Each night he returned to their bungalow covered in abrasions that had no time to heal before he returned to the field the next morning.

"As well as you think," he said, walking over to the stone and sitting beside it. Shara crossed her legs and lowered herself before him. He was quite handsome, she thought, not for the first time. Most Orbian females swooned over the Tolbas-sized warriors in the Tribe, but Ketern seemed molded to suit Shara's ideal form: not too imposing, yet certainly strong enough to scoop her up. Her body blushed. She pushed away the thoughts quickly, hoping he would not draw attention to her outburst, when he spoke.

"I am not strong enough to fight in the Tribe." He didn't look at her.

"Why should you have to fight? Did you talk to your father?"

He snorted. "The general would not tolerate his firstborn enlisting as an observer. House Wollen carries the blood of warriors," he boomed, voice carrying across the grove, "not little sneaks who creep through trees."

"You didn't answer my question."

He didn't answer right away. "No."

"Why not?"

"He'd never—"

"Your brother is more suited for fighting than you." He looked wounded, so she leaned forward. "Ketern, I am the quietest Orbian I know—"

"Except when you attempt cooking. The words that come out of your mouth..."

"—and yet I could never sneak the way you did a few minutes ago," she said, raising her voice and giving him a warning look.

He winked, then looked down. "My brother meets my father's expectations."

Gathering her courage, she reached forward and took his hand. "But not mine." A soft glow suffused her. She let it.

Ketern's grin almost split his face. They talked for a time, Orba's gaze growing fainter and fainter around them. Eventually Ketern yawned and pulled his hand from hers to stretch. "I should sleep. Training continues tomorrow, and I need rest if I am to top today's spectacular failure."

Shara nodded, smoothing her features to hide her disappointment. Her hand felt so cold and empty without his. "You will talk to your father, then?" she asked casually.

He grimaced, then shot to his feet as the trees across the grove rustled. "We need to leave."

She started to rise, then paused. "No."

"No?"

"Not until you agree to talk to your father."

"Shara," he said, then glanced back as the sounds grew louder.

She took his hand again. "Please. For me ."

He studied her, then squeezed. "All right." Then he pulled her up—she squeaked, but only half in surprise—and they darted into the trees just as two priests stepped through from the other side and looked around stupidly.


Four weeks later, Shara crouched near the marriage stone at the edge of Orba's gaze, waiting, listening. The air whispering through the trees carried no sounds of celebration, only silence. A sound behind her made her spin around. She wanted to call for Ketern, but he had said not to. She would listen. She trusted him.

Then he stepped into the light and without thinking she rose and threw her arms around him. When she pulled away, she forgot her fear at the sight of the wooden tree pinned to the breast of his uniform.

"You're an observer," she said, beaming.

"Thanks to you," he said, drawing her out of the light and glancing around.

She shook her head. "You were born for it, Ketern. I knew it, and your father now knows as well."

Ketern ran a hand over his face. "He went on quite the tirade when I told him I intended to enlist as an observer, but he came around quickly."

"Oh?"

Ketern chuckled. "Oh, yes. My final challenge involved sneaking past the great general and my newly christened brother. I'm surprised you didn't hear Father curse. He grew so angry he almost felled a tree."

She clasped her hands in delight. "I'm proud of you." She accepted his hand and let him guide her to the ground where they sat side by side. "What shall we do to celebrate?"

His face grew contemplative. "A feast, perhaps. You don't even have to cook it."

"Thank you."

"No, thank *you*."

She jabbed his arm. "And when shall we hold this grand feast?"

His smile faded. "Probably not for a while, I'm afraid."

Fear came rushing back, though his presence dulled it. The grove suddenly felt small, as if the trees inched forward to surround them. She shivered. "What news?"

"My skill was not the only reason Father acquiesced to my will to join the observers. The Tribe needs them." He took a breath. "Reports say invaders have entered the forest."

She waited to speak until she felt calm. "Where?"

"From the south. Four parties of observers leave early tomorrow, each in a different direction. We're to send word of their largest gathering. The Tribe will attack at night; these invaders can't see as well as we can. Then—"

"We?" she interjected, and now her voice was anything but calm.

"Yes." His voice shook too. "I will join the regiment heading south. My father's lieutenants say I have the most promise they've seen in centuries. Only then did the general become a believer," he finished bitterly.

She placed a hand on his shoulder. "I believed in you."

"I know. I've known you two cycles, yet you believed in me before someone who has known me my entire life."

She tried to speak, but her throat constricted. Suddenly he was on his knees before her, his strong hand cupping her cheek.

"We will be fine, Shara."

"I know," she said. Her voice firmed. "I know. I have you to protect me."

He leaned in and she did not pull away. When he removed his mouth from hers, she was breathing heavily, as was he, and her body shone as brightly as Orba herself. Part of her wanted to dim her light, but she didn't know if she could. His fingers traced their way down her neck, watching her with star-flecked eyes as he ran his other hand through her hair before both hands stopped on the clasps of her robe. She pulled back.

"Oh," he said, panicked. "I—"

She pressed a finger to her lips and studied his eyes, seeing the same desire that burned through her. But was she ready? Then he kissed her finger lightly, and the memory of his lips pressed to hers came rushing back.

"I'm sorry," he said softly. "I was just—"

"I know what you were just," she said. He read her tone and grinned.

As the night wore on, Orba moved with it, politely averting her gaze.


The forest burned. Screams rose above the roar of the flames as they feasted on flesh and wood, stretching into the night sky like searing fingers. Shara burst into the marriage grove, eyes stinging, throat raw, coughing and sputtering as she stumbled to the ground and crawled. One hand, inflamed and searing, pawed the ground, feeling its way toward the marriage stone as she blinked away a mask of stinging tears. The other hand, a balled fist wrapped around her belly, clutched parchment stained with soot and ash and bearing the first words she had received from her husband since he'd left her almost three full cycles prior.

*Grove. Safe.*

Heavy footsteps grew louder behind her as an invader crashed through the ring of trees. Grunting, he grabbed her and flung her onto her back. She tried to cry out but managed only a hoarse whisper. The man struck her and her ears rang louder than the bells on Orba's Eve. Then he was on her, groping at her robe, tearing it away.

Suddenly his eyes bulged and he slumped, growing impossible heavy. A hand, small but strong, clutched at his shoulder and pushed him away. Then the hand grabbed her and she beat at it until a familiar scent washed over her: bark from the trees he scaled so effortlessly. Herbs from the wash she made for them each month. Sweat. Smoke. An acrid, salty tang.

Ketern touched her cheek with a hand that felt warm and sticky but she took it and held it there. Then he collapsed to the ground and she saw the blood oozing from a hole in his belly the size of a fingertip. She watched him fall in a daze, and her mind wandered off. *How could so much blood come from such a small hole?*

He whispered her name and that shattered her trance. She fell beside him and fussed at his robes, tearing off a strip of cloth and patting his belly with it, trying to ignore the high note of panic in his voice as he babbled her name over and over and the way his wide eyes clung to her as if she were the only branch on the forest's highest tree.

She pressed the cloth against his gut as hard as the red hands clawing at her arms, but the blood soaked through. She looked around desperately. "Help!" she cried, but her voice dissolved in a fit of coughing.

He called for her again, fainter now, and she cradled him close, crushing him against her to stop his shakes. She called out again and again, willing her voice louder and louder, but still no one came. She rocked him, talked to him, telling him her special news that she had waited to reveal to him in person, until her eyes fell on the shaft of soft light from above, cool and imperturbable as ever.

"Please. Please don't take him from us. I'll do anything. Please."

It was not a proper prayer like the ones her mother had made her intone over and over, but it was *a* prayer. Orba would hear it.


Four nights later, Shara knelt within the light that cradled the marriage stone, one hand resting against her protruding belly. She was alone, and not just in the grove. The priests had gathered all surviving Orbians and embarked on a journey out of their forest and to another. If another forest even existed. No one knew for certain, but the priests had told them to go, so they went. Mother had insisted Shara come along but gave up after Shara refused, migrating with the rest of their people and leaving her daughter behind in a land ruined by the invaders' onslaught, one the Tribe had only just managed to turn away. The invaders would return, the priests said, but Shara didn't care. Only smoking stumps hid her from prying eyes, but no eyes remained alive to pry.

Shara was alone. So there was no one around to scream, to faint, to chastise, or to beat her when, after hours of quiet reflection, she looked up at Orba and said:

"I hate you."

The goddess, she had decided, worked in mysterious and cruel ways. All her life she had worshipped Orba not because she'd wanted to, but because she'd been told to. She had followed her people's laws and customs not by choice, but by heavy-handed command. Then, on a night not even six cycles before, her mother had practically dragged her to the marriage grove to give her to a husband she had never met. Custom demanded it. Orba had chosen Ketern for her, and her for him, and that was that.

And *that* had worked. Shara squeezed her eyes shut, but the memories of her short time with Ketern played against her eyelids as easily as they played against the forest's blackened carcass. Marriage was not a path she had chosen, but it was a path she had come to love. And then Orba, the one who had pushed and prodded her down this path, had apparently changed her mind.

Or had she? Did she have as much control over her Orbians as the priests believed? Shara thought back to something Ketern had said the night they were wed.

*Orba, in her infinite wisdom from her place high in the sky apart from all our thoughts, feelings, and struggles, has chosen us to be together.*

Ketern was right. What did Orba know of their lives? Did she have a plan for any of them? She gave Ketern to Shara, then took him away. *So sorry, Shara, dear, but I made a mistake. We'll just start over somewhere else, hm? Now be a good girl and go wander off into the unknown for awhile.*

Shara braced herself on the stone and hauled herself to her feet and looked around at the charred remains of trees that had stood for thousands of years.

"What path do I walk now, goddess? Do you even know?"

Predictably, Orba did not answer. Shara turned away to leave—not sure of where she would go, exactly—when light glinted off a small object near the far side of the stone. Curious, she went to it and gasped. As quickly as she was able, she stooped and retrieved the crest of House Sonta, the House of her maiden years.

It looked the same as when she had given it to Ketern the night Orba had joined their Houses, but marred by a small patch of blood. Ketern had taken it with him at her insistence. He said he would place it next to hers again when he came home to her.

Grief welled anew. She shoved it down deep and focused on the crest. As she turned it over, Orba's light took hold of it, giving it a sheen her mother would have envied. Mother had worked tirelessly to prepare the crest for her daughter's wedding, cleaning and polishing and—

The crest stopped moving in her hands. She stared at it, concentrating, until the rest of what Ketern had said to her on their wedding night crawled up from memory.

*Orba, in her infinite wisdom from her place high in the sky apart from all our thoughts, feelings, and struggles, has chosen us to be together. Or perhaps I simply polished my crest more. Either way, we are married. We had no say in that, but we have say in other things.*

Holding the crest in a white-knuckled grip, Shara smiled as her thoughts drifted through her life since that night. Had he burnished his crest more painstakingly than her other suitors? She thought it likely. He was as fastidious an Orbian as she'd ever met, even drawing nods of approval from Mother at the way he helped her keep their bungalow despite her comments regarding his small stature.

More importantly, Ketern, she had learned, was not one to leave anything to fate. She believed he had chosen to set his crest apart from the others; just as they had chosen, together, to grow as friends; just as she had chosen to give herself to him completely; just as she had chosen to support his dream to become an observer; and just as he had summoned the courage to follow that dream.

But perhaps their fates had been predetermined. Perhaps Orba had maneuvered them to the marriage stone according to some grand plan. If that were true, Shara counted it a blessing— but a blessing that didn't change what had happened thereafter. They, not Orba, nor her mother, nor his father, nor anyone else, had made their choices, and they were the ones who bore their consequences for better or worse.

Kneeling in Orba's light, Shara let the grief bubble up and over her. When it passed, she entered the forest, found the prints made by her people as they slinked into the unknown, and went in the opposite direction, making her own path.

# SMALL SEVEN'S SECRET

By Billie Milholland

On the pond the full moon's reflection wrinkled each time fish lips disturbed the surface. Sister Four, watching the moon and the fish, sat still as a statue. Her small feet in embroidered, satin shoes were tucked beneath an over-sized, bamboo chair that could have held two of her. Sister Four's face was tranquil, but Small Seven, standing just inside the moon gate, noticed that her sister's hands were clasped tightly in her lap. Sister Four was afraid.

Small Seven wanted the bamboo chair replaced after Sister One died in it during Master Wu's first moon experiment. Her father, Lord Zhang, had agreed, but Master Wu argued the chair was not at fault. He said Sister One had not practiced her rituals properly; she refused to call down sufficient Moon Power. She had been disobedient. The chair stayed.

Sisters Two and Three also died as a result of Master Wu's moon experiments, but their deaths were not as mercifully sudden. Sister Two endured exceptional agony for a week before she crawled out one night into the east courtyard and with her poor little hands, dug up enough Woman's Bane root to poison the whole household. In her weakened condition, a few bites from one root were enough to release her from suffering.

Before Sister Two was buried, all the offending plants were removed and burned, in order to deflect bad luck that might otherwise settle upon the great trading House of Zhang.

Sister Three did not become ill until she had endured several weeks of Master Wu's moon experiments. Master Wu insisted she would have survived her illness had she not, in a fit of unreasonable hysteria, sliced herself open with a broken tea cup and bled to death under his favourite peach tree.

Before Sister Three was buried, a rumour emerged within merchant circles that the unfortunate girl had fallen victim to Gudu sorcery. The reason: jealousy from an unnamed rival who resented favours bestowed upon the House of Zhang from within the Forbidden City. Because no merchant wanted his name connected to accusations of sorcery, great gifts of sympathy and condolence poured into the House of Zhang from every quarter of the city.

Master Wu assured Lord Zhang that Sister Four was not in danger. Had he not proven that Moon Power, bestowed by Heaven upon the unworthy daughters born to the House of Zhang, became naturally more concentrated as it passed from one sister to the next? He reminded Lord Zhang that he had three robust sons that would carry on his name and his business. These were gifts from Heaven that not all his rivals enjoyed. After that, Lord Zhang did not need to be reminded that it would be impractical not to use, for the benefit of his business, daughters of which he had plenty to spare. Lord Zhang finally commanded Sister Four to contribute her moon skill to Master Wu's science.

In a stone vault, two levels below the courtyard, Master Wu's steam engine gathered power. The rhythmic ticking of a large, foreign clock at the far end of the courtyard beat like demon heart into the quiet night. Small Seven held an ebony box against her chest. She had copied and miniaturized the precise, mechanical movements of the ungainly time piece in order to operate the delicate systems embedded in each of the tiny, ceramic heads nestled in the silk lining of her box.

Master Wu called her creations sing-songs, and when he noticed her, which wasn't often, he patted her head indulgently as she sat quietly in the corners of his workshops fiddling with discarded gears, chains and springs.

When Small Seven was still an infant, Sister One carried her in a basket into the maze of Master Wu's workshops. There Small Seven learned to walk, tottering among the mechanical wonders created therein, and because she was a quiet child, she became invisible to all who hunched over their workbenches, soldering and brazing with their air-hydrogen blowpipes. There she learned to read and to write among the long, dusty columns of shelves that held Master Wu's library. There she learned to use files, punches and mainspring winders, but most of all, it was there she learned how to think.

Since the moment she opened her tiny fist to the first full moon of her first lunar year, Small Seven was in full possession of her Moon Power. No one noticed it then, and no one noticed it now as she strode across the courtyard to stand beside her sister and to set her box on a wooden table, gleaming dark with Ningpo varnish.

All the daughters of the House of Zhang were moon-touched, but, because of the last great famine, there had been no other moon-touched left to train them. Only Small Seven learned to train herself, but because she was the last born, no one valued what she said.

So she stood beside her sisters as they bowed to the will of Master Wu. She watched and she listened and she learned how to command and increase her Moon Power with the help of her sing-songs. Each experiment added to her knowledge and she kept each sister alive longer. But it had not been enough. Three sisters had died.

This time Small Seven had a different plan, a bolder plan. This time Small Seven would intervene before Sister Four sacrificed her life's essence. If she succeeded, she would then reach beyond the walls of her small city and into the Forbidden City itself. She would fly on the wings of Master Wu's small idea and release a bigger idea.

Before sun-down Master Wu instructed Sister Four. He told her precisely what he believed she must do this night. As she listened, she kept her head bowed as was proper, and when he finished, she covered her face with her hands to subdue her fear.

To Master Wu, she said, as Small Seven had bid her to say, "I am not afraid." Thankfully the tremble in her voice was not enough to alarm Master Wu.

Far away in the Imperial City, the woman in command of the Dragon Throne also sat beside a pool, watching the moon's reflection. No sound marred the stillness of the night, save the ticking from the large foreign clock Master Wu had sent last week. It sat at the far end of the courtyard, a giant, metal-clad toad. Not a pretty thing. She'd ordered it draped with fabric so it would not offend the eye with its brash ugliness. She was not surprised at the gasps of horror from attendants uncovering it just before sundown this evening. The homely lump made disruptive sounds, but she would endure them, because of what Master Wu promised.

While she waited, she thought of her exquisite water clocks, the elegant way they divided each day into suitable parts. She especially loved Su-Sung's ancient clock tower with its five doors, each opening to reveal a figure that rang a gong and held a tablet that described a special time of day. There was no question in her mind which civilization was more advanced. She felt immediate pity for her western sister who sat on a barbarian throne ruling the ungainly and remarkably uncivilized British Empire.

According to Master Wu, the foreign clock did more than click and whirr. What it did worried her advisers and they cautioned against listening to a man who had spent so many years living with foreign devils. She allowed herself a slight smile at their plight, shut away from her tonight and ordered, on pain of death, not to come to her until she summoned them.

Foreign devils had their uses and she would not let revulsion for their cultural crudeness prevent her from enjoying the entertainment of their good science. Tonight, with assistance from foreign science, the Dowager Empress would exchange pleasantries with the faraway Empress of India, monarch to monarch.

Her interest in communicating with the distant Empress was not born of an urge to forgive foreign devils for the war and strife they had brought to the Middle Kingdom. She would never do that. She merely wanted to take the measure of a foreign female, who, like she, commanded a sprawling empire with admirable success.

The Empress Dowager knew there was nothing significant to be gained from this exercise. She was curious, that's all, and it amused her to observe Master Wu's workers scurrying like rats in the dungeons beneath the Forbidden City constructing his monstrous devices. Only eunuchs and women, of course, were allowed to work within the great city walls, so it also amused her to watch Master Wu stretching his spleen to train those unaccustomed to handling delicate mechanisms.

He knew the honour he gained from her favour was better than gold. She knew he would not fail. It was his head on a pike tomorrow if he did not make good his claim. He insisted that by means of his hot engines, his annoying mechanical devices and the cold power of Lady Moon she would see the face of and exchange words with her sister ruler even though separated from her by a continent of deserts and mountains.

In Balmoral Castle, dwarfed by the mechanical apparatus that surrounded her, Queen Victoria sat next to a copper tub filled with enough water to bathe an elephant. She had sent her attendants away, even her loyal daughter, Princess Beatrice, who had persuaded the others that no harm would come to their monarch from her toying with Chinese superstition and magic.

The Queen liked Master Wu. For an Oriental he was surprisingly advanced in both education and civilized rhetoric. She admitted that his communication device sounded far-fetched and his science, mixed with liberal doses of moon myth, sounded silly, but she was an old woman, wearied by relentless responsibilities of state. Should she not be allowed some simple amusement?

Small Seven did not concern herself with either old lady. They were women near the end of their lives, therefore vulnerable to the deeper workings of the moon. Master Wu with his Teslascope, his steam engine and other apparatus, would unwittingly open the way for her to enter the minds of two aging monarchs. Perhaps the barbarian mind of an Empress who commanded a sprawling empire of foreign devils would be of little use to her. That was irrelevant. It was in bending the will of the Dowager Empress that she had a chance to save herself and her remaining sisters from the exploitations of Master Wu.

Sister Four was a dutiful daughter. In spite of her fear she was willing to sacrifice herself for the good of the House of Zhang. Small Seven was also a dutiful daughter, but she had come to believe it was not necessary to sacrifice lives to advance the House of Zhang.

As vibrations far below increased and the smooth grey tiles in the courtyard trembled under her feet, Small Seven smiled. It was time.

She whispered to her sister in her smallest voice. "Are you ready?"

As she had been instructed, Sister Four turned her palm up in agreement. Small Seven could feel her sister's fear. Before she could make a movement to sooth her, their father passed through the courtyard on his way to his apartments.

"Are you wearied, Small Seven?" Concern wrinkled deep into his forehead.

"I am refreshed, thank you, Father. I rested earlier."

"Is it truly necessary that two daughters expose themselves to the night air for this thing to happen?"

Sister Four grabbed for Small Seven's hand. "She calms me, Father." The alarm in her voice unmistakable.

Had this experiment the same purpose as the others, her father would have disallowed it, his trading company already expanded beyond his most ambitious hope. But this time, Master Wu's science would be executed at the command of the Dowager Empress. No man would dare refuse the whim of the woman who ruled the Middle Kingdom.

He nodded and Small Seven watched his back disappear through the round moon gate. He did not have the courage to observe the exertions that, in spite of what Master Wu had promised, might kill Sister Four.

As the power built beneath her feet Small Seven was relieved to be rid of distraction. Corresponding energy rose within her as Lady Moon inched ever nearer, cooling the hot rays from the sun that beat upon her pale, pock-marked surface; condensing them for harvest by the moon-touched below.

The steady thrum of the steam engine pressed against the soles of Small Seven's feet, pushing energy up through her body. The foreign clock, calibrated to the interval she required, ticked strongly. She heard Master Wu enter the courtyard.

"Is it time?" He did not disguise the excitement in his voice.

Sister Four gripped the arms of her chair. "It is time, Honourable Wu." She stood slowly, as she had been instructed, and stretched her arms up toward the moon. Then she shrieked, bent clutching her stomach and collapsed to the cold, stone tiles.

For a moment Master Wu did not utter a word, nor did he move. He stared at Sister Four like someone had tossed a pile of silk and satin at his feet for laundering.

Small Seven tugged on his sleeve. "Remove her, Honourable Teacher. Quickly. I will take her place."

He swung around. "You? How can one such as you do anything? You are not prepared."

"I am prepared." She looked at him directly.

Shock at her impertinence widened his eyes.

"Go. If I fail, you can have me executed. You can blame me however you wish."

Panic flooded his face and he did not move.

"Go." She shoved him. "The moment will be wasted."

He bent and lifted Sister Four's slight body easily. Without looking back, he stumbled through the moon gate.

Small Seven opened her box and when the moonlight had illuminated the little faces she stood and lifted her arms, letting the pulse below flow through her. She breathed deeply for a few minutes, using the measured beat of the foreign clock to pace the surges of energy she felt from above.

She lowered her head and watched the moon's face in the pond waver and become that of the Dowager Empress. Small Seven had never seen the venerable ruler before this, very few had, but she did not doubt the identity of the fierce-faced, old woman glaring up at her.

"What is this? What concubine dares mar the surface of my pool?"

How she answered was critical, but Small Seven didn't hesitate. With head bent so her eyes would not meet those of her ruler, she responded.

"It is only an insignificant insect you see. For one breath or two. Across the back of which your foreign sister will travel to you."

In that moment, a deep thrill shook Small Seven, and the angular face of the Dowager Empress was joined by the round visage of the one who called herself the Empress of India. Her hair was parted in the middle, just like that of the august lady in the Forbidden City, but her forehead had not been plucked, giving her a disappointing, common appearance.

Nevertheless, Small Seven held steady while the two, old monarchs took each other's measure. She kept their images sharp and clear. The sounds they made as they spoke to each other were transported, just as Master Wu had predicted, by Teslascope, its radio waves having travelled into the heavens along the connection she created with the moon. From there they leapfrogged off the moon's surface, split in half and travelled toward two destinations.

Small Seven ignored the awkward translations made by the complex clockworks in each court. As the elderly voices moved through her, she stroked them and stretched them and stored them in the tiny, ceramic heads in her box. From emotions that rose to the surface of each old woman, Small Seven spun spider threads of memories full of victory and loss, full of successes and failures, full of triumph and regret.

When the formal communication ceased and each old woman settled back in her chair to ponder the wonder of what had just happened, Small Seven wound the thin threads she had extracted around the anchors she had created inside the little heads. After she secured her connections and duplicated each one for insurance, she closed the lid and clutched her box lovingly to her chest.

Master Wu stumbled into the courtyard.

"Did it… did you…"

Small Seven bent her head as if in weariness. "It is done."

"Will the Empress be pleased?" Desperation thinned his voice to an unattractive squawk. She grabbed the back of the chair as if to steady herself.

"Only she can answer that. Only she."

She let her voice fall to a whisper and tottered towards her rooms as if in a daze. Master Wu would think her at the point of collapse. She knew the Empress had been more than pleased, but she would let Master Wu's stomach clench like a fist for the time it took the Empress to indicate her satisfaction. Small Seven hoped his discomfort would be severe.

As she expected, Master Wu did not interrupt her departure, nor was he curious about what was in her box. She would take to her bed and languish prettily until Master Wu lost interest in her. That would not take long.

Once assured of Celestial favour he would continue his subterfuge with Princess Der-Ling, the foreign-educated First Lady-in-Waiting to the Empress Dowager; and with Princess Beatrice, the long-suffering, youngest daughter of the other monarch. Together they would complete various trade agreements, communicating by means of Master Wu's ponderous electromagnetic devices that required thousands of li of wires strung over desert and mountain and under the deep oceans.

While he was diverted by commerce, Small Seven would travel butterfly soft and lightning fast across the moon threads she had woven into the mind of the one known in the Middle Kingdom as Suh-shee, and perhaps even to the far-away one known as Victoria. Soon their thoughts would become known to her and her thoughts would become their thoughts. It would be easy then to protect the daughters of the House of Zhang. That she would do first.

Of other things she could not be certain, but it was possible that as long as she lived, so would the old rulers live. It was possible that she could extend their lives by decades. If that was true, she had her own experiment in mind. An experiment wherein control of nations would flow naturally like a spring freshet away from the heavy hand of men to the light, but courageous and therefore more ruthless hand of women. It was an experiment wherein not only moon-touched women like the daughters of the House of Zhang would direct their own destiny, but other women as well. She set the box on the table beside her bed and lifted the lid. She touched each head with a fingertip.

"Rest well, little treasures. Tomorrow we begin to stitch up the rents in the world with silver moon thread."

Small Seven yawned as she snuggled under her rose-red satin quilt.

# HUSKS

By Isabella Drzemczewska Hodson

A spider skitters along the forest floor, winding its way through the maze of debris with quick, sure steps. It heads straight for a bush so lush its leaves tangle. A bush that springs with life, its riot of leaves full of shadowed corners and hiding-spots.

The spider lifts a spindly leg onto the woody stem of the plant and, once partway up, winds its way carefully, slowly, looking for the perfect spot. Its burden glistens in the moonlight: a soft, delicate white sac. The spider, brown and sparsely furred, stops on the underside of a leaf and deftly plucks her cargo from her abdomen. She shoots a wad of gummy silk from her spinneret and attaches the egg-sac to the leaf. She pauses and looks at her work.

A stray moonbeam finds its way past the dense foliage and lights the little spider. She touches her sac with one leg, as though sad to leave it there, hesitates, then turns and skitters away. Her steps slower this time, lazy almost, as though she has nothing left to worry about.

She walks a little ways from the leaf where she left her eggs, perches, and waits. Her eyes watch the world around her—the great trees skimming the sky, the muted mat of undergrowth against the forest floor, the smaller plants and bushes in between, and the moon that casts its light over everything. This night humid and warm, the spider's eggs a tiny sac of hope against the leaf. The spider's movements slow and her eyes dull. By the time dawn's grey light peeks into the sleeping forest, only a husk of the spider remains, empty legs clutching the stem of the bush.

The children sleep during the day. April thinks them strange, with their pale skin and pointed teeth, wiry limbs and dark eyes. These children have no colour. Twins—a boy and a girl, abandoned on the doorstep six years ago. Their mother didn't even give them clothes. Two naked, howling, newborn babes left at the door of the orphanage at dawn. She remembers their arrival—how she woke at the sound of a cry, a soft wail coming from outside. Padding softly down the stairs, opening the door, discovering the babes, their moon-white skin goosefleshed as they trembled and wailed. Overcome with a panicked love, plucking them both from the step, wrapping them in her robe. She'd been so fearful for their lives, with their skin so pale and cold, that she hadn't thought to look around for a mother who might be hiding and watching somewhere nearby. No; she'd just pulled the babes right on in and walked straight up the stairs to Mother Rachel's room to wake her.

Tom and Ava—that's what the nuns called the little ones— don't fit in with the other children. The other children run, scream, play. They fight and scrape their knees. They shriek and push each other down the stairs sometimes, or sing softly to themselves in bed when their little hearts burst with loneliness. April knows it all. She grew up here, abandoned on the doorstep in a cradle made from green willows. She tells herself that's why she loves the little ones she found—they're just like her, lost and alone, abandoned. Here for life, no doubt, like April herself, unless some kindly souls take it into their hearts to adopt them and take them far from this place. That would be good, she thinks, because no matter how hard she tries to persuade them to play with the others, to lift themselves out of their shells and join a children's game, they keep to themselves. Almost as if they don't want to belong.

She keeps her eye on them, even as she goes about her daily tasks—slicing the buns that the baker's boy brings, mopping the kitchen floor, washing the endless river of linens that comes her way. Those children walk around as though they are asleep. Small shuffling steps, vacant eyes, heads nodding off onto shoulders. While the other girls take turns hopping over the skipping rope, Ava curls into a wiry little ball and sleeps. While the boys leapfrog over one another's backs or play tug-of-war with a sheet borrowed from the laundry basket, Tom finds a dark corner and tucks his head between his knees. April can't help but notice the little bodies tucked into corners, behind boxes, curled into basketfuls of linens. Books, teddy bears, even a stray dog used as pillows. Mother Rachel and the other sisters don't seem to ever notice these little bundles of sleep, so quiet and always keeping to themselves. The nuns are too busy. But April knows.

She tries to coax the twins from their daze. Tries to lure them out of the shadows with treats and promises. Tugs at their dirty little clothes, trying to pull them outdoors into the sunlight. She knows it will do them good. Yet every time, without fail, Tom and Ava find their way inside again. For every minute of sunlight that touches their skin, they spend an hour indoors, asleep. As though they wish to sleep through their young lives.

Night. The moon beckons. Its beams spear through the window and the thin white curtain. Inside the girls' dormitory, two small feet touch the floor and pad softly to the window. A thin, narrow face looks out. Ava's eyes shoot straight to the moon's wide beaming face. Not a sound escapes her thin little lips with the strange pointed teeth hiding behind them. She stares up, up, up at the moon, entirely transfixed, oblivious to the dark dormitory around her and the two-dozen other little girls sleeping in their hard, lumpy beds.

The leaves lie still in the forest. They curl inward as though from the cold. An owlet calls from a tree, practicing his call. Two spiders walk along the forest floor, picking their careful way through the debris with thin, strong legs. They inch apart around fallen leaves, chunks of wood, twigs, deer and rabbit scat, bits of bone. They spread apart and come together again, tiny brown bodies invisible against the dark earth. They explore, winding their way up trunks of trees, along blades of grass, through the moss. Their progress slow compared to that of a larger animal, but sure. Exploring the world in the light of the moon.

April wonders why their skin won't break. Such pale skin, pale as moonlight. Translucent almost. And those dark eyes. Even in the sunlight, they shine black as a beetle's back. She's seen Tom fall. Pushed into the dust by the bigger boys, falling on hands and knees, spitting sand from his mouth. Yet he will not bleed. Any other child's skin would burst open and spill a stream of red, but not Tom's or Ava's. Their skins hard, like a shell.

When she cannot sleep, April wanders. She lifts the cloth that covers the bread and inhales its scent. Takes a sip of cold milk— never enough to be noticeable; just enough to soothe her stomach. More often than not she finds her slippered feet flitting to the bedrooms, to the rows of boys and girls.

She has noticed how Tom and Ava disappear. She knows that neither hides in the bathroom, that she will not discover them below the stairs. At first April thought they might sleep together in a cocoon of blankets, but she has never found their spot. They cannot leave—every door is double-locked, every window shut tight. The cracks under the doors and in the walls the only entries and exits, but even a mouse would have trouble fitting through.

She knows now that every time the moon is out, the children disappear. A half-moon, full moon, even just the faintest sliver— the moon wakes the little ones and steals them from their beds. But if it rains or clouds cover the moon's light, they stay sleeping, blankets tucked all the way to their chins. April has thought about reporting this, but has never breathed a word. She gives the children these nights—let them sleep during the day, then, if they may wander together at night. She sees no harm.

Summer turns to autumn, autumn to winter. Winter to spring, spring to summer. Again and again. April worries now, more than she used to. She feels like a mother to her little orphans, all growing too quickly. Still her twins wander the night, just as sure as the baker's boy brings the daily bread, but now her heart beats quicker. Six years later and still she has not discovered their hiding-spot.

She sits with Ava one day. She looks at the peculiar girl whose limbs are too long for her body and realizes with a shock that Ava may never find herself in the arms of a man either, unless she grows into her woman's body and blossoms. But she worries, so she asks, *Ava, where do you go at night?*

Ava looks up, eyes befuddled by the sunlight, and looks entirely lost. Her lips purse. *What do you mean?*

*Come now, you can tell me. I know your secret.*

Ava rubs her eyes and locks her gaze with April's. *I have no idea what you speak of.* She rubs her eyes some more, as though to wake herself from her confusion. *Why would I go anywhere at night?*

April runs her hand over Ava's braided hair. *You never sleep in your bed, little one. Where do you go with Tom?*

Ava looks at her with such profound confusion, such utter befuddlement, that April knows she speaks the truth. *I go nowhere. In my dreams I walk the forest, sometimes, or fly with the wind on a cloud of silk, but I stay right here, asleep in bed.*

April nods. *I wonder where Tom goes?* she mutters.

Fourteen is magic. Tom, always too tall for his age and far too thin, begins to grow into his frame. Muscles spurt beneath his skin almost overnight, new hairs stubble his face. He must earn his keep now. He wanders the woods with an uncanny knack for knowing where he is, and chops wood for the nuns. His axe plunges into the tree trunks and severs branches, slices trunks.

When he has chopped enough wood for the orphanage, he trades his extra lumber for coin. The maidens look at him now, as he walks to and from the forest each day, shooting admiring glances at his sinewy arms and legs that sprout dark hairs. None of the other children at the orphanage see him as a boy anymore; they look to him as a man.

Ava blossoms. The quiet, gangly, peculiar girl so easily forgotten by the nuns and overlooked by passersby disappears. A wild beauty replaces her. Her black eyes soften to a becoming gray. Hips flare from her narrow waist so her skirt pools around her ankles. The rosy petals on her pale chest blossom into rich mounds. Her cheeks flush and the features on her once-hard face soften. She becomes a beautiful stranger seemingly overnight. Gone is the timid girl who hid in dark corners. A gentle confidence steals into her bones. No man can keep his eyes off her now; she transfixes with her smile and enchants with her laugh. Still, April thinks, Ava is too tall for her own good, and continues to dislike the sun's rays. She walks around half-groggy, as though drunk on lack of sleep.

Though friends and strangers alike now notice Ava through the orphanage gates, she has eyes for only one man: Ewan, the baker's boy. Every day for as long as she can remember, he has come to the orphanage with his father's loaves and buns. And every day, he has offered the bread with the excuse that his father baked too much. Everyone here knows better, though. They know his father's kind heart and generous nature, and they've come to depend on his offerings and Ewan's sunny smile.

Ava noticed him long ago. Even when no one else spotted her as she hid in her dark corners, behind doors and curtains, he knew where she stood. He'd find her and pluck a fresh apple danish or sugar-crusted cherry pie, wrapped in wax paper, from his pocket. She knew he saved one every day especially for her. She liked that. He made her feel special. And she liked him.

Ewan noticed Ava's transformation right away. The softening of her features, the widening of her hips. He pulsed for her. He grew into manhood himself and he wanted her. He dreamed of her at night, pictured her smiling just for him, her strange pointed teeth protruding past her gums, accentuating her fine features. He imagined her in the moonlight—he pictured her naked, garbed only in moon-glow.

He lingered now, on the days when he didn't see her right away. He went out of his way to walk by the orphanage and peer through the gates while completing his delivery rounds. His eyes always seeking their prize, the beautiful young woman with limbs long as a spider's.

*Ava,* he'd whisper through the gate, *Let me show you the sun.* He'd hold out his hand. Come with me.

Always she'd cast her dark eyes his way and shake her head. *I like it where it's dark.*

He brought her new presents, pulled delights from his pockets. All of the pastries his father was teaching him to make. Buttery crescents filled with thick custard, spiced apples wrapped in puff pastry, handfuls of pie filled with sweet cheese and marzipan. Ava delighted in the morsels, bursting with excitement as she wondered what Ewan would bring her each day, but she never went with him when he asked.


His pastries worked like a potion in her blood. She could think of nothing but Ewan. He awakened her. Those lightly muscled arms, fuzzed with new hairs. The way his thighs filled his breeches. The earnest smile on his face, always with a hint of hope that she'd join him on his excursion.

She no longer dreamed of the forest at night. Instead she dreamed of the forest with him in it. Showing Ewan her special places—her favourite spots to perch, to sit and wait, to bask in the glow of the moon. The space between her legs grew moist and she found her hands wandering to the rosy buds on her chest. She felt the stirrings in her body.


Ava knows when he reaches the gate. She knows his step as well as she knows her own. That sure, quick pace so different from her shuffle. In the day she shuffles, she knows it, but in her dreams she walks with a practiced pattern of feet through the forest.

*Come with me, Ava,* he whispers, her name a blessing on his tongue.

Ava looks at him and her lips part, exposing those exquisite teeth. *Ewan,* she whispers, her voice just a breath, so laden with want. *Show me the day.*

His smile splits open. It blazes wide and bright as a sunset. He takes her long-fingered hand in his moist, warm one and she opens the gate to stand beside him. April watches and smiles for her little charge; this girl will find love after all. She will not die alone.

Ewan leads Ava down one street and then the next. She follows him blindly; she hardly knows the world outside her little home. Ewan holds her hand firmly as he guides her through the cobbled streets, steering her out of the way of carriages and piles of horse manure. Ava looks with wonder at the stalls they pass: baskets of fruit all the colours of the rainbow, clothes and tapestries, rosaries and prayer cards, statues of the Virgin Mary, tobacco-pipes and fish and dead pigs hanging from hooks. Live chickens squawking, clucking, tussling one another in their cages. Stray dogs pleading for morsels of food. An acrobat who plies his trade for spare coins. Ava marvels at each and every sight, and Ewan must tug her along to make her follow. She does not know this world by day.

The path leads to the outskirts of the forest and suddenly Ava is home. *Come,* she says, tugging Ewan with a twinkle in her eye. *Follow me.* And then she runs, free as the wind, her long legs carrying her through the thickets and briars. She jumps over scraggly bushes and loops her arms around tree trunks and low branches, grasping and flying, deft as an acrobat. Ewan struggles to keep up. Thorns and brambles scratch his legs and tear his clothes. *Where are you going?*

Ava runs, her skirts dancing around every fallen log and outstretched branch. She knows her way.

Ewan trips and falls. *Ava!* he calls out. He scratches a tear from his eye and sucks in his breath. *Ava, you'll get lost. And I could never live with that.*

From far ahead, Ava hears him. She stops her sprint and turns back. She slowly picks her way back to Ewan's side. *I'm sorry*, she says, a tentative smile playing along her lips, *I was free*.

Ewan looks at her as she speaks, from his sorry perch on the ground, shirt torn and stockings in tatters. *How do you see in this dark?*

*I want to show you my favourite place.* She holds out her hand and pulls him up. She walks next to him as he gingerly picks his way through the brambles and moss. He does not ask how she knows the forest so well; he merely follows, his pride a little hurt, knees a little bruised.


Sunlight dips through the canopy and the trees thin. Ava and Ewan emerge in a clearing. *Here*, she breathes. She lies down on the grass, a few rocks and dried leaves scattered around her. The sun hits her skin and Ewan is transfixed by its pallor. She does not belong to the realm of the sun.

*Sit beside me*, she says, tapping the ground, and Ewan forgets his every thought. He sits and his body trembles. He feels himself rising and he cannot look at her face. Instead he fixes his eyes on her wrist.

She brushes her hand over his thigh and he jerks away. *Ava*, he murmurs, voice no more than a hoarse croak.

*Ewan.* She leans forward and Ewan looks up. He can't help but notice the swell of her breasts beneath her blouse. He pulls his gaze to her face and loses himself in those gray eyes. Her lips part. She leans closer. *Ava, I—*

*Shhh.* She touches a finger to his lips. *Will you kiss me?*

His pulse hammers in his throat. *Kiss you?* he repeats.

*Kiss me.*

He hopes she does not see his trembling as he presses in and touches his lips to hers. Awkward, simple, beautiful.

A breath escapes her lips. She touches them with a finger, exploring the place where his mouth touched hers. She looks at him, a smile playing about her face. *Ewan, will you one day make me your wife?*

His eyes light up. *I wish to make you mine.*

A stream of naked want hums through her body. She feels like a torch ignited; she needs to be consumed by the flame. *Ewan*, she murmurs, hands running the breadth of his shoulders. *Make me yours.*

*But Ava—*

She stops his protests with a finger to his lips. Please. She traces her hand down his torso, inches it across the softness of his belly. *Touch me.*

He reaches a trembling hand to her neck and hesitantly runs it down her throat. The skin strangely hard. He can feel her pulse, quick as his own. He pauses, swallows, then quickly cups a hand around a small breast. She gasps, then smiles encouragingly. Ewan explores her body then, and the fire within her flares.

By the time the sun's rays slant sideways, afternoon just beginning its metamorphosis into evening, the two youths lie naked in the clearing, wrapped in each other's arms, Ava's legs curled around Ewan's. She clings to him possessively in her sleep, clutching his torso and holding him tight. His arms, muscles bulging gently from their frame, cuddle her to his body. His manhood, spent now, exposed to the sun's touch. They look both beautiful and strange together—this tall, thin girl with skin like fog, intertwined with the peach-pink, soft-skinned, stocky youth. Their eyelashes dust their cheeks as they rest, the air growing colder as the sun arcs west.

The moon comes out and still they sleep. Ewan breathes softly now, his chest rising and falling in a deep sleep, even as the sun sets and the owls begin to hoot. Ava's breaths soft but quick—shallow pulses, as though she waits to wake. And then she does, when the moon rises higher and casts its light on her shape. She looks to Ewan then, still sleeping, and she blushes. She studies his naked body with her eyes—every inch of his beautiful skin, so soft and wondrous. The soft stirrings of love tug at her heart.

She looks to the moon, then, almost full, hanging heavy, and she feels a different kind of hunger awaken inside of her. Not the urgent pulse that sang through her body before, where she could think of nothing but Ewan and her need to couple with him. No, not anymore, not now that he has spilled his seed inside of her and she can feel it warm and hot—alive—inside. This is a different hunger entirely, and Ava recognizes it.

She looks to Ewan now, deliciously naked. She smiles and runs her tongue along his throat. He stirs but does not wake. Ava's teeth hum. She bends her head to Ewan's chest and breathes in his scent. Her eyes turn inward and she sees. She remembers breaking open the sac, a slow gnawing process with her pedipalps, pushing tiny new legs into cold night air. Tom behind her. She remembers flying on a filament, lighter than air. Catching the wind all the way into town on that first night. Landing on the doorstep, legs first. Naked.

By the time someone heard her cries, she was no longer herself. Instead, she held a new shape. A vulnerable, pale, peculiar shape. A shape that never fit, even after all these years. She could only hold her real form at night, under the moon's beams. Scuttling down rickety bedframes, flitting through cracks and under doorways, catching the wind with filaments of silk and flying with Tom to the forest. Where she belongs.

She opens her mouth wide now, above Ewan's throat, and pauses for only a relished second before she ducks her head and bites him open.

Ewan wakes as blood gurgles out of his throat. His eyes open wide with fear and see his love with blood circling her lips. He tries to cry out but blood spurts from his neck, spittles from his mouth. His fists pound Ava's shoulders but they do nothing against the hard shell of her skin. Ava lunges forward and seizes his throat between her teeth, too intent on her task to notice Ewan's urgent eyes, frantic sobs.


Tom knows when his sister does not return. He knows that she is gone. April whispers into his ear, *She eloped with the baker's boy.* But he knows this is not the right story.

A lone spider roams the forest. He crawls up and down the trunks of trees, searching. He knows when he finds it. He can smell it. He crawls up the tree trunk and stands sentry all night.

No sign of her; she's gone like a spider on the wind. He waits all night, listening, staying perfectly still, invisible against the bark of the tree.

Morning casts its light into the forest and he drops from the tree to the ground. Naked, human. He is afraid to open the earth. But he summons the courage and pulls apart the freshly-churned soil beneath the tree's roots. And there he finds what she hid, and he knows without a shred of a doubt that she is gone. Bones, gnawed by pointed teeth. Cracked open, the marrow sucked out. Fresh bones. Too many bones. A complete skeleton. Tom throws the bones back into the earth and retches. He spits on his palms and wipes the blood away. He grasps the earth in handfuls and casts it back where it belongs. When his task is complete, he pats the soil under the tree, hiding his sister's secret.


A spider skitters across the forest floor. She carries a white sac on her back, eggs heavy inside. She searches for the perfect spot, wandering through the foliage of each bush she comes across. And then she finds it.

Carefully, she pulls her egg-sac from her abdomen and attaches it to the underside of the leaf. She nudges it, making sure it's safe, then skitters away, an intoxicating freedom in her step. She finds a spot on the branch of a nearby bush and waits the night, moonbeams shivering down onto her back. She rests, her task complete. By morning, only a husk remains.

# SUNSET AT THE SEA OF FERTILITY

By Tony Noland

The edge of the sun turned purple-green two days before sunset. They crowded into the Pasture to watch as the discolouration bled across Sol's sinking face. Under the dome's layers of polarized polyaluminum, they muttered and swore, tromped the carbongrass and scared the rabbits until Jacob forced them to leave. For a few hours after Sol was gone, the stain of the coronal mass ejection lingered above the craggy horizon as a luminous glow.

*Like a halo for the angel of death*, Jacob thought. *The question is, do you pray to God to protect you, or pray to Sol for mercy?*

He came in from the Pasture and laid down the sleeping rabbit, another one of the big females. He secured the strap across the chocks, pinning its head in place. Before he could hit it with the shockstick, Captain Donnelly stepped into the abattoir with Dr. Irina Kolevsky and a thin, nervous-looking man Jacob didn't know. They looked around at the dozens of skinned, headless rabbit carcasses hanging in their racks, each a pink and gray anatomy lesson.

"It's about time you brought him, Donnelly," Jacob said. "I've got to get another thirty-two rabbits culled to meet the carbon dioxide balance numbers the committee gave me. I'm taking all the matriarchs first."

"Um, won't that disrupt the breeding cycle?"

With one big hand on the rabbit, the other holding the shockstick, Jacob turned toward the newcomer who'd spoken. "Yes, that's right," Jacob said, "The females eat like locusts when they're in full breeding mode. Without the matriarchs bossing them around, all the young females will get pregnant in a matter of days. Growing embryos soak up lots of carbon." He paused. "You are Terry Jardin, aren't you? The biosystems guy from Farside?"

The other man flushed. "Um, no. My name is DeSilva."

Donnelly said, "Enrique DeSilva, meet Jacob McHenry-Xiang, chief biosystems engineer for Nearside Base." Donnelly waved his hands back and forth as he made the introductions. "DeSilva here is an expert in plant physiology."

"I don't give a damn who he is. Where the hell is Jardin? I need his expertise—we've got calculations to run."

"Dr. Jardin had a suit malfunction during the evacuation," Donnelly said. "A fatal one. I'm sure DeSilva here will be able to work with you. He was Dr. Jardin's assistant."

"Ah, not an assistant, exactly," DeSilva said. "I'm a postdoc from the University of Florida. I came up here to study -"

"Yes, that's fine," said Donnelly. "Jacob, he's going to assist you in rebalancing the biosystems to handle the increased load. We've got three days until the plasma storm hits and we're going to need to be creative in how we address this crisis. I expect you two to make it happen ASAP. To that end, Dr. Kolevsky here will go over the atmosphere numbers with you again." Donnelly turned to face the woman. "As we discussed, Dr. Kolevsky, please make Jacob fully aware of the situation and help him to revise his figures. I want you to bring the new numbers to the emergency committee briefing this afternoon. Is that clearly understood, Doctor?"

"Yes, Captain," she said, "I heard you."

Without waiting for a reply from anyone, Donnelly left.

There was a moment of silence, interrupted only by a scrabbling sound from the rabbit's nails on the table. Cursing, Jacob applied the shockstick to the base of its skull and it went still.

"I try to shock them before they wake up," Jacob said, "so they won't feel it." He hung it by the feet on the next set of hooks over the collection trough. "The gene-enhancements make them go into hibernation when the sun goes down, but this stainless steel table is so cold..." With one hand on the rabbit's neck, Jacob picked up the big loppers, the ones with the long, curved blade. "I hate it when they wake up." He held the tool, but made no move to use it.

The silence returned.

"Um, listen," DeSilva said, "Dr. Jardin showed me how to do that. Can I, ah, help you?"

Jacob sighed and said, "Yeah. Apron and gloves are in that cabinet against the wall. Go find something that fits." His eyes still fixed on the dead rabbit, Jacob heard DeSilva walk over to the equipment locker.

"Jake?" Irina had come close, her voice low and quiet behind him. "Are you OK?"

"Is that how you were told to begin? Soften me up by asking me if I'm OK?" The blade crunched through the rabbit's neck. With three snips, the head was free; he tossed it into the reprocessing bin with the others. Jacob watched the blood pulse into the collection trough, errant droplets arcing high and wide in the lunar gravity.

She said nothing.

"No, Irina, I'm not OK," he said. "We're all gonna die if we do it their way."

"You don't know that."

"It's the outcome with the highest probability, and that's as good as I've got. You have the atmosphere numbers, you know what we're dealing with here."

"Of course I do. I helped write the original recommendation, remember?"

"Then how can you help them? Knowing what you know about how the biosystem works, how can you possibly be going along with them so blindly?"

"Jacob, for the last time, I'm not blindly going along with anyone. I don't want to kill all the rabbits any more than you do, but we are running out of options. Yes, the rabbits are a source of protein for us, but the fact is, air is more important than food. It'll take us months to starve to death, but without air we all die in a week. It's that simple."

"Dammit, Irina, there's nothing simple about it. I could kill every rabbit in the warren and our oxygen consumption would only go down by two percent."

"Why do you insist on using the most pessimistic assumptions about -"

"And having killed them all, we not only lose the only means we have of converting cellulose to useable food calories, but the carbon dioxide capture efficiency of the Pasture goes right to hell. Without the rabbits in there grazing them down, the carbongrass goes to maturity in five days and full dormancy in nine."

"Don't lecture me, Jacob, I know how it works."

"Yeah? Did you forget that dormant grasses don't fix carbon dioxide, don't make oxygen and don't transpire water?"

"They don't shut down completely during dormancy and you know it."

"Efficiency drops so low they might as well. We're gonna need every fraction of a percent if we're to make it until a rescue comes. Look, forget about the rabbits as a food supply, OK? Without them, the Pasture can't replenish the air or filter the water. Did you people even read the report?"

"Oh, so now I'm 'you people'? What the hell is that supposed to mean?"

"Ah, excuse me?" DeSilva stood off to the side, shifting his feet. "I don't mean to interrupt, but, um..."

Irina crossed her arms and turned away. Jacob turned to snap at him, then stopped himself, and drew another breath before speaking. "Yes?"

"I just wanted to let you know that I'm all set," DeSilva said. "If you could show me which females I should bring in, I can get out of your way. Leave you to your, uh, discussion."

Jacob glanced at Irina, then said, "Right, let's go." He stepped away from the table, toward the door to the Pasture.

Irina put a hand on his arm. "Jacob," she said, "we need to talk about this. Seriously, I mean. I have to be able to tell them something."

"Tell them... tell them I'll be consulting with Dr. Enrique DeSilva, a subject matter expert who worked with the chief biosystems engineer at Farside."

"Hey, um, listen, I'm not really an expert in -"

"Will you do that for me, Irina? Just tell them I'll have a revised estimate by nine o'clock tomorrow morning?"

She shook her head. "Tonight, Jacob. They'll be deciding this tonight."

"No!" He slammed the table. "They don't 'decide' anything in here! They don't know what they're doing! When it comes to the biosystems, they only advise and request—I decide!"

"Jacob, please! Things are different now. The system is stretched past the breaking point. They're scared. We're all scared." She rubbed her eyes, red-rimmed with fatigue.

After a moment, Jacob took off his gloves and lightly stroked her hair. "I know, Irina. I'm sorry," he said. "I'm just trying to keep them from doing something stupid, something that looks like it might buy some time but will kill us all in the long term."

Irina reached up and pulled his hand to her cheek. "Is there even going to be a long term, Jake? Is there?"

He caressed her and said, "I don't know. But we have to act like there will be, don't we? Or we might as well give up now."

She held his hand, cupping it to her lips before kissing his palm and letting him go. As she straightened, she said, "I'm sorry, Jake, really, I am, but I need to give them some kind of concession. Something, anything. Please."

Jacob sighed, then pulled his gloves back on. "Fine. Tell them we'll do all the rabbits the committee originally advised, plus an additional fifteen. Will that be enough to hold them off? Can you get them to see reason?"

Her mouth twisted into a half-smile. "That's asking a lot of military administrators, but I think it should calm them down. For now, anyway. After the storm hits, though? It'll just depend on what happens." She walked past DeSilva, but stopped at the door. "Jacob, rational calculations took a backseat to emotions after the last rescue shuttle left. They're not going to start asking for volunteers when there's even a single rabbit still breathing. It's just not going to happen." With that, she left.

Jacob leaned against the table and closed his eyes.

"Um, hey, I'm sorry for interrupting you two. I didn't mean to cause any trouble."

"Forget it."

"Listen, can I ask something?" DeSilva's voice was a little unsteady. "What did she mean about asking for volunteers?"

"It means that some of us are going to be heroes before this is all over." Seeing that DeSilva didn't understand, he said, "This coronal mass ejection is the biggest solar plasma storm we've ever recorded, by a factor of at least ten million. It's bad enough that it's headed right toward us, still worse that it would hit when it was nighttime here at Nearside. Farside Base is a much bigger facility, outnumbering us three-to-one."

"Right, because of the radio astronomy station and the helium mines."

Jacob nodded. "It would have been much better for us to be able to evacuate over to your place instead of having all you guys come here. The radiation and ion scouring from the coronal plasma is going to make Farside leak like a punctured tire, so we are all stuck, crammed together here. Have you done any calculations of Nearside's life support carrying capacity?"

"I've been trying," DeSilva said, "but I don't even know how many people came over."

"Well, there's been a lot of reassuring blather from the emergency committee in the Base Administrator's office, but I've seen the numbers. I know better than anyone what kind of a load our biosystems can handle." Jacob waited for DeSilva to ask, but his expression made it plain that he feared the answer. "Under starvation rations," Jacob said, "the food will hold out longer than the air. That's assuming the rabbits keep the Pasture at peak photosynthetic capacity and the chemical carbon dioxide scrubbers hold out. After that, we suffocate."

"So the volunteers she's talking about are -"

"- are people willing to go outside and vent their suits." He pushed aside the skinned and gutted carcass. "The sooner they start asking people to make the ultimate sacrifice, the greater the chance the rest will survive until Earth can send another shuttle."

"My God. But how long will that be? When will they be able to launch?"

Jacob opened an equipment cupboard and set up a second workstation on the steel table, a few feet away from his own. Chocks, loppers, gutting knife and hanging rack, all standard issue.

"That depends on how many people are left alive on Earth after the storm passes, if they still have launch capability and if we're anywhere on the priority list."

"What if they can't send a shuttle for us?"

"Then we'll need more volunteers."

"And if they don't get enough willing volunteers?"

Jacob walked to the curtainwall and held it back for DeSilva. After a moment, the younger man went through and Jacob followed him into the Pasture.


Days later, when the coronal mass hit, the Sun's superheated plasma swirled around the moon like a stream flowing around a rock, leaving Nearside Base in a relatively sheltered calm. The dome was lit with swirling colours, interrupted by bright electrical discharges, each the size of a continent. Jacob heard a stuttering whine from the intake vents and smelled the warm, fetid air as it poured into the Pasture.

"The rabbits are awake," said DeSilva. "I think they're sick, though."

"No, they're just groggy," Jacob replied as he continued to work through calculations at a whiteboard as he spoke. "The light from the plasma woke them early."

"Oh." DeSilva looked up, then looked away. The view was hypnotic, but behind the glowing cloud was the Earth, now suffering an unknown fate. He said, "I think I liked it better when we could see what was happening back home."

"You mean like watching those giant lightning storms stretch from pole to pole when the Earth's magnetic field lines started to compress together?" Jacob said. "Or when the upper atmosphere began to stream away into space?" He stepped away from the board, frowning. "It's just as well we can't watch."

DeSilva sat in silence, trying not to look up. "Jacob?"

"Yes?"

"Are we safe in here?"

"You mean here in the Pasture?" Jacob nodded. "On emergency power, the fans are moving the air, but everything else is more or less shut off. We're not going to have full power again until sunrise, still more than seven days away." *At least we'll be able to store power from the solar arrays,* he thought. *If those power surges had fried the nuclear lattice batteries, we'd only have power during the fourteen days of sunlight. We'd be dead at the next sundown.*

Jacob returned to the board, revising his predictive model for the life support system. When the solar plasma short-circuited everything, electrical fires had consumed some of their oxygen, but eleven people died from electrocution, another fourteen from asphyxiation before they got the fans working again. He worked and re-worked the numbers.

"Well?" asked DeSilva.

The light from the dome flashed overhead. Horrific, tempest lightning, but without the thunder, punctuated only by the sound of the irregular blowing from the vents.

"Losing twenty-five people extends our food and water significantly," Jacob replied, "but it only extends the air by two days."

"Oh."

"What about you? Are you making any progress?"

DeSilva put down the luminometer. "It's only about four percent as bright as normal sunlight."

"The carbongrasses are as heavily gene-engineered for the lunar environment as the rabbits are. There's enough light from the plasma storm to trigger some level of photosynthesis, isn't there?"

"Maybe, if it's the right spectrum," DeSilva said. "If the wavelengths are wrong, the plants won't photosynthesize no matter how bright it is. I wish we could run the overhead flood lights to supplement it, but that takes power."

"Which we don't have." Jacob felt more tired than he could ever remember. "I didn't expect to get even this much light from the plasma. It's just that I was hoping it would push the numbers more."

"So we're screwed?" said DeSilva. "We just wait until we all start passing out?"

Jacob paused, then straightened. "No," he replied, "we don't just wait. We take action."

"What do you mean? What more can we do?"

"I don't have time to explain it in detail. I need you to go over to the tool room by the loading bay. There's a crate of equipment marked 'condensors—manual operation'. Find it and bring it back."

"Tool room, loading bay, condensors. Got it. I'll be right back." DeSilva hurried from the office.

Jacob sighed. He closed the door then twisted the manual override lever on the control panel. Heavy bolts shot home, locking the door and preventing access to the office from the outside. There were four entrances that led directly into the Pasture; walking around the perimeter, he secured them all.

"Jake?"

*Irina*, he thought. *She suspected me all along. I wonder why that doesn't surprise me?* He turned to face her.

She held the anti-personnel taser gun up high, aimed at his chest.

*Has she been crying? Or is that just a trick of this light?*

"You son of a bitch," she said. "You sent him out there to die."

"I couldn't let him stay here. They would have broken down the doors to come in after him. If it's just me in here, they might not come in. I might be able to talk them out of it."

"You would have left me out there to die, too."

Jacob shook his head. "No, Irina, that's not true. DeSilva is... look, I'm sorry about him, OK? I'm sorry that it's come to this for all of us. But in here or out there, when they start drawing up lists of who's essential and who's not, he's not going to make the cut."

"And you are? You're so damned important that you get to live while DeSilva and who knows how many others don't? What's it going to take, Jacob? How many have to die so the rest can live? And all that while you're safe in here with your precious goddamned rabbits?"

"Without the Pasture, everybody dies. And without somebody to maintain it, the Pasture dies. Believe me, I wish someone else could do this job. I was expecting Jardin to come over from Farside in the evacuation. We could have, I don't know, flipped a coin or something, made it fair. But as it is? The emergency committee is going crazy out there, only pretending to be rational. I have to keep them from destroying the Pasture's ecology, or the sacrifices the volunteers are going to make won't be enough. Please, Irina, I have no choice. "

"But you chose not to tell me you were going to barricade yourself in here. You were going to abandon me."

"I wasn't abandoning you. I knew you'd be safe. You're their expert for the nutrient recyclers. The committee wouldn't ask you to volunteer, they need you."

She lowered the gun. "No," she said, "they don't. I saw the new list before the power went out. You're safe. I'm not."

"No. I don't believe it."

"My name won't be in the first round of volunteers. If I'm lucky, it won't be in the second round, either. But by the third?" She shook her head.

Jacob sagged against the wall. "You were supposed to be safe. I was sure of it." He looked up at her. "But you're safe now. You're in here, with me."

She shook her head. "No, Jake. I'm no different from DeSilva. If I stay in here with you, they'll come in to get me, and once they're in, they'll kill the rabbits and then they'll kill you. I can't let them do that." Irina tucked the gun into her waistband and approached him. She tilted his face down and kissed him. "Make it work, Jake. If the Pasture keeps the air and water clean, they won't have to start drawing names." At one of the doors, she undid the manual override, opened the hatch and stepped out into the hallway. "Lock this after me, Jake. I'll do what I can to keep them from breaking in."

"Get the power back on, Irina. Drain the batteries, use the generators from the rovers, cannibalize the transports, anything. If I can get the flood lights on and push up the photosynthesis rate, we might have a chance."

She nodded, touched her fingers to her lips and closed the door. He re-engaged the manual locks and sealed himself in.

For the next hour, Jacob sat in his office, numb. The rabbits emerged from hiding and moved across the Pasture, nibbling the carbongrass beneath the shifting, spectral light of the sun's wrath.


Days passed in the silent, stinking dimness of the Pasture. After the solar storm moved on, the Earth was all but incinerated. Jacob searched its surface for hour after hour. Wherever his telescope was able to peer through thick, dark clouds, he saw no trace of green on any continent—only brown, white and black. All the forests of the world had burned to the ground, filling the skies with soot and ash.

Right on schedule, the sun, once again pure and bright, rose over the eastern limb of Mare Fecunditatis. When the thin blade of light hit the leading solar arrays, the dim floodlights under the dome flickered and strengthened. Through the walls and the floor, Jacob heard voices cheering as systems returned to full power. In a few minutes, the sunlight would touch the floor of the Pasture. The grasses would grow, the rabbits would feast; Nearside would have a chance.

The phone rang.

He jerked at the sound. It had been dead since the power surge.

"Yes? Hello?"

"This is Enrique DeSilva. Open those doors, you son of a bitch."

"Who? DeSilva?" *He's alive?* Since he'd locked himself in, Jacob had heard only threats, shouted at him through the heavy doors. He hadn't known who had volunteered, or had been sacrificed. *But if DeSilva is alive, then did anyone have to die?* "Listen, DeSilva, is Irina... is she..."

"Yes, she's alive, as alive as any of us are out here. Irina told me what you planned, why you did what you did. She and I convinced them to divert power from all the other systems to feed your lights, to just hang on until sunrise. Now, the power is coming back on, to the ventilation, the lights, water pumps, everything. But, dammit, we're half-dead out here! We need fresh air, we need to see something green and growing. Open the damned doors, Jacob, now!"

*We made it,* Jacob thought. *This far at least, we made it.* "I will, DeSilva, I will. But the rabbits need some time to adjust to the sunlight. I'll open up in twenty-four hours, I promise, after the base is flushed with fresh air and everyone out there has a chance to get some rest." *Plus, I don't want you to kill me as soon as you come in.*

DeSilva was quiet for a moment. Then he said, "There are pockets of survivors on Earth, but it's bad down there. Real bad. We can hear them on the emergency-band radio , but they aren't paying any attention to us. There isn't going to be a rescue, not soon. Maybe not ever."

Jacob said nothing.

"If we can cobble together a second dome with what we can salvage from Farside," DeSilva continued, "can we establish another Pasture? Are there enough rabbits and carbongrass to transfer some? The committee is trying to make plans for the long term."

Sunbeams glinted through the uppermost panes of the dome, angling downward onto the Pasture and the grazing rabbits, males and females sniffing each other.

"Yes," Jacob said, "we can do that."

# BITTER HARVEST

By Jay Raven

The banging at the cottage door was insistent, impatient—as were the voices of my confederates.

"Open up, Josiah. It's us. Open up, Man, the moon's full on. The wagon's ready. It's time to get to work."

Swallowing hard, I laid my clay pipe by the grate and got up from my rocker. The bangs continued but I ignored them, peering worriedly through the dusty glass at the full, fat orb blazing high in the sky, its brilliance pushing back the darkness.

It was as bright a night as I could ever remember; an unwelcome amount of illumination for the furtive task we had to perform.

"Please, my love, don't go. I'm begging you." Mary's voice was taut, eyes moist in the candlelight. "Tell them you want no part of this. They can keep the money. We'll make do, scrimp and sacrifice a little more. We'll get by somehow."

I shook my head. I wasn't going to allow our children to go hungry another day; to pretend not to notice as Mary, gaunt and weary, took what meagre victuals were on her plate and stuffed them in the mouth of our youngest. I wasn't prepared to go on confronting my haunted face in the looking glass, the expression of self-loathing and helplessness tearing my soul apart.

They said the famine was an act of God and no man should feel he'd failed, but that didn't make me feel any less wretched.

What pathetic kind of man couldn't provide for his family? I had to do something, even if it was against the law and risked me dangling at the end of a noose.

Besides, even if I had wanted to pull out, I couldn't. Not with these stone-hearted men. My new companions weren't the kind you let down. I had only been acquainted with them for a few days, knew them only as Daniels and Lafferty, but in that time I'd witnessed enough to comprehend the unspeakable pain and cruelty they could inflict if I displeased them.

"I won't tell you again, Farm Boy. Don't vex me. Open up or we'll break this bloody door down."

Squeezing Mary's sagging shoulder, I pulled back the metal bolt and let in the sharp, dry, Autumn air.

"What's your game, Matey?" Daniels pushed his gangly frame past me and grinned darkly at Mary, making no attempt to hide his appraising gaze. "What kept you? Having some slap and tickle with the lovely wife?"

"No," Lafferty corrected, slamming the door shut behind him. "He got cold feet. Thought he'd just leave us outside and we'd quietly go away. That it, Carrot-cruncher? Planning to welch on your side of the bargain?"

I gasped, unprepared for the beefy fingers that grabbed my throat and dug in viciously.

"Nooo... no... it wasn't like that," I tried to say, but the pressure was agony, my neck burning, my tongue tasting coppery blood as I spluttered and coughed.

"Cos we'd take it right badly if that's what you thought, friend." Lafferty's plump unshaven face came close and I was assailed by the stench of raw onion and cheese. "There's too much at stake," he hissed, "to let some frightened, gutless bumpkin ruin it for us."

"I wasn't backing out, I promise..." My words rasped, barely comprehensible, yet the trepidation they contained seemed enough to satisfy him. With a shove, he released his grip and I dropped to my knees, retching.

"You are nothing but villains, cowards— " Mary cried, but I signalled her to be silent. Defiance could only make things worse. After an anguished moment, she acquiesced, but stared at both with undisguised loathing, fists balled.

"Ma-ma, what's going on? What's all the noise? Who are these strangers?"

My heart chilled. I'd prayed that the children would stay deep in slumber in the other room. Tom rubbed his eyes with the heel of his hand, frowning, as he came fully into the front room.

"It's fine, Lad," I told him. "Go back to bed, Son. This doesn't concern you." But he remained rooted to the spot, puzzled, blinking at me prone on the floor.

"What's wrong with Pa-pa? Is he ill?"

"Tom, do as you're told. Bed. Now." Mary bustled towards him anxiously, shooing the child away.

Daniels bared his tobacco-stained teeth in a snigger, waving his hands in a mocking pantomime of Mary's gesture.

Yet, Lafferty didn't laugh. He remained deadly serious as he took a step to block her and commanded: "No, wait. Let me look at the boy."

Taking Tom firmly by the chin, he jerked my son's face to the side and grunted. Then he felt Tom's arms.

"Seems a strong lad," he murmured, in a tone that increased my dread. "How old are you, Boy?"

"Sir?"

"What is your age?"

"Ten, Sir. Ten years and eight months."

I leapt to my feet. "Leave him be!" I ordered, sounding more brave than I felt.

Lafferty made a sour face. "I'm simply showing an interest, Friend Josiah," he said, feigning innocence. "Almost eleven, hmmm? Nearly a man. And keen for some adventure, eh Sonny?"

Tom nodded slowly, uncertain how to respond.

"Then you shall have it, Fair Lad. Tonight you shall accompany your father as he helps us carry out our lucrative chore. Another pair of hands could be of great benefit."

Mary stiffened, mouthing: "No!"

"It's out of the question," I barked. "He is not to be part of this. I forbid it."

In an instant I realized resistance was useless. Lafferty didn't answer, but slowly let his greatcoat swing open to reveal the flintlock tucked in the waistline of his britches.

"Please!" I looked deep into his unyielding eyes, trying to discern any glimmer of mercy or understanding. "He's my only son. He is precious to me. My greatest joy."

"And that's why he shall accompany us, to guarantee your full co-operation."

He paused for a heartbeat. "Unless you'd prefer Daniels to remain with your wife while we toil. I'm sure he'd find that a very appealing notion."

His rat-faced sidekick winked lewdly.

I let my head droop. "There is no need for that," I mumbled. "Tom will come. We'll do whatever you say."

Ignoring Mary's pleading look and distressed intake of breath, I told my son: "Go dress, and be swift about it. And wrap up well—it's as cold as charity out there."

The wagon bounced roughly over the rutted ground, as we travelled through the empty, dormant streets. No-one spoke, careful not to waken those in the many thatched cottages that lay between us and our goal—the deep, wide village pond. We couldn't allow anyone to witness our deeds, lest they question why we were abroad at such an ungodly hour, or why our heavy cart was loaded with long, large wooden rakes.

Being jostled in the back, I pulled Tom tight to me, hoping beyond all hope that the night's nefarious business would pass without calamity.

For the umpteenth time I asked myself why I had been so unforgivably reckless as to let these rogues talk me into this madness. Had it only been a short week ago that I'd encountered them? It seemed like they'd always been part of my life, like a gnawing ache.

I'd been in the tavern in the nearby town, half drunk, trying to find solace in the bottom of an ale glass, when they'd approached and asked how well I knew the community of Devizes.

Foolishly I'd blurted out that it was an amazing coincidence, for didn't I hail from that very village—born and brought up these 40-odd years in the Wiltshire hamlet.

They'd already known that, of course, and had been watching me all evening, waiting until I was addled before making their move.

"I hear times are harsh round here, my friend," Lafferty said, all bonhomie as he pushed another foaming pint under my nose. "Folks are suffering right severely, barely able to put enough food on the table."

I'd snorted, and told him he didn't know the half of it. I'd not worked in months, the barren fields testament to the blight that had ruined the crop and left us farm labourers bereft and desperate.

"Well, this could be your lucky night," he confided, with a mischievous grin. "Because I and my companion have work—good paying work—for the right man. Someone who isn't afraid to bend his back, who can keep his mouth tight shut and knows Devizes and all the quiet lanes and byways leading from it."

Even in my stupor, I sensed that this work was trouble; that the kind words pouring from their lips like over-ripe honey were dangerous lies.

But the money... oh Lord, the thought of sovereigns in my money bag, paying my mounting debts, was all it took to overcome my apprehension and niggling doubts.

They described themselves as transporters of rare and much sought-after wares, but I knew they were smugglers. In a conspiratorial whisper, Lafferty explained that they'd been due to collect a consignment of contraband French brandy being brought up secretly from the South coast by mule train. The handover was to have been just five miles from my home. From there, it was to be ferried North by wagon, to the sprawling, thirsty towns of the Midlands, the casks hidden under a deep coating of straw.

Without paying the hefty duties charged on such imports, my newly acquired comrades were guaranteed to make a comfortable profit.

That had been their plan. However, it had all gone awry. Acting on intelligence, His Majesty's Customs men had been scouring the countryside, backed up by troops from the Fifth Company of Foot.

"The fools we were supposed to meet caught sight of the Revenue men, panicked and dumped the barrels," Daniels said in angry disbelief. "Rolled them straight into your damned village pond."

"And now we need to recover the submerged casks," Lafferty went on. "And you, Josiah, are going to assist us."

I gasped as the icy water surged up my thighs. Shivering, I halted, balking at wading farther out into the dark, chill foulness.

Feet away, I heard Daniels curse, as he too was soaked through.

"What's the hold-up?" Lafferty hissed from his dry vantage point on the bank. "Why have you stopped, you imbeciles!"

"It's perishing," Daniels snapped back, teeth chattering. "It's bloody freezing in this God-awful piss-hole. I'm going to catch my death."

Until this point I had thought of them as brothers in crime, inseparable. Now I realized their bond was only financial, lacking any vestige of camaraderie, as the large man scowled and replied ominously: "If you don't stop screwing around and get the barrels sharpish, I'll make sure that you do."

Daniels jerked as though slapped, before spitting into the water and staggering onwards, muttering as he grasped his unwieldy rake even tighter.

I followed, carrying my rake carefully across my body for balance, swaying with each slow, precarious step into the deepening pond. I didn't need to be threatened. I could see Tom huddled on the wagon's running board, alarm on his face, hostage to my good behaviour.

Soon Daniels and I were up to our chests, feet squelching in the soft, treacherous sludge. Without warning I felt something hit against my leg, the object big and hard.

"I've found them," I declared.

Splashing awkwardly, Daniels came to my side.

He kicked the barrel, then grinned and gave Lafferty the thumbs-up.

We plunged the unwieldy poles under the surface, the teeth of the rakes scratching across the wood as they sought for purchase.

I tugged and felt the submerged barrel start to turn, but it didn't dislodge. I pulled harder, putting all my strength into it, but it still refused to budge.

Daniels swore, having the same problem.

"What is it now?" Lafferty demanded.

"The bloody tubs won't move," his accomplice explained, giving another nerve-stretching pull. "They've stuck fast. The mud's holding them tighter than a miser's purse."

"Then pull harder!"

"I've tried, damn you. They won't give. Ask the bumpkin, if you don't believe me."

"He's telling the truth," I agreed. "The ooze has them in its grasp."

I willed the crooks to accept that it was hopeless and cease their futile enterprise. But, in my soul, I knew it was a vain hope. There was too much gold at stake.

It would require more power to break the casks free and I supposed that the scoundrels would have to return another night with more men, and chains to tie around the heavy containers. Chains that could be attached to the horses, employing their strength to haul the barrels to the surface.

However, the fat man had other ideas.

"The boy," he said.

"What!" The word exploded from my lips.

"We'll use the boy. He can dive under the water and dig them free as you pull with the rake. He has nimble fingers. He'll have no trouble breaking the suction."

"No," I snarled. "It's too perilous. I won't allow it."

I felt confident. Lafferty couldn't risk using his flintlock. The noise would attract unwelcome attention.

The sharp pain in my side told me I'd underestimated the pair. Daniels had a switch-blade, pressed hard against me, the point digging in. He'd moved more swiftly than I'd have dared imagine. His rake, now abandoned, floated idly, bobbing on the angry ripples dancing under the moonlight.

"We aren't asking for your permission," he growled. "Tell the lad to get into the water. Quick now, before I slice you up like a pig."

"He's a poor swimmer," I protested.

"Then this will be a good opportunity for him to improve."

"It's okay, Pa-pa. I'll do it. I don't mind," Tom whispered, but I knew it was bravado. Fear made his voice shake.

A shove from Lafferty, an explosion of spray and Tom was in, crossing the murky surface in short, laboured strokes.

"It'll be fine, Son," I said with a reassuring nod, as he approached. "Just take a deep breath and hold it as long as you can."

With that, he was gone, head ducked under and feet kicking, pushing downwards.

I gave Daniels a long, threatening stare. "You'd better pray that he comes to no harm," I warned.

He had a sneering reply ready, but didn't get to utter it. His mouth fell open as he glanced at something over my shoulder and went rigid at the very moment that I heard several loud clicks—familiar clicks—the unmistakable sound of musket hammers being cocked.

"Well, well, well. Here's a picture to behold. What do we have here?"

Spinning round, I saw the owner of the voice. He was short, dressed in a full-length riding coat, scuffed, dirty boots, and a three-cornered hat. He had no weapon, but the Revenue Man didn't need one. The ten tall soldiers by his side in their red tunics had more than enough firepower, rifles raised and ready.

Horrified, I watched Lafferty's hand instinctively go towards his own gun, then let out my breath in relief as his movement froze just an inch from the handle.

Like me, he'd rapidly analyzed our predicament, deducing that to resist was suicide. He might bring down one or two of our ambushers but there'd be a replying salvo of lead, cutting us to pieces.

"I asked you, what do you think you're doing?" the Customs man repeated, irritation clear.

My head whirled. I had to think of an answer, some plausible innocent explanation, before my accomplices tried to bolt, or blurted out something that would condemn us.

I opened my mouth, not sure what words would pour out: "My Lord, don't shoot. Don't shoot. We're honest men, simple farm labourers."

The Customs Inspector grunted. "I didn't ask who you were, Oaf. I asked what you were doing."

"Fishing, Your Honour."

"What!"

I don't know who was more surprised, the Excise official or the smugglers, who glared at me as though I'd lost my senses.

"We be fishing," I said, making my rural twang more pronounced, and giving him a wide, foolish grin.

"In a village pond? Don't talk soft. What kind of fish do you cretins think you'll catch in a mud pool?" His voice dripped with sarcasm, suspicion obvious. "Unless, of course, you are fishing for something more valuable. Like some smuggler's booty."

I frowned, and flashed him a bemused expression, as though the very idea was beyond reason.

"Booty? Smuggler's booty? Oh Sir, I don't know what you're referring to but it sounds fanciful indeed."

I was about to say more but a petrifying thought struck: Tom. In the commotion, I'd forgotten about my son. He was still under the water!

Frantically, I scanned the still pond. He should have surfaced by now! I gulped back the bile filling my throat.

My instincts clashed. I yearned to dive down and rescue him, but another part of my brain—rational, emotionless, calculating—counselled that to do so would doom us all to the gallows.

Abruptly, Daniels flinched, jerking his head towards a faint disturbance in the water behind him. Lord be praised, Tom's small head popped up, eyes wide in panic, mouth open and greedily gulping air. I almost swooned, but my joy disappeared as the smuggler reached backwards and grabbed Tom by the hair, forcing him back under before the child had chance to make a sound.

It was over in a heartbeat, so fast that our captors were unaware what had transpired.

Guts twisting, I spoke to the Revenue man with renewed urgency, holding my hands wide in submission. "Truly, Sir. I cannot fool you. You have seen through our harmless deception. There are certainly no fish to be caught in these waters. We be after a much bigger prize."

And lifting my rake, I dragged it across the pond towards the ball of light shimmering on its surface.

"The moon," I announced. "We be after capturing the moon."


The night echoed with laughter. Even Lafferty and Daniels, stunned and unable to comprehend what gibberish I was uttering, chortled.

The Customs official doubled over, slapping the side of his britches, tears of mirth rolling down his wrinkled cheeks.

"See, see," he spluttered to the troopers. "I told you. I told you these yokels were witless buffoons. Capturing the moon! Ha, I've never heard anything so idiotic in all my life."

I feigned puzzlement and annoyance. "Your Honour, I don't see why you should find such merriment in our enterprise. It will make us all rich men. There are many grand ladies and fine men who will pay handsomely to own this wondrous white globe. Even his Majesty the King would surely desire to have it hang behind his throne."

This made all laugh even louder.

"Pay handsomely for the moon! Do you hear what he said? It's hilarious." The Revenue agent shook his head pityingly. "You bumpkins aren't even blessed with the common sense the rest of us are born with. It's no more than a reflection, you clown. You can't snatch it from the water."

"Sir? Are you sure, Sir?"

He jerked his thumb upwards. "It's up there in the sky. See. Miles above us."

I frowned theatrically, careful not to overdo my performance. "Then what is that?" I enquired. "At the end of my rake. Surely, there cannot be two such dazzling orbs."

He rolled his eyeballs, muttering: "God almighty, just how pig-shit stupid can these inbred peasants be?"

He came to a decision in seconds.

"C'mon men, we're wasting our time here," he declared, his finger mockingly circling the side of his head to signal that I was clearly a lunatic. "They're obviously too brainless to be smugglers. Our quarry lies elsewhere. We need to get moving. We have a lot of ground to cover before daybreak. We'll leave our deluded rural friends here to their cretinous endeavours. Much good may it do them."

I bowed with mock solemnity, as did my two now-smirking companions.

With a last disbelieving backwards glance, the Government man snorted and led the contingent away, back into the darkness from whence they'd come.

For a full, agonizing minute, I watched them go, my whole body trembling, my nerves screaming, wanting to yell with delight and shock that my outrageous dupe had worked.

"You did it, you bloody well pulled it off, Carrot-cruncher. You pulled the wool over their eyes," Lafferty gasped, heaving with hilarity—this time at the gullibility of those who'd sought to trap us. "They swallowed your fairy tale like babes in arms."

But there was no time for celebration or back-slapping. I had more pressing business to attend to. Frantically, I surged across to Daniels, hissing: "Let him up. Let Tom up. Take your hand off his head."

He didn't reply. Didn't move.

"I said, let him up, you bastard. Let him breathe."

Daniels' pained expression made me gasp, in icy realization. A cry formed in my throat as I saw that both his hands were in clear view—and had been for ages.

I fell to my knees, splashing, thrashing, grabbing through the water like a man possessed, as the single word "Tom!" screeched from my lips.

They say our exploits have become the stuff of legend, the talk of the taverns. Many chuckle, marvelling at our cunning and audacity, and predicting that Wiltshire men will be forever known as Moonrakers.

I care little.

All I know is that night I lost my son and my soul. And learned just what evil and depravity I am capable of...

Mary swore that none of it was my fault, I had no choice and should not blame myself for our darling Tom's death, but she hasn't been able to look me in the eye since, or comfort me as I weep.

Every night, I see my son's poor, bedraggled, frail, drowned body in my nightmares. He is light as I pluck him from the chilly wetness and cradle him to my bosom, squeezing tight... so tight.

I have a hazy recollection of what occurred next that accursed evening; mere glimpses, fragments seen through a crimson mist of violence and rage.

I recall grabbing Daniels with both hands, pushing his foul frame towards the water, intent that he too should drown. Struggling wildly, he cursed and thrashed, fighting to break my inhuman grip as I forced him face first far into the freezing darkness.

However, I was robbed of the satisfaction of watching the precious air leaving his lungs, for a sharp crack exploded near my ear and Daniels shuddered and went still.

The musket ball, meant for me, lay embedded in his broken back, ruby blood dripping copiously into the water.

Letting his dying bulk sink, I began slipping and sliding my way towards the bank, roaring, splashing chaotically. Lafferty, visage pale, nostrils flared, raced to reload. Despite my fury, I made slow progress and the cur must have thought he had time.

But I had Daniels' knife and years of experience throwing blades at the vermin in the barn.

It landed square between his incredulous eyes and he crumpled to his knees, mouth falling open lopsidedly. He wasn't dead... not then. That came dozens of frenzied stabs later, as I vented my crazed grief.

Many seasons have passed, the barrels of brandy long since gone, removed and sold, the proceeds the only thing that saved so many families from starvation during that cruellest of winters.

Yet, our village pond still holds secrets.

And each month, I stand alone by its edge and softly say a prayer, staring downwards until I glimpse the bleached, white bones held in the greedy mud—bones that fluoresce and shine, gleaming starkly under the light of the accusing moon.

# A MOON RISE IN SEVEN HOURS

By Lori Strongin

## Midnight

This is not a fairy tale. No one will hang their bodies in the sky when they die.


The city slumbers under dark shadows cast from a wandering crescent moon. Oz, six stories up, presses his face against the smudged glass window. He feels as if he's just run a marathon with something squeezing his heart until he can't breathe.

He knows It is coming, the *thing* that will break down the door and destroy him even if he surrenders. Its endless hunger will leave him broken and battered like the girl in the bed behind him. She feasts upon an apple-flavored split end as she turns off the alarm clock.

The coffee mug he holds slips from his fingers, crashes to the floor. He stares at it for a minute, the blue liquid spreading, seeping into the rotting floorboards. Slowly he kneels, fingers wrapping around a shard of cool, broken ceramic. He holds it up to his face, examining the way the porcelain cracked in a straight line, jutting sharply into a pointed edge.

The white of the glaze looks like bone, and Oz wonders if this is what her skull looks like. Sharp angles, harsh fault lines, jagged edges.

Oz looks at the shards on the floor, knowing that the mug can never be put back together. There are too many pieces, like an unsolvable puzzle. The mug is no longer a mug, just broken glass.

Like her.

Oz loves her. He *loves* her, but he doesn't know if he can do this. He's afraid. Of himself, of what he'll do, what he's done. He's never been one to handle responsibility well. Oz is the one to lash out, to put up his defenses, to push others away.

Not her. Never *her*.

And still, he can do nothing to stop It from coming for her. For them both.

"Do you ever feel like…however hard you try, you can't get it right? No matter what you do?" he asks.

She is too far gone to answer.


**One a.m.**


*Oz would never forget the way Tsuki Yomo looked, felt, tasted, smelled that night as they worked together on a Sudoku puzzle in his living room. He peered over her shoulder, the girl framing the numbers slowly as she tried to keep up, muttering sums under her breath. She was slow in everything she did—waxing, glowing silver-white, before fading into the waif again. But it didn't really matter when her body was a mass of warmth pressed against his chest as she shifted in his lap. He tongued the bubble gum from her mouth and tasted her upon the candy, all the time bending her closer to the floor.*

*The next morning, they found her mother hanging from the red maple in the backyard, like a monkey swinging on a vine.*


**Two a.m.**

Oz's eyes grow heavy, but every time he thinks about dozing off, the choking uneven cough from the tangle of blankets on the ratty mattress startles him back to wakefulness. His head is foggy and his tongue clings to the roof of his mouth from not having enough water.

Determinism, he knows, is an idea that has been around for centuries, millennia. It came from Mayans who could speak the language of the moon. Everything is predetermined, they said. Free will doesn't exist. And thus if you recognize all the factors beforehand, you will know everything that will happen, how it will happen and when. Not the details, the minutiae, but the big moments, the important moments, the moments that count.

But if that were true, then Oz would have understood the meaning behind his inability to breathe the day he met Tsuki, would have expected the feeling of being punched in the stomach, been unsurprised by the world glowing brighter and more beautiful out of the abyss of nothingness whenever she was near.

If it was pre-written what he would say, what he thought, what he would do when the moment came, then couldn't that tiny rebellious part of him have argued, "I don't have to do what you say. I can break the mold. We can be free."

But he didn't.

If there were any truth in the world, then he could have saved her from this.

The waiting makes his hands shake. Or perhaps that's the fear, the uncertainty he's lived with for twenty-eight days as the moon waned and waxed and waned again.

He can taste It, like fire and thistle.


**Three a.m.**

*Every time Oz closed his eyes, he'd see Tsuki's grandfather—an old sea fox—sitting low in his chair, dragons of smoke wafting from his rice paper cigarettes, sipping sake from a snifter that reflected candlelight rainbows around the room.*

*Just as the ancient mariner sat every night since the day his only child took her life, now more ghost than man.*

*"You're the only one left now," he told Tsuki. "The old traveler, spinning tales. He took your mother; he'll take you, too."*

*Oz tried to soothe her, Tsuki with her dark eyes and perfume that smelt like her grandfather's garden where the old fox spent hours on end, sifting through soil, giving birth through his fingertips, now sleeping beneath his prized Japanese maple, buried under the light of the full blood moon.*

*That night a grieving girl found relief in a boy, a needle, and a vial of Dark Side of the Moon.*

*Oz never knew if she mourned the old man, or what his death meant. He was too afraid to ask.*

### Four a.m.

Staring at the dim lights of the alarm clock, Oz wonders what a.m. and p.m. actually stand for.

And why he bothers to care.

He feels It coming.

His skin peels away from his bones and tries to crawl away through cracks in the floorboards, but eventually snaps back into place. He takes his pulse to remind himself that he's still living.

Alive…alive…alive.

A mantra in his mind. Something to startle himself from sleep because he can feel his eyes drifting, drooping, closing, slamming open, like a lullaby he can't stop humming.

The blankets shift and Tsuki's hair settles like moon rocks on a polished mirror.

### Five a.m.

*Oz knew all about falling.*

*He had watched Tsuki's little sister tumble down the stairs at the age of five; saw the way her blood stained the rug while Tsuki screamed. Saw her mother's shaking hands, the wildness in her eyes as she stumbled before finally hitting bottom at the end of a hangman's noose two weeks later, the half-moon her only witness.*

*And so Death claimed the first, the monkey.*

*Her grandfather followed a fortnight later—he, the witness, the watcher, the patient one, the keeper of the tale. The old man fell on a bullet from a .45 Remington, straight through his heart.*

*This time, Death took with him the fox.*

*And then there was Oz...taking the plunge that night when Tsuki, desperate to escape the past of future's present, pressed herself against his cold, chapped mouth and slipped Solid Courage through a newly exposed vein. If it wasn't so messy and clumsy and perfect, it would have been laughable, but nothing amused him much these days.*

*Oh yes, he could write a whole book on falling. Which was why, when the sliver sliced the sky once more and he knew the old traveler would come to complete his collection, Oz didn't give Tsuki the chance to say Yes.*

## Six a.m.

Her breath rattles to a stop; her face, swollen and edged with purple, is relaxed, jaw slightly open, only the slightest crease between her eyebrows. The bed beneath her grows cold.

Oz kneels next to her, takes her in his arms, never wants to let her go.

The silence of the apartment is crushing. It wraps around his throat and seeps into his pores, completely overwhelming him. His breathing grows ragged as his thoughts fracture into nothing. Or maybe he's thinking about everything. Oz can't even tell anymore.

Without her, everything feels off-balance. There is no counter weight to hold Oz up. Nothing will be able to stop his fall now that she is gone.

Then, he hears It.

A knock at the door, but Oz won't answer it. He's wrapped up, stifled, consumed. He lurches to his feet, panic racing in his veins. He looks around, desperate to escape.

But there's nowhere left to run. Nowhere to go. No one is left.

The door creaks open and footsteps pad into the room, then pause. The old traveler stands there, muddy duster dripping on the floor, peaked judge's cap brushing the doorframe. Marks line his face, one for each of the roads he's traveled.

There are many marks.

"I thirst," he says. "Will you not offer an old man a drink?"

All Oz has to give is the bottle of cyanide he'd given to Tsuki, cruel in his kindness to save her. It was the only way.

"No? Then please, give me something to eat."

Unless the traveler wishes to gorge himself on ecstasy and cocaine, Oz has nothing to proffer.

"Let me rest my weary bones, good sir?"

The only furniture in the decrepit apartment is the rotting mattress where the corpse of his girlfriend now lays.

The first rays of the new day rise in the east. A thin silver sliver of moon peers over the horizon, fading as the light bleeds into the apartment through the broken gray windows.

He creeps closer, the Shinigami, the Reaper, the God of Death.

The dark side of the moon.

He stands beside Oz, wraps bone-thin arms around his shoulders. For a brief, hopeful moment, he imagines it's her. Her, who was always so good at comforting, who knew exactly what to say, how to make him feel worthy of basking in her light.

But it's not, it can't be, it never will be again.

"Monkey gave me the blood of her daughter to feast upon," the traveler whispers in his ear. "Fox, the tears of his heart to drink."

His voice rasps like chains on a rusted steel floor. The sound makes Oz want to scream.

"But the Rabbit withheld her sacrifice." Clank, rasp, clank. "She did not throw herself upon the flames for my comfort. What will you offer in her place?"

Oz's heart beats so fast, he's afraid it's going to leap out of his chest and explode. There has to be a better way to go.

**Seven a.m.**

*Once upon a time, long ago, a monkey, a rabbit, and a fox lived together as friends. During the day, they played upon the mountain; at night they returned home to the forest. All creatures sang of their unbreakable friendship, of how they lived their lives with bushido, with honour. Their lives were simple and unfettered from greed and hatred.*

*Until the Moon came down one night to test them.*

*He appeared disguised as an old traveler. "I have wandered through these mountains and valleys many days. Please, would you honour this old man with the comforts of something to eat and drink while I rest?"*

*The monkey went off at once to gather tree fruits, the sap staining her hands bright red. The fox brought river water he squeezed from his bushy, heart-shaped tail.*

*The rabbit, though, ran through the fields in every direction, hunting and scrounging with all her might, but came back with nothing.*

*Monkey and Fox teased her, "You are good for nothing."*

*The little rabbit, not to be shamed, asked the monkey to gather some thistles and requested the fox to set fire to them.*

*Once done, Rabbit said to the old traveler, "Please, eat me," and threw herself upon the flames.*

*The Moon was pierced to the heart by the rabbit's sacrifice and wept. So touched was he by Rabbit's loyalty and obedience, by the way she valued honour over life, that he restored the rabbit to her original form and took the little body to be buried in the palace of the moon, where her face would always shine for all to see.*

This is not a fairy tale. No one will hang their bodies in the sky when they die.

# ALOHA MOON

By Shereen Vedam

*The goddess Hele ordered her youngest daughter to marry a Hawaiian prince with whom she was well pleased. The young goddess, who loved a fisherman, refused and, crying, ran away to live on the moon. The story goes, Lani, that one of her teardrops landed back on earth and splashed a sea dragon's forehead. Over time that tear formed into a pearl that could influence the moon's gravitational pull.*

Maia raised her four-meter long sinewy neck and extended her jaws past the protest of tendons and muscles. Blinking away the rain of blood flooding her eyes from the jagged gouge on her forehead, she then howled her protest at the loss of her soul stone.

Her tormented cry bounced off the water-smoothed granite of her underwater shelter and rippled through the Pacific Ocean, until the note burst into air and bathed the moonlit sky with tremors of pain.

Lightning answered her cry with mirrored anguish and thunder threatened retribution. Far above the earth, the moon's darker half shifted with disapproval.

On the southern edge of Vancouver Island, the Victorian streetlights, artfully decorated with lush hanging baskets, flickered. Lani studied the lamps with suspicion as her unease flared. Raindrops bounced off her hardhat and splashed her face.

*When the Kai Kelekona calls,* her mother said before Lani left Hawaii, *even if you run halfway across the world, mark my words, you'll hear it.*

Lani shook off her disquiet. Wielding her stop/slow sign, she safely moved cars past her road crew finishing a bike path and sidewalk adjacent to a grassy strip. Sea dragons were a myth. This job was real.

*No one in our family has been called to action in over a century, Mama,* she'd said. *And I'm eighteen, not eleven. Fairytales aren't true and I refuse to waste years waiting to be of service to a mythical beast. I want my freedom. I want a life.*

*In Canada?* Her mother's response still made Lani smile.

Dark clouds hid the rising moon and the twilight sky turned pitch-black. She shivered beneath her reflective safety vest. The air fairly sizzled with angst. At the next thunderclap, her every nerve quivered as if someone had flicked a switch

Her silver ring, a family relic with a milky white stone, shot a burst of energy up her finger. She switched the traffic sign to her left hand and flexed her right inside her work glove.

"Focus, Aloha!" her boss shouted.

She scowled at the nickname more than the reprimand, and then motioned to oncoming cars. She raised her flagging sign and fought an absurd urge to drop the stupid sign and race toward *makai.*

*Yup, definitely seaward.* Something out there pleaded for her help. *Am I losing it?*

Her boss's murderous expression as he sidestepped a vehicle that brushed by him said, *Yes.*

"Can we hurry up?" she asked. If this kept up, she'd be permanently finished in this job. "It's raining."

"This is Victoria. Get used to it."

Grace stretched out on her sofa and caressed her latest find—a legendary gold armband from India. She'd searched for this bracelet with its mystic runes for over two years. Finally, it was hers, a fine addition for her collection.

Ignoring the sudden patter of rain, she checked the TV. The interview had started. Her fingers trembled over her prize, reluctant to release it, even for Ace Stanton. Gripping the band, she reached for the clicker and turned up the volume.

"We're holding an emergency response exercise in two days time," Ace said in his precise tone.

Her pulse sped up. Two years apart and still his deep voice affected her.

He stared into the camera as if he spoke directly to her. "This will be a joint effort involving the airport, ferries, and local fire departments, as well as the island's health authority and Coast Guard. All coordinated through my office at the new emergency preparedness centre in downtown Victoria."

Lightning lit the sky as if daylight blinked. Thunder rumbled and the frames on her mantelpiece shook. One tumbled, smashing onto the hardwood floor. Grace went over and picked it up. Ace kissed her behind broken glass.

"We interrupt this program for breaking news."

She returned to her seat, cradling the frame.

Ace had left. The host read from the teleprompter. "Reports are coming in of massive flooding on the west coast of Vancouver Island. Evacuation orders have been issued for Port Renfrew."

The armband clattered onto the table. Ace was ambitious enough to risk using a dragon's pearl. She should never have told him about that monster sighting along the West Coast Trail!


Well past midnight, Lani finally got off work. She rubbed her temple to ease a headache. All night long, *the call* had sounded like an annoying trick-or-treater with his thumb planted on the doorbell. Ignoring it was no longer an option. She left a message for her roommate at the university's housing complex that she wouldn't be home, got into her ancient Fiat and headed west.

She was on the West Coast Road when flashing lights ahead indicated traffic was being re-routed. With a grumble, she pulled over and ran into the woods.

She fought past overgrown prickly blackberry bushes and prayed she wouldn't run into a racoon out for a nightly prowl. Soon scratches stung her face, neck and hands. She finally stumbled onto a narrow deer path only to sink her right foot into a squishy pile that released a waft of rotting fruit. Bear scat. "Yuck."

Worries about running into an irritable black bear overtook concerns about crossing a mean-spirited racoon. Despite the increased risk, she shook her foot clean, pulled her hood up, and followed *the call* toward the salty scent of beached kelp.

At first, this compulsion had been an imposition. The long hike, however, had given her time to come around. For years, she'd denied she had this gift to hear a sea dragon's wail. Now, denial gave way to excitement.

All those stories her mother told her, ones about which she'd drawn pictures to cover her bedroom walls, could be true. She now sorely regretted shredding those crayon-coloured masterpieces the day she turned thirteen and a boy laughed at her because she'd shared with him her "secret."

She could still hear her response to him. *Sea dragons do exist. My family is their guardian. One day I, too, will serve one.*

The trail opened onto a cliff and the ocean's roar drew her toward the edge. She looked down. Way down. Only the occasional break of sea stacks and giant white driftwood distinguished shore from sea.

"Of course, the tide would be in." She absently twirled her ring. "Mama, I sense a watery grave in my future."

Pulling out her cell phone, she pressed one for Hawaii. Her mother's line was busy. She left her tenth message since leaving work. "Call me!"

She clicked the cell shut and shoved it into her back pocket. The idealistic child she used to be was back with a vengeance. "I hope I make you proud, Mama."

She cautiously sought secure footfalls to the unseen beach below. Her descent quickly turned into a slip-sliding free-fall. A boulder punched her back. Her left elbow struck a sharp rock and she cried out as her funny bone strummed a painful note. She landed with an icy splash, neck-deep in stinging, salty water.

She coughed and spat out a slimy piece of kelp. Shivering, she scrambled to find her footing when something whipped around her legs, trapping both ankles.

In a panic, Lani kicked out. In seconds, the vine had bound her legs, hips, waist and chest, and then rose up her neck. Heart thundering, Lani took a deep breath before her mouth was covered.

*I'm going to die!*

Her face was wrapped and she was yanked underwater and out to sea. She was being lassoed toward *makai* in the truest sense.

After a minute, she couldn't hold her breath any longer. She gulped. To her surprise, in came air instead of water. The vine had created an air bubble.

*I'm not going to drown.* That certainty was quickly followed by the incredible idea that she was being taken to the one who summoned her. Except that sea dragon introductions normally occurred on a beach, not underwater.

The ride could have lasted an hour or a minute, but abruptly, it ended. Her binding loosened and she bobbed up inside a luminescent cave.

Taking a deep breath, she crawled onto dry ground, scared that the vine would capture her again. Pulse hammering, she paused to take in her surroundings.

No sounds except for the lapping water. The cave roof was so high it appeared to be a black hole. Then something scraped along the floor. Lani yelped and hurried back to the pool's edge. Something big was coming.

Dread mingled with excitement. This was it. She was about to meet a real live, non-crayon drawn, sea dragon!

The creature didn't step closer though.

Controlling her rapid breathing, Lani fought to remember the greeting phrases her mother had drilled into her but the right words eluded her. So she said the only thing that came to mind. "Aloha."

The creature moved forward then.

Lani gasped and looked up, and up, and up. Unlike the scaly, squat creatures she had crafted on paper, this giant was all smooth skin, long limbs and folded wings. Or were those fins? Like its granite abode, the dragon looked as if it, too, had been worn smooth by water and time. What caught and held Lani's gaze, however, was the lumpy patch on its forehead—directly above the windshield-sized glasses resting on its rounded nose.

*I hurt.*

Lani's forehead twitched in sympathy. "What happened?"

*Someone stole my soul stone. It's your fault. I was perfectly safe among the Hawaiian Islands, but you had to come here where it's colder and people are nosy.*

The dragon gave an exasperated *harrumph. You're supposed to protect me. Yet you've never come to visit. And in case you're interested, my name is Maia.*

Lani digested that mouthful of bitter accusations and stunning revelations. She felt like a simpleton, but had to ask. "You wear glasses?"

The long tail swung forward and slammed the floor. The bright stonewalls quivered and a shard broke off to crash beside Lani. *I'm old! Eyesight fades with time. It's a fact.*

She sounded so like Lani's boss whenever anyone asked him a lame question that she smiled. Then the third surprising thing about this dragon dawned. "You followed me?"

*You're my guard! If I'm in Hawaii and you're only-the-Moon-Goddess-knows-where, how are you supposed to watch over me?*

Each answer generated more questions. Lani focused on the most pressing one. "Who hurt you?"

*A man crept in at moonrise while I slept and cut it out.*

Lani choked on her next question, afraid to insult this short-tempered dragon. But how could anyone attack a big, ferocious dragon—glasses notwithstanding—and get away?

"What do you want me to do?"

*Find my stone! Or else.*

"Or else what?" She was already doomed...there was no way to return to land. Not without help and Maia didn't seem in a helping mood.

*Or else the island you've chosen to live on will be no more.*
"What?"

Maia shrugged. *The water pressures have shifted. The land above will be underwater by moonrise.* She tilted her head upward. *The southwestern tip's already flooded.*

The roadblock! "How much time is left?'

*Maybe six hours. Not my fault. Who took a long time to get here?*

Lani scrambled for her phone and pressed one.

"Aloha, Kaikamahine." That age old mother-daughter greeting chimed the sweetest note.

"Mama!" Lani spilled the entire story and then pointed her phone camera at Maia.

The sea dragon extended a claw and waved.

Lani clicked send. "What should I do, Mama?"

"Get everyone off that island."

"How can four million people evacuate in a few hours?" Who would believe her? She had no proof.

"Surely they have an evacuation plan? Most islands do, dear. Even way up there."

"But there's no time."

"Well, there is another way. If the dragon's pearl, that's Maia's soul stone, is returned to a sea dragon, legend says that could mitigate the weather effects caused by its removal."

"Will that stop the flooding?" Lani asked Maia.

The dragon's shrug was startlingly unconcerned. *Might. Might not.*

"You must place it on her forehead before the moon sets," her mother said. "Fail, and not only will the island be flooded, but...Maia could die."

"The moon rose just after sunset." Lani checked her cell clock. "That leaves less than five hours. How can I find this stone that quickly?"

"*Ko'u aniani,*" her mother and Maia said.

The familiar words reverberated. As a little girl, Lani had daydreamed about this ritual that involved a guardian and a dragon mingling blood. The cuts could be on hands, feet or any other similar parts. *Ko'u aniani* literally meant "my mirror."

Her mother indicated they should speak privately.

Lani moved to the pool's far edge. "What Mama?"

"Take another look at Maia's wound."

She checked over her shoulder. Though the kelp patch had crusted, at its lower edge blood still dripped. She touched her forehead. "Everyone would see it."

"It will save hurting her a second time. More importantly, it will give you the strongest connection to that stone, making it easier to locate. But there is a dire consequence, Lani."

"The scar?"

"The parts used define a bond, Kaikamahine." Her mother's voice gentled. "Using the spot where her soul stone rested will bind your souls far past this current crisis. You will never be truly free again."

Lani's world closed in and she disconnected the call. This is how she'd felt a month after high school graduation. As if all those who loved her clung like lodestones. She knelt and skimmed a finger in the water. In her reflection, her boss checked his watch and then snapped, *Focus, Aloha*.

How odd that she'd run four hundred odd miles from home, yet ended up taking on a similar role to the one she'd abandoned. Guarding others. That's because she hadn't run from the idea of serving. Rather it was the idea of serving something that did not exist. But Maia was real enough. As were her co-workers and everyone else on the island who needed her now more than ever.

In one swift move, she stood and returned to Maia. Without hesitation, she tapped her forehead. "Slash me here."

Maia did hesitate, her pain-filled gaze widening behind her glasses. Then, without a word, she used her sharp claw.

Lani cringed but the pain was minuscule compared to what Maia had gone through, was going through.

The dragon shifted backwards before crouching. She then ripped off her patch and lowered her head.

Maia's rounded nose was slippery to climb. Lani grabbed the glasses to steady herself and leaned toward the jagged bloody depression. Her stomach churned with acrid rage at whoever had injured this gentle creature. And then together, they became *Ko'u aniani*.

Maia dropped Lani off near where she'd abandoned her Fiat. From there, Lani's new connection to the dragon's pearl drew her straight to downtown Victoria. Once she passed Sooke, the roads were bare except for emergency vehicles.

Even though they'd physically parted, Maia's presence remained as a shadow on Lani's soul and the tiny scratch on her forehead throbbed like the stump of an amputated limb, proclaiming she and Maia were now one. What hurt the dragon hurt Lani. She could also sense exactly which secluded cove the sea dragon had retreated to in order to await Lani's return and knew the dragon was worried.

"I'll get that stone back to you, Maia, I promise."

Lani's newly formed link transmitted other odd sensations. Air pressure shifts. Waves crashing all across the island. Most disconcerting of all, the moon's magnetic ebb and flow was like the slow *thud-thud* of a heartbeat.

She turned on the radio to distract herself. The stations warned people in Sooke to head for higher elevations but there wasn't anywhere on the island high enough.

She stepped on the pedal, running every stoplight from uptown to downtown until she screeched to a halt by a three-story brick building that shone like a beacon to her heightened senses.

Maia's stone was somewhere inside this place, the city's new emergency site. She cruised looking for a free parking spot. Was that a helicopter pad in the back? Why the pearl would be here was a mystery. As was a clear plan on how to retrieve and return it to Maia in... two hours and twenty-two minutes.

Giving up on this last chance to perform a law-abiding gesture, she double-parked near the front entrance behind an apple-red SUV hybrid. The parking spot was labelled "Commander Ace Stanton."

Hoping to look official, Lani shrugged on her safety vest and hardhat. It worked. People rushed in and out the front doors but paid her no attention. She raced for the back stairs. Her connection guided her like a built-in GPS.

She stopped before a half-glass door. The brass plate read "Command and Control." Past the glass were two men and a woman arguing loud enough to be heard outside.

*Too much to ask that the stone be stored in a deserted basement?*

She tried the handle. Locked. She rapped three times.

The harried middle-aged man and a coiffed woman ignored Lani in favour of getting into each other's face.

A younger guy, two inches taller than Lani and wearing a tailored suit that hung loose on his slender frame responded. He opened the door a sliver and his gaze went straight to her wounded forehead.

"I need to come inside," she said.

He met her gaze with a frown. "Mr. Stanton can't be disturbed."

"This can't wait." Lani shoved the door open and strode in. He stumbled back giving little resistance.

Inside, she found a desk, steel filing cabinets and a waist-high chart table with numerous cubbies that housed charts. She sensed that in one of those openings was one pissed-off treasure. The stone thrummed an "about-time" welcome. Apparently, it had inherited Maia's temperament.

Lani had taken less than four steps toward the table when Mr. Suit blocked her. "You're not allowed in here."

"Cody, stand down." Stanton came over to confront her. "What's this about?

"I'm here for the dragon's pearl."

He turned to the other woman with a frown. "Grace, is she your friend?"

The woman hurried over. "I've never met her before, Ace. How do you know about the pearl?"

Cody edged toward the chart table with a guilty slither and Lani's blood pressure shot up. She clenched her fists to keep from thumping this ignorant fool for what he'd done to Maia.

"Give it to me," she said in a soft tone that she hoped promised mayhem if he didn't instantly obey.

"Wait a minute." Stanton extended a protective arm. "What makes you think this pearl is here?"

"I feel its presence."

"Then you must be a guardian." Grace spoke in an awed voice. "You're a descendant of a fisherman, aren't you?"

Lani ignored her in favour of the commander. As angry as she was, she had little time to waste. "That stone is causing the flooding, sir. If you want to save this island, give it to me and let me leave."

He weighed her words and then turned to Grace with a raised eyebrow.

"I believe her, Ace," she said. "I'm sorry I accused you of stealing the pearl, but you're the only one I told about the dragon sighting."

He gave Cody a grim look. "And I told you. You actually stole this stone from a sea dragon?"

Lani grabbed Cody's arms. "There's blood on your hands."

A picture of shame, he looked at his hands. Seeing his spotless fingertips, he pulled back. "You're trying to trick me." He sounded brave but his wide eyes suggested fear. "One thing is true, Ace. That stone does affect the weather." He inched closer to his boss. "Imagine if we could figure out how it works. We could become famous. I brought it here to show you."

"Our role is to help people, not endanger them so we can be heroes. If you don't believe that, you don't belong on my team." Ace shoved him back. "Now, give her the stone."

Cody's shoulders dropped. He swallowed, then turned and reached into the chart table and pulled out a large cloth-covered bundle. The sea's pungent aroma wafted from the bloody material. After a slight hesitation, he handed it to Lani.

She hugged the heavy stone, inhaling the salty scent of Maia, and sweet relief overwhelmed her. Then doubt crept in. She pushed the cloth aside to reveal a gorgeous breadfruit-sized pearl that easily weighed ten pounds. How could this scrawny young man have gouged out this treasure? "You didn't steal this, did you?"

He gave a surprised start and then shook his head. "Ever since Ace told me about the dragon, I've been combing the west coast beaches. Last night, as it grew dark, I was about to leave when a creature rose up. So cool, it wore glasses!"

"Oh, really?" Grace said.

"Go on, Cody," Stanton said.

"Then it reached into its forehead and tore out that stone. Blood spurted everywhere. When it thrust the pearl into my hands, I panicked and came here. I wanted to tell you, but I didn't think you'd believe me that I didn't hurt that animal."

"I don't believe you," Grace said. "Why would any creature harm itself?"

"She did it for me." Lani touched her forehead. *To connect with me.* She swung around. "I have to get this back if we're to save this island." *And Maia.*

"Let me fly you!" Stanton ran after her. "It'll give us a chance to talk."


The moon was dangerously low on the horizon by the time Ace, along with Grace and Cody, flew Lani to where Maia waited. The moment she spotted the dragon, the helicopter dipped and Lani leapt out. Maia caught her before she hit the water and settled her on her nose.

Lani placed the soul stone over Maia's wound. Instantly, the hole sucked the pearl inward and the surrounding skin contracted until only a sliver of white winked in dawn's first light.

The constant ache on Lani's forehead eased. She stepped back and repositioned the glasses she'd dislodged.

*As bonding gifts go,* Maia said, this is decent. *Better even than your great-grandmother's gift of my spectacles.*

"I'm glad." Lani turned her ring, recognizing its hum as an echo of Maia's stone. So many things suddenly made sense but one concern remained. Maia had almost destroyed Vancouver Island.

*I'm sorry.* The dragon's words sounded heartfelt.

"For what?"

"For endangering your people."

Lani breathed a sigh of relief. So she did understand that what she did was wrong. "I'm sorry, too. Am I forgiven for not visiting sooner?"

*Depends. Can we go home to Hawaii?*

"To visit, maybe, but this island is now my home." The whirring helicopter above drew her gaze.

Grace and Cody leaned out to wave. Ace saluted her.

"Maia, if you're truly sorry, there is a way we can make amends."

*How?*

"There's been lots of media chatter lately about weather disasters around the world. With your ability to perceive oncoming weather changes, we could warn people to prepare for an emergency. Save lives. It would mean more travelling, though."

Maia didn't hesitate. *Where Lani goes, so does Maia.*


Overhead, clouds drifted apart to reveal a brightening blue sky. Low on the horizon, the moon's dark side shifted into a more contented position.

# CHERRY BLOSSOMS

By Amy Laurens

Ambrose sits alone in utter darkness, no one but fear for company as he prepares for the culmination of his ambitions. It's been years since he felt fear; it's been years since he felt anything. That was one of the demands of the quest: let nothing distract him from his single-mindedness, not love, not hatred, not regret, not fear. So in a way, it's nice to feel again, even if it does set his teeth on edge and send his pulse racing.

There's no reason for the fear, of course. He knows the potion will work. Years of research and millions of dollars have ensured that. But the moisture that should coat his tongue and throat still slicks his palms and forehead instead. Ambrose scrubs his hands on his bare thighs; his grip must be firm, sure. The timing of this experiment is so crucial to its success; the merest half-millisecond hesitation caused by a slip of the knife would be disastrous—and he doesn't want to die.

Which is entirely the point. He sits here, naked and alone in the dark of night in a house nobody wanted on a rug nobody loved because he is about to reach the pinnacle of his ambitions, and finally, at last, escape the clutches of death forever. Shame he has to die to do it.

Ambrose takes a deep breath and feels for the knife to his right and the stone goblet to his left. Careful not to spill the precious liquid, he raises the goblet to his lips, fingers wrapped around stone so smooth it feels wet. Or is that sweat again? In his other hand he clutches the knife, simple wooden hilt roughing his skin, and presses the blade to his throat. It's cold and somehow it tickles.

Fear leaps in his stomach but he catches it, moulds it, hones it until it's as sharp as the blade and is just another weapon at his disposal. He tilts the goblet until the liquid meets his lips, presses the blade into his skin until he feels the sting of blood. This is it, the moment when he will end his life and begin it, the moment when he will grasp his immortality. On the silent count of three, he draws the knife across his throat and swallows down the potion.

Hot fire grips him, and whether from the wound or liquid, he can't tell, and it doesn't matter, because the pain sears down into his belly and he can't breathe, can't scream, and his heart stutters. He's dying. His muscles cramp, arching his spine until he knows his bones must shatter from the strain, and it burns, flames under his skin that light him up like a candle.

The fear bursts from his grip and floods through him on a tide of adrenalin. Everything's done, everything's over, and it was all for nothing, and the only thing he can think of is Lena's eyes and a spray of cherry blossom in the moonlight. In despair that overwhelms even the pain, he passes out.

When he wakes, the fire has died down, and only the embers of pain are left. They flare in his joints and limbs when he stirs, and at first he is too groggy to realise what they mean. Ambrose strains open his eyes and stares vaguely at a stone goblet lying on its side, rim chipped, the sticky residue of black, tar-like liquid pooling underneath it.

The memories come flooding back and he wonders how long it's been. Will Morris have missed him yet and realise what it means? He struggles to his feet, biting back moans as his muscles catch and clench—but then he grins. He's standing. He died, and now he's standing, and he feels... Ambrose stretches and twists, staring at his body, wondering exactly what it is he feels. He's happy that it worked, of course; he's achieved the

175

ambition of several lifetimes, and beaten all the others who raced against him. But it's a quiet sort of happiness, reserved, not at all the elation he'd expected. And underneath it all, he realises, there's still the stink of fear. What if they don't believe him?

Suddenly frantic, Ambrose strides to the corner of the room and his bundle of clothes. He dresses, not worrying over minor things like buttons, and hurries from the room. Downstairs, out in front, his car is waiting and in it is his phone, left there so he wouldn't be disturbed. He punches in the speed dial for the office and fidgets as it rings. Morris will know; his elder brother always understands.

The secretary—Sarah? Sara?—answers the phone and Ambrose snaps for Morris. An awkward silence fills the end of the line. His stomach sinks. "What? What is it?" he demands.

"He's dead, Ambrose," the secretary says. "They found him in his flat three days ago. Suicide. We... He had no idea where you'd gone, Ambrose. He thought you'd left us."

Ambrose leans back against the seat as the world reels around him. "Three days? How long have I been gone?"

"A week."

Numb, Ambrose hangs up. He's achieved immortality, only it doesn't matter, because he was going to share it with Morris. Not that he'd ever told Morris that, not in so many words, but the promise was there, implied. And now it's too late.


It's a month later, and still the mobs haven't died away. They never use the doorbell, just lie in wait around the front steps of the old, unloved house that's now his refuge, waiting for him to appear. When he does, it's all flashing lights and questions, microphones in his face. He's tried his best to ignore them, but they're persistent, and they want to know his secrets. It's enough to make him wish he'd never publicised his findings, never made it known that he'd finally won the race.

Even at night they wolf around the steps, and it's hard for him to spot them because the moon has disappeared. To be sure, the moon has always been sporadic. Despite rumours that centuries ago the moon was constant in its cycle, in all of living history it's been inconstant, full one night and new the next. But never has it been gone so long.

Morris is gone, the moon is gone, and even Lena, the lovesick moony-eyed girl that used to follow him everywhere, is gone, and he feels utterly alone. Outside, the mobs catch sight of his shadow through the frosted panes of the door and begin their restless murmurs. He needs food, needs to walk—but he can't face the mob again, not alone. He leans his forehead on the ice-cold glass in the door. He's got everything he ever wanted, but no one told him the emptiness would feel like this. Even though he can remember the taste of Lena's lips that night under the last full moon, even though he can remember losing his focus for a split second in the pleasure of holding another warm body, of her skin pressing against his in the moonlight—it's not enough.

She'd tried, of course. All she wanted was to be with him, to love him. But immortality was a harsh master and he couldn't afford to become entangled, to be distracted from his research. All he'd wanted was some fun on the side.

Only now she's gone, and he's standing here, barricaded in his own house by mobs of reporters and spies and conspirators, and he can't leave, can't go outside, and all he can see is the pain and confusion in her eyes as he'd turned and stridden away. He'd never meant to hurt her.

The whirr of something moving quickly through the air cuts into his memories and he jerks away from the door. Where his head had rested only instants ago, the glass now sprouts a crossbow bolt that fizzes and sizzles. Ambrose laughs, which turns into a sob. He's immortal, don't they understand? But it's obvious that they won't stop trying. He reaches out and bolts the deadlock. He'll order in groceries, find some way around it. Either way, he won't set foot outside again.


It's an ordinary night when Ambrose pelts down the hallway to answer the bell, sprinting so he doesn't have a chance to change his mind. For the last month without fail, someone has left cherry blossoms on his doorstep, and he knows it's Lena. She told him once—or maybe twice—that cherry blossoms were her favourite, that they reminded her of everything good in life and how fragile and ephemeral it all was. And no one else ever rings the bell.

The reporters left not long after he swore himself to hermitism, and the snoops and gold-diggers followed a few months later. The assassins took the longest to give up, but it's been at least a year now since the last attempt, so he feels confident flinging the door wide open and peering left and right, hoping for any glimpse of Lena. As always, he's greeted by an empty street—only tonight is not so ordinary after all. It takes a moment for him to realise what's wrong, what's different, and when he does, he falls back a step, eyes wide: the moon is shining.

He'd always had the sneaking suspicion that it was because he'd died that the moon had gone, but here, hanging above the darkly-silhouetted trees, is proof that he was wrong. A quiet sort of relief fills him; it wasn't his fault after all.

Feeling as close to cheerful as it's possible to get when you gave up on feelings a decade ago, Ambrose leans down to retrieve the spray of blossom, and a thrill runs through him. The blossom is there, of course, pale pink petals drenched in silver light, the branch a sharp shadow beneath—but there is more. Tonight, the spray rests on a stack of letters, envelopes hand-folded from thick cream paper and addressed in fluid, loopy writing that's Lena all over. His pulse skips as he snatches them up and carries them inside.

Why letters? he thinks. Why now? For a month she'd come to visit every night, and for a month he'd been too anxious to answer the door until she'd gone. Is she giving up? He doesn't know how he feels about that, and he stares at the bundle apprehensively. On the one hand, he never professed to love her; never bought her roses, never sent her chocolates, never wrote her cards on Valentine's Day or birthdays. She'd been a bit of fun, a bluebell in the middle of an icy winter, and nothing more.

But on the other hand, she'd been sweet, and innocent, and every bloody thing he'd let go for immortality. And she'd followed him past death, the only person from his former life to make an effort, to pound against the wall he'd built around himself.

Ambrose sits down in the armchair and pulls at the silky pink ribbon that holds the bundle together. It comes away, spilling cherry petals in his lap. He lifts what remains of the spray, feeling somehow responsible for the flowers' death.

Which is stupid, of course. Lena is the one who picked them, who killed them, and if she intended for him to keep them she should have brought something more robust, like chrysanthemums or lilies or sunflowers. She always was impractical.

He sets the branch aside, conscience prickling as he tries to avoid comparing Lena to a cherry flower, wondering if something might make her wither, and if it might be him. Morris had always said that it was selfish to lead her on, to dance when he never meant to stay.

Ambrose cracks the seal on the first letter and unfolds it. He stares at it for a moment before realising that it details their first encounter, and a phrase catches his eye:

*Why the Fates have chosen you as my target, I cannot untangle. But if you need me, I will persist as long as they require it.*

He frowns. She had targeted him? Or, more precisely, someone had targeted her *at* him. Who? One of his competitors, trying to distract him? Ambrose grits his teeth then forces out a laugh. It doesn't matter; he won in the end.

Restless, he flicks absently through the rest of the letters, and only towards the end does he realise that they all begin the same way. "Today, Ambrose stood me up, and there was no moon in the sky", or, "Tonight we walked through the park for hours, talking about our dreams, and the full moon was bright"; always a brief summary of what had happened and a description of the moon, right up until that very last full moon, the night he kissed her. Strange.

He scans back over the letters, noting how their best dates always coincided with a full moon, and the nights he'd left her

179

hurt the sky had been dark. Curiosity piqued, he reaches for the last letter, unfolds it, and begins to read.

*Today, there is no moon. There has been no moon for twenty-one months now and I wonder if you know why.*

A shiver finds his spine, and Ambrose rubs the goosebumps from his arms. It's been twenty-one months since he died. Is the moon's disappearance his fault after all?

*You're a shadow, but because you were human once, it's enough; life clings to you like oil to water.*

*I cannot die—but I cannot cling to half-life either. So tonight, there'll be a moon again.*

You were human, she says. What is she, then? Absently, he brushes his fingers against his lips, feeling the ghost of hers, and he remembers the light flooding his front step just now. "There will be a moon again," he murmurs, and his heart contracts. Who is she, that she can predict the moon?

Then again, so what? He brushes his nerves aside. She'd no doubt penned the letter right before she came, probably by the light of the very moon she claimed to predict—hardly some feat of prophecy. No. It's nothing to worry about, and he is the only immortal, he knows that without a doubt. She's trying to mess with his head, nothing more, and he won't let her.

*I don't need you. I never needed you, and certainly not in the way you needed me. But I did love you.*

What does she mean, she didn't need him? She shadowed him everywhere, hung on his every word! He was everything to her. He'd *meant* something to her. The paper crumples in his hand as he presses his fist against the chair, anger clogging his throat. And to say that *he* needed *her*? He'd never needed anyone less. She'd nearly ruined everything.

*I'm going home, now. You wouldn't be dissuaded from your goals, and the Fates have decided my job is done. I disagree; I think you'll see the point in time. After all, you have time illimited now, and I think you know that what you sacrificed will always haunt your dreams.*

And there it is: she's giving up after all. Good, he thinks, vindictive. Then he reads the paragraph again and is kissed with disappointment. She hadn't loved him after all, despite what she may say. Someone had hired her to draw him away from the quest for immortality. He swallows down the sourness. This is a good thing. It means he didn't hurt her, isn't responsible, because she never truly wanted anything more.

As for the last, well, he has no dreams now. He hasn't dreamed of love or guilt, kindness or anything other than sheer and bloody-minded determination in years. At least, that's what he tells himself in the early hours of the morning when he wakes, drenched in sweat. Ambrose scowls and pushes the image aside.

*You won't hear from me again,* the letter continues. *In a few years, you'll probably forget that I ever existed. But I'll be watching you. Because I do love you. You're never alone.*

All that follows is her signature, embellished with a sliver-moon. "Watching me," he mutters, scrambling to his feet. It doesn't occur to him that she might be lying, because that's not the kind of thing she does. Instead, he paces in a circle, wondering where she might be hiding.

But halfway round it hits him: Lena doesn't lie. She's gone, she's never coming back. Tonight, the night he'd finally answered the door for her, she is gone. He clutches for the curtain and it slides aside. Moonlight floods in and alights on the table where letters and petals are strewn.

Moonlight on petals, the last thing he remembered before he died. Lena in the moonlight, bright-eyed and laughing; Lena in darkness, a figure half-glimpsed over his shoulder as he walked away. The moon was always bright when Lena was and always dim when she cried.

A hazy memory struggles into view. It's that night in the park when they confessed secrets to each other and he said things he'd never said before, and never should have then. She'd tried to tell him something, a story about a young woman who was the moon, and he'd laughed, and done like he always had, and brushed her words aside.

Now, he glances between the letters on the table and the full moon in the sky. From here, he can just make out her signature and its adornment—and the shadows on the moon that look like blossoms.

Blood racing, Ambrose holds his breath all the way to the front door and rests his hand on the knob. "I'm watching you," he whispers. "You're never alone." Palms sweaty, mouth dry, he opens the door. He's cut himself off from everything because he can't bear to walk alone, but perhaps isolation isn't the answer. Perhaps he ought to try to live—he has so much life left after all.

The street sprawls before him, bathed in silver and black, everything sharp, everything clear. Cherry blossoms wither, but the moonlight is forever. He takes a deep breath, closes his eyes, and steps out into the night.

Perhaps, if it was a more sensational world, the moonlight might burn his skin and the trees might burst into song. Instead, when he opens his eyes, nothing has changed—only now he knows he doesn't have to face forever alone, imprisoned in an unloved house with an unloved rug. Lena may be gone, but she will always be there, just as she always has, and the sky will never be empty again.

# THE BLACK MERMAID AND THE MOON

By Chrystalla Thoma

Semor surveyed the quiet streets, his heart thumping against his ribs. Everyone with a bit of sense would stay indoors tonight. It was a full moon, a dangerous and ill-omened time when everyone and everything showed their true face.

But if he turned back now, his life was forfeit, and he'd never see Adelia again.

He stalked the narrow streets of the town, stacked high with stone buildings, crowded by whispering trees. The moon silvered the cobbles and gave the foliage voice. A bird flapped down from a roof and he pressed himself to the shadow of a doorway as it writhed and grew, scales forming on its legs and curled claws and it screamed, taking off, black against the moon.

The black mermaid, the sea goddess, lived off these shores, in the haunted waters of the bay. While traveling around the world, seeking answers, he'd heard rumours that she collected the souls the currents of the world brought her; that she kept them in oyster shells and clams and nursed them.

Semor didn't believe in gods or fate, but in desperate times one did desperate things.

Unlike other creatures, the black mermaid did not transform, and did not exist at any other time; it was the full moon that brought her to life, carved her out of water and darkness.

So here Semor stood, mercenary fighter and faithless man, in search of his lost soul.

A calm pond of water reflected the moon. He leaned over it, knowing what he would see—or rather what he wouldn't: his own reflection. It was six months back when he'd first noticed it, after a hard battle up north; when he'd picked up a fallen man's shield and found his soul gone. He'd looked for his own face in every polished surface since then, hoping against all hope that he'd been mistaken, but nothing ever stared back from shiny metal or still water.

Without a soul, he was a dead man walking.

A winged horse galloped by and took off into the sky, dragging its hapless rider who hung from the saddle, whimpering. Semor slid along the groaning walls where old bones and flesh embedded for centuries clamoured for release. He inched across the street, keeping an eye out for any other transformed creatures, and followed the sound of the crashing waves towards the beach. The smell of rotting seaweed and fish was getting stronger and the creaking of boats sitting on the sand and rocks filled his ears.

He was perhaps the only being in this town not affected by the moon—because he had no soul for it to drag in its ripping tides. A growl to his right stopped him and he crouched low, watched as a woman crawled by, flesh hanging from her bones, her face a skull. The dead were awake now too, and he cast a worried glance in the direction she had come from. A cemetery so close to sea?

Semor gripped the handle of his dagger, but didn't unsheathe it, not yet. The woman passed, leaving smears of flesh and gore behind, and the yowl of dogs rang out. They jumped after her, eyes glowing, huge fangs bared, made again into wolves of old that haunted children's tales.

At least she was already dead. He had to make it alive until he found his soul, or else he'd never see Adelia again, and without Adelia, what was there to live for?

He skulked along the crumbling houses, the sea a pulsing presence ahead, calling to every fiber of his being. All souls were water, rolling and retreating with the tides, moved by the planets and the comets, controlled by the forces of the cosmos.

His soul was out there, and the black mermaid could give it back to him. *But at what cost?* his mind screeched in fear.

*At whatever cost it takes.* He'd seen men destroyed by the aftermath of war, empty shells waiting to fade. Men with no purpose. No beginning. No end. Haunts that didn't know they were dead already.

The memory of Adelia's face, her body, the way she spoke his name, that was all he had, all that grounded him on earth.

Semor raked a hand through his hair. He'd fought enough battles and had gathered enough money to propose to her, to marry her. He had to live. Because he finally had something to live for.

The ground shook, tendrils of green shooting up to curl against stone facades and twist around fences and iron gates. The moon would soon be at its peak, at the summit of the sky. Not much time left. Cursing, he started to run.

Mouths snapped at him as he exposed himself at last. Snakes flew by, beating huge leathery wings. Crabs advanced in hordes, mounted one on top of the other. Fish crawled on the sand, mouths opening and closing as if about to speak.

He could see it now, the path painted by the moon on the water. The sea moaned and heaved, but the path remained calm in its midst, leading deep.

He threw his dagger to the sand, toed off his boots, and jumped into the frigid water.

*Adelia.* Her face filled his thoughts as he swam out into the sea, every strong stroke taking him farther from the safety of shore. The moon awoke everyone, and the sea was full of life.

Something swam beneath him, long and dark, and he sped up, his breath coming in pants. A tentacle wrapped around his leg and he tore at it with his bare hands, sinking. He managed to slip out of its hold and swim back to the surface. The pale lunar light showed him swarms of fish under the surface, swirling in liquid silver. They scattered as he reached them and then burst all around him, fluttering on translucent butterfly wings, skimming the surface. He batted at them, then dived under and surfaced some way off.

The cold was starting to slow him, and his heart hammered so hard it might break a rib, when what felt like claws grabbed his waist and dragged him down, kicking and squirming.

Down to the deeper blue.

Deeper and deeper they sank, past twisted scaled bodies that transformed before his eyes into winged birds and back into their serpentine nature, past corals that sprouted leaves and flowers then retracted again, past dolphins that grew legs and arms as they swam by, long hair sprouting from their heads.

He writhed and tried to see what had got him but he only caught glimpses of fins and huge tails. His air was running out and fear pumped his blood faster in his veins. He kicked and pulled but couldn't get free.

*Adelia*, he thought, every thought now wearing her face, her smile, every form he saw becoming her, surrounding him. "Adelia!"

Maybe this was dying. Maybe without a soul he'd just dissipate in the clear water.

The descent slowed and a dark silhouette rose before him, at least thrice his height, all black in the milky water. The dark face lifted and pale eyes the colour of clear skies found him.

The black mermaid.

She reached out, clamping her hands on his arms, and they shot upward, to the surface. They broke through in a fountain of crystal. The water fell with tinkling noises around them, drop after sparkling drop, as if time had slowed. A glittering eel flew against the moon on wings of gossamer.

He drew breath, his lungs burning. She released him, then, and they floated facing each other, he a fleck on the shield of her face.

"Semor of Twenor," she said in an echoing voice, as though they were still underwater, and his heart boomed in fear.

"You know my name."

"I know all names under the firmament." Her form diminished, shrinking before him, until he saw her eye to eye.

Her long black hair, entwined with green weeds, trailed on the calm sea and her black tail lashed, breaking the mirror of the sky. "I am a collector of souls. I steal them, bargain for them, catch them in my nets. All water currents lead to me. And they have brought you." The moon reflected in her eyes like twin coins. "What have you come to ask for?"

"My soul." As far as the eye could see, the sea lay flat and shimmering like metal, and haze curled on its edges. "Have you seen it?"

"Seen it? Smelled it? Felt it?" Her mouth smiled, her eyes flashed. "I have. It looks like a moth with mottled wings. It smells like a field drenched in the first rain. It feels like a pebble caught inside a wound."

"You know where it is then?" Relief filled him.

"I do. It is in a place dark and warm, fluttering against another." Her tongue, black and thin and long, crept out of her mouth and licked her chin.

"Can you give it back to me?"

"The currents have not brought your soul to me."

Despair gripped his chest in a vise. "Then can you help me find it, get it back?"

She bowed her head for a moment that stretched, her high cheekbones glimmering, still wet, her tail beating a rhythm on the water. Voices rose, singing, sighing, laughing. She shook her head, her weed-tressed hair slithering.

"It is not in the sea, not in the water. It must be on land. Someone, a witch, stole it from you as you slept and breathed and lived." She smiled, a bronze curling of lips, a drum rolling in the deep. "What do you want to do now?"

He nodded, and wiped water from his eyes. "I want to know who took it, where this witch can be found. How to get my soul back."

The mermaid raised an ebony arm, sleek and sculpted, and with her fingertips raised his chin toward her. Flames jumped in her gaze, swallowing the reflection of the moon. "I can do that. But you must pay me back."

He swallowed a seed of fear that stuck in his throat. He'd do anything for a life with Adelia. "Yes. What do you want?"

The mermaid's smile stretched, sharp teeth flashing. "I want the witch's soul. For my collection."

*Fair enough.* "What must I do?"

"Take seawater in your flask. After you free your soul, throw the water on the witch and I will take her soul away."

"But how can I free my soul?"

She clucked her tongue and the water around her shivered. "As she stole your soul from you, you can steal it back. The water in your flask will show you the way. I will be guiding you; remember: I am the sea, I am the water."

He nodded. "I shall do as you say."

"Just remember..." The mermaid's gaze slid sideways. "Without a soul inside you, you cannot break this deal. Without a soul, mortal, soon you shall pine away and die."

His heart hammered and he nodded again. She spoke as if he needed a soul, any soul, inside him to break the spell, to keep alive. But he wasn't a witch to steal a soul like his had been stolen.

The mermaid laughed then, and spread her arms wide. Mermaids and mermen swarmed from the deep to swim around them, blue tails and silver fins and long green hair.

*Adelia...* "How much longer do I have left?"

But he got no reply and the world went dark as the moon set.

Semor found himself flung on the beach like driftwood. The fish had returned to the sea, the dead to their graves and the stones to immobility. He filled his flask with seawater and followed its tug during the days that followed.

The mermaid's words echoed in his mind. The short length of his remaining time was like a noose around his neck. He feared he wouldn't see Adelia before he died.

His feet trod familiar earth and he realized he was passing close to her village. Surely he could sidestep from his mission for a moment and see her. After all, he might not set eyes on her again.

Strangely, the tug of the water in his flask didn't resist, but instead dragged him toward the village. With a terrible suspicion souring his thoughts, he wasn't that much surprised when the pull of the water led him to Adelia's door. Not Adelia, that couldn't be. She wished him no harm. She was no witch.

Was she?

He hesitated, gathered his courage around him like battle armour and knocked.

Adelia answered the door, dressed in her favourite blue dress, her gaze lighting up when she saw him. The sight of her took his breath away, reminded him why he clung to life despite everything. When she flung herself into his arms and he inhaled her scent of jasmine, he had no need of the mermaid's magic to feel his soul in her touch or to know he'd do anything for her.

"I love you, Semor," she whispered. "I knew you'd return."

He'd traveled around the world to find his soul, and it was here–she was here. And suddenly, in his heart of hearts, he knew. Maybe it was the mermaid's binding that revealed to him the powers at work, but he finally realized what had happened.

Adelia hadn't stolen his soul–he'd given it to her freely. She was no witch—she was the owner of his heart.

But now what could he do?

The mermaid had bound him with a promise and a threat. He had to give her Adelia's soul, and that was unthinkable. But if he didn't get a soul back into his body, he'd die soon. Yet, without a soul inside him, the mermaid had said, he couldn't break the deal.

With a soul, he could. Even if it was another's soul.

He traced Adelia's face, the fine features, the beloved mouth, and turned all he knew over in his mind.

A kiss of love, that was how he'd given Adelia his soul. Because, in love, one shared more than one's body.

What if Adelia gave him her soul in return? What if he broke the deal and they both lived–carrying each other's soul, side by side?

A roar tore through the air and the ground rippled like a great wave. The flask shook in his hand, spilling seawater to the ground. The mermaid's displeasure echoed in his bones. *A good sign.*

"Adelia." He had to trust himself or all would be lost. "Please listen. I gave you my soul. It's yours to keep forever. Will you now give me yours? I promise to cherish it and keep it as my own."

She nodded, her eyes wide. "Is this a pledge? I waited so long for you to say it." She smiled, and he saw something of his own fear and sadness in the tilt of her lips. A mirror of himself. "Take it. It's yours."

Had she understood he really meant it? He shook his head. No need to fear. He really couldn't take it by force—if she loved him, she'd offer it freely.

And in the end that was the only thing that mattered.

So he kissed her.

The flask fell from his hand and shattered.

# JE ME SOUVIENS

By Edward Willett

The hopcar soared over the crater wall and settled to the rock-strewn floor just a few meters away. Its bright-green metalwork, only slightly dulled by the dust its landing had raised, gleamed in the Earthshine.

Years of trudging across the crater floor from my habidome to the shrine had turned my own moonsuit the colour of old bones. Recently, my skin had begun to take on that same skeletal gray, as though, like the legendary chameleon of old Earth, I was beginning to blend in with my surroundings. Nevertheless, with both gloved hands I brushed away the fresh layer of dust the hopcar's arrival had deposited, wanting to look my best for my visitor.

After all, it had been most of a decade since the last one.

The dust settled, and the hopcar's airlock slid open, revealing my visitor, her own moonsuit so spotlessly white that it glowed almost as bright as the smooth pearl-white globe of the Earth, hanging above us.

"Welcome, Ms. Chai," I said into my helmet microphone. "I am Brother Damon."

"Then you really do exist," a woman's voice came back in my ears. "I admit I half-expected I'd get out here and find the whole thing was an elaborate joke by my friends."

191

I didn't know how to respond to that; I didn't know what she meant, then. Instead I said, "If you'll follow me, Ms. Chai, I'll show you to the shrine."

"Lead on, Brother Damon. And call me Tia, please."

"Very well, Tia." I waited until she joined me, then led her across the crater floor toward the shadowed wall where the shrine is buried.

"I don't see anything," Tia said.

"Wait until we step into shadow," I said, which we did a moment later. "Now turn off your lamp and wait for your eyes to adjust."

Her lamp went out; I had never turned mine on. We waited in silence for one minute, two; then, "Oh!" she said.

From the darkness ahead of us emerged the ghostly image of a door, a simple, arched doorway outlined in faint, glowing silver. Words in a thousand ancient languages and alphabets surrounded it on all sides, always the same words, whatever the language, whatever the script. "Je me souviens." "I remember." "Ich mich erinnern." "Recuerdo." A faint path outlined in the same luminescent silver wound through tumbled rocks to the door.

"Now we will go in," I said.

The door swung outward at our approach, and closed behind us. We stood in a chamber walled and floored in smooth, black rock. Overhead, a single glowring, set in a golden sunburst, struck sparks of fiery light from thousands of tiny crystals embedded in the rock. For the short time we stood there, as the pumps filled the chamber with air, we might have been floating in space, surrounded by stars.

"Cool," said Tia.

The glowring changed colour from silver-white to a golden-yellow, and I removed my helmet. Tia followed suit, and shook out long black hair that proved to me she seldom visited airless worlds; those who often wear vacuum suits keep their hair cropped short, as I did, when I still had hair.

She smiled at me, dark eyes flashing in a heart-shaped, almond-coloured face. She was younger than I had anticipated;

but then, perhaps I was older than she had anticipated, for the first thing she said was, "How long have you been here?"

"I have kept this shrine for almost fifty standard years," I said, aware, as I had not really been in a long time, of my own balding pate and lined face, thinning now toward gauntness. A part of my mind chided me for my vanity, while another part, forever young and foolish, lamented the fact this dark-haired beauty would never find me attractive. Until a few weeks ago, the chastity drugs silenced that part, but the medirobot stopped providing those drugs after my last physical examination.

I stepped forward and lightly touched the inner door, and it opened, admitting us into the shrine itself.

We might have been in one of the ancient churches of Earth, familiar to me from the archives of the Order. Carved from billion-year-old moonstone, the shrine is a long, high-ceilinged vault. Pillars march down both sides, carved in the shapes of trees, their branches blending smoothly into the gothic ribs of the ceiling and twining across the walls in a profusion of stony leaves and twigs. Set among the branches, like strange fruit, are globes of red crystal, each containing an oil lamp. Their soft light spills like fresh blood across the polished floor, offering the only illumination apart from the silvery glow of the nave.

There stands a great basalt sphere, ten times the height of a man, the oceans and landmasses of old Earth molded in high relief upon it. Billions of photon emitters prick the surface, individually too tiny to be seen, one for each human being still living on the Earth when the great asteroid slammed into the North Atlantic, cracking the crust like an eggshell, boiling away the oceans, shrouding the dying world in steam and gas.

The light is siphoned down from the moon's surface through fiber-optic threads. As the featureless white Earth waxes and wanes, a translucent, sourceless glow likewise waxes and wanes across the basalt globe.

I waited for Tia's reaction. The last pilgrim, all those years ago, wept. Even though I visit the shrine every day, changing the oil in the lamps, sweeping the already spotless floor, polishing the globe, reciting the prayers that have been said every day in this place for most of three centuries, I occasionally find tears in my eyes, too.

After a long moment, Tia spoke. "I can't believe this is still here." Her voice was too loud for that silent place, yet she raised it even louder, as though trying to raise an echo.

There are no echoes in the shrine; reverberation suppressors built into the pillars ensure it.

"Where would it go?" I said.

"I guess what I really mean is, I can't believe *you're* here." She looked around. "For fifty years, you've been tending this place? For what?"

"For the Order."

"What's that?"

"Let's sit down. Even lunar gravity, I find, wears at a man my age." I was feeling every one of my years at that moment. I slid into a pew, and she slid in beside me. For a moment, I looked at the globe.

"Three hundred years ago," I said, my voice hoarse—except for the daily prayers, I spoke so little—"the Earth was destroyed. Yet, by the grace of God, humanity survived. Here on the moon, on Mars, elsewhere in the solar system. Barely self-sufficient, the colonies struggled. Some failed. Many more people died. But humanity survived. And since then, we have conquered the stars themselves. Now there are a hundred worlds, where before there was only one."

"By the grace of God?" Tia gestured at the globe. "Eight *billion* dead. Where is God in such a calamity?"

"Had the asteroid hit a century before, when there were no self-sufficient colonies, humanity would have been destroyed," I said. "God gave us the time we needed to develop the technology we needed to survive...just as He gave Noah time to build the Ark."

"Even if that's true, why this shrine? What purpose does it serve?"

"If we are to remember the grace of God, we must remember the catastrophe from which we were spared—and the billions who were not," I said. "In the years after the destruction of Earth, my Order was formed, an Order dedicated to serving God in remembrance and honour of all those who served God on Earth in all the myriad religions humanity's God-given sense of the divine had spawned. With the support of all the colonies of the Solar System, we built this shrine, and we have kept it ever since, saying daily prayers for humanity's dead. Humanity's leaders came here to dedicate it. People from all over the solar system made pilgrimages to it. It inspired poetry and artwork and literature and music for decades. It inspired humanity itself, inspired it to a rebirth and rededication; focused its efforts on surviving and prospering."

"But...surely that would have happened anyway."

"Maybe, maybe not." I looked at the globe. The Earth was near full and all the globe's landmasses glowed with light. "This place reminds us of where we came from, and all those for whom our ancestral home became a grave. For the Order, it became a sacred trust. And though we serve God in many other ways throughout the Hundred Worlds, we have always kept a brother or sister here, to keep the shrine and greet the pilgrims who visit it."

Tia bit her lip for a moment, then burst out, "But...nobody really cares any more, do they?"

"You do. You cared enough to make the journey here from...wherever you are from."

"Oskana," she said. She must have seen my incomprehension, for she added, "Alpha Centauri IV."

"An unusual name."

She shrugged. "I'm told it's a word from an ancient Earth language meaning 'the place where the bones are piled.' Oskana only has plant life now, but giant animals lived there millions of years ago. You can hardly take a step without tripping over a fossil."

"The place where the bones are piled." I nodded at the globe. "It would be a fitting name for Earth."

"I didn't come because I care," she said then. "I came on a bet."

I stared at her.

"A friend bet me this place was real; he'd read about it in some old history. I bet it was a myth. I was coming to Luna on business, so I decided to see for myself. And here I am."

My stomach churned; my heart fluttered. How could this holy shrine, meant to last forever, have become a myth in less than thirty decades?

I looked back at the globe to give myself time to gather my wits. Perhaps she felt that way before she came, I thought. But I could not believe that anyone could fail to be moved by the shrine. "And now that you have seen it?" I ventured at last.

She stared at it a long moment more. "It's smaller than I imagined." She stood, smiling at me. "Thanks for the tour. I have to catch a ship, so I'd better be going."

I wanted to shout at her, argue with her, cajole her...but we have strict rules against proselytizing; those who come to us must come of their own free will. I could answer questions, as I had, but that was all my vows would allow.

Silent, I led her back to her hopcar. I didn't watch her leave; instead, I turned away and trudged across the crater floor to my habidome.

In the main room, between the dining table and my narrow bed, the medirobot's casket-like diagnostic chamber still yawned open, just as I had left it after the checkup two weeks ago that had changed everything.

I sat at the table and stared at the chamber.

For fifty years, the medirobot had found nothing wrong with me beyond the usual ravages of time. My heart was strong; my bones, after so many years at low gravity, were not, but there were effective treatments for that, once I returned to a planetary environment.

The results of my last physical had been...different.

Perhaps I had missed a scheduled check-up; it seemed likely. I passed my time in ritual and work, each day the same as the one before. And my days, governed by Earth's rotational period, bore no relationship to the alternating sunlight and darkness that crept across the eternal lunar landscape. I might well have misplaced a month; perhaps even a year.

And perhaps the habidome's shielding was not what it should have been; perhaps it had not stopped as much of fifty years of sleeting radiation as it should have.

Whatever the reason, I had gone from being healthy on my second-last checkup to anything but on my last one. This time, the nanoprobes that searched every nook and cranny of my body, like the spies the children of Israel sent into the promised land, brought back report of giants in the land: an explosively metastasizing cancer that had already colonized much of my body.

It meant the end of my time at the shrine. Within 24 hours, the automated hopcar that brought me supplies would arrive, and I would ride it back to Apollo City, to see what modern medicine could do for me. Perhaps nanotechnology or gene therapy or some new treatment could keep me alive for many more years, even decades. Perhaps not. Either way, my time here was done.

In a way, I felt relieved. I did not regret joining the Order; I did not regret the hermitic life; I did not doubt my decision to serve God. But I had wondered, in the years since the last pilgrim had visited, if perhaps I could not have served God better on my own world, perhaps in the monastery whose white walls, looming above our farm, had so fascinated me as a child.

Tia's visit made me question my devotion to the shrine even more. If most of humanity no longer knew the shrine existed, or cared, why should I?

I took off the gold-trimmed, dark green vestments I had donned for Tia's visit, and climbed into the medirobot's chamber. The robot stabbed me in the arm, dispensing a little of the pain medicine that helped me sleep. I climbed stiffly out, dimmed the lights, lay down on my bed, and slept.

In the morning, for what I thought would be the last time, I followed my usual routine. After a simple breakfast of reconstituted cheese, bread and fruit, I donned my moonsuit and made the trek across the crater floor to the shrine. The Earth had reached full, and its perfect white ball threw my shadow in sharp relief across the crater floor even though the sun itself was out of sight beyond the wall. I wondered who would take my place; what brother or sister, young and idealistic as I had once been, would make this trek next.

That thought stayed with me as I swept the shrine free of the dust Tia and I had tracked in, refilled the red lamps with oil in the hope they would burn until my replacement arrived, then opened the stone chest before the globe where I kept the holy symbols of Earth's religion, swathed in black velvet, and began the two-hour litany of prayers.

Once I had had to refer to the red-bound book that also lay within the chest for the words of the prayers and instructions on how to spin the prayer wheels and burn the incense. But the litany had long since become second nature, a calming ritual that seemed to take both no time at all and all the time in the world.

Today, though, I stumbled over the words, as the constant thought intruded: "This is the last time..."

Relief mingled with my sadness when I finished. I packed away the holy items, bowed to the shining globe, donned my dust-stained moonsuit, and went out through the black stone airlock.

A silver hopcar waited near the habidome.

Its profile looked odd. As I got closer, I realized the hopcar did not carry the usual crates of supplies. Instead, there was only a small black octagonal chest, a light in its lid blinking green: a message capsule from the Order.

Puzzled by the absence of supplies, but not overly concerned, since I intended to leave the shrine anyway, I took the message capsule inside. It contained a small silver datachip nestled in thick red padding. I removed the chip and slipped it into my computer.

"Greetings in the One whom all humanity serves," began the message, which appeared only in text, without voice or vid. "I write to tell you that your long and worthy service has come to an end. The Order has decided that the Shrine to Home, which you have tended for so many years with such faithfulness, is to be abandoned. It seems clear to us that humanity no longer feels the need of worship or meditation in that once-holy spot. Our resources are limited, and constantly shrinking, as human spirituality fragments among the Hundred Worlds; and so we feel it best to close the shrine.

"This car will remain at your disposal until you are ready to leave, then will return you to Apollo City. We have arranged passage back to your homeworld of Manor, where you are to report to the monastery at your convenience. In the Service of the One, Henri Michaud, First Secretary."

I sat and stared at the message for a long time. Here was official permission to do the very thing I was preparing to do: leave the shrine and return to the mainstream of humanity. But it had never crossed my mind that the shrine would be abandoned, that I would be its final keeper.

I should have been excited, happy, ready to drop everything and seek out the medical attention that might prolong my life. But instead, brought face to face with the impending closure of the shrine, my thoughts did not turn to the length of my life, but to its purpose.

For fifty years, I had lived to tend the shrine. Abandoning that purpose to save my own life would make those fifty years, the greater part of my life, meaningless. It would mean Tia had been right, and this place no longer mattered—not to the vast crowd of humanity spread among the Hundred Worlds, not to me...perhaps not even to God.

And who even knew if my life could be saved? The medirobot was not optimistic, and it was a long journey to any place that would have the latest medical technology; certainly Apollo City, an interstellar backwater now, did not. I could be dead before any ship I might board could reach any place that might have a hope of saving me.

I put on my moonsuit and stepped out into the crater; but instead of going to the shrine, I stood just outside the habidome, looking up at the pure white pearl of the Earth.

The asteroid that slammed into humanity's home had been unexpected, devastating, and fatal. But humanity lived, through God's grace; and in a way, the Earth, too, lived on, in images, words, thoughts, beliefs—and in this shrine to its memory.

My cancer was just as unexpected, just as devastating, and just as fatal. But if the shrine closed, nothing of me would live on beyond my death; my years in service here would be forgotten, a footnote in the Order's archives, nothing more.

I could do nothing to make the Order keep the shrine open; but I could, perhaps, reach beyond my death to those who might someday come here after me, just as the shrine was meant to do.

I sent the hopcar back with a reply acknowledging the message from the Order, announcing my resignation, and letting them know I would not be returning to Manor.

Then I began my final vigil.

For days now the pain has been constant. I will no longer let the medirobot dispense the drugs that could ease the discomfort. The pain will end soon enough, and in this place of mourning, pain is appropriate.

I no longer follow my ritual of cleaning and prayer. Instead, I spend most of my time in the shrine, gazing at the globe. I let its silvery light wash over me like water, light from eight billion fitful ghosts...soon to be joined by one more.

The last oil has burned in the blood-red lamps, so the shrine is darker now. Soon, the last of the food will be gone, or the water will run out...or perhaps the pain in my cancer-ravaged body will become too much for me to bear. And then, my waiting will cease.

I have programmed the computer that controls the shrine's functions to open the inner and outer doors together on my voice signal. When the time comes, very soon, I will enter the shrine, hang my moonsuit by the door and make my way to the altar. I will surround myself with the holy items of a hundred faiths, open the red-bound book and place it on the floor, then prostrate myself before it. And then I will command the airlock to open.

Open to vacuum, sheltered in the crater wall, the shrine may last a million years or more. The fiber optics that cause Earthlight to play across the basalt globe may fail, but the globe itself may endure long after humanity itself has vanished from the galaxy.

But if, someday, a human or whatever humans have become returns to the Moon and finds the shrine, they will also find, prostrate before the globe, one faithful man still honouring the billions who, unable to flee into space, died on humanity's ancestral home—and the grace of God, through which a remnant of the human race survived.

We each must find the purpose for our own life.

This is mine.

# MOON LAWS, DREAM LAWS

By Ada Hoffmann

I was in temple, mixing libations for the Lady of Blood and Stone, the night the moon did not rise.

Even here, where we worship the moon, it took too long to work out what happened. We are too used to the Un-God, his demand for knowledge and order instead of worship. We talk to each other on phones with his bright little screens. We forget that all the gods but him are still wild as beasts.

It was an overcast night. We chanted the Moon's Awakening unknowing, with nothing but a blur of cloud on the projection screen at the temple's apse. The ceremony was long over when Friana, the Acolyte of the Telescopes, ran in.

Friana is always running, tripping over the hem of her blood-red robe, her hair in disarray. It's usually nothing. But she ran past the sub-altar where I was measuring wine and oil, and her panic cut through me. Sharper than Friana's usual panic.

She ran all the way to the High Priestess. I put down my sacrificial dishes to watch. She spoke breathlessly, and I couldn't make out the words.

The High Priestess's voice was clear: "You what?"

And then, "You checked every instrument? The radio telescopes? The laser optics?"

Friana bowed her head, mumbled.

Then, "That's impossible. You've mixed up the coordinates again."

"No." This time Friana was loud, shrill. "I double-checked that! The moon didn't rise. It *disappeared*."

Everyone looked up at that. The High Priestess glared around, then picked up her robes and swept off with Friana. "Back to work. We'll sort this out."

Terrified chatter burst out in all directions.

The Lady of Blood and Stone *is* the moon—in a way. She is also a stern maiden, and also... Well, with gods, you could never finish counting the things that they are. But the moon is what we weave in our tapestries, praise in our poetry. The moon is our livelihood.

That is why the others were worried. It is not why I suddenly had trouble breathing. The world blurred, and the libations ceased to matter. All I could think was a name.

*Trulia.*

I remember saying goodbye to Trulia. I clutched her in my arms and kissed her, on the launch pad, breathing her sharp scent while her separation anxiety tangled painfully with mine.

"It's only a year," she protested. "Then I'll be back." But no one had tried to live on the moon before. Anything could happen.

"Call me whenever you can. And dream of me."

"Yeah."

She didn't mean it. Even waking up next to me, arguing over breakfast about what we remembered, she had trouble believing in dreams. I had tried to teach her to travel that world, but there hadn't been time. At least we had phones.

I let her go. The Un-God's rocket flared to life, and she flew away.

I called Trulia over and over again. All I got were error messages. A few priestesses gave me sour looks, which I felt more than saw—I ought to have been readying the wine and oil for the next ceremony. I didn't care.

When the High Priestess strode back into the sanctuary, she had changed clothes. The silver-and-white diadem of the Highest Days crowned her head. Blood-red ribbons draped her limbs, and new crimson lines—real cuts—stood out on her face. Her fear was even worse than Friana's. It startled me, feeling that sting from someone so outwardly serene.

Her amplified voice echoed in every niche. "There is no reason to panic. Remain calm."

There was no calm. Hysterical murmurs rose at the corners of the room.

"I have gone into trance and spoken to our Lady." The High Priestess's voice was crystalline, betraying no trace of the fear underneath. But that is how we choose High Priestesses: they must be cold as space, celibate, queenly and unshakeable. "She is hidden for a time. She is angry, but not at us. We will continue our duties. That is all we need know."

*That is all?*

She knew about Trulia. She did not meet my eyes.

Voices rose in chaos as she swept out. But only I was reckless enough to follow.


Trulia didn't mean to go to the moon. She disliked my Lady, even though I could see a resemblance, a moonlike hardness in Trulia's eyes at times. Her supervisor guilted her into adding her name to the recruitment list, promised she'd be a fifth-string backup at best, just some quick training and a prestige point for the university. We didn't think anything would come of it.

Then exotic-materials engineers started bowing out—family concerns, sudden illness—until Trulia was the only good candidate left.

"I can't go," she blurted when the colony's recruiters came knocking. "We're having a baby."

"You're what?"

We weren't really. We'd talked about it, decided we wanted it, even though Trulia would be barred from my Lady's temple for nine months. We'd drawn blood for the Changing God's rites—turning my woman's cells into something that could burrow into

Trulia's womb and make life. But those rites, like anything of the Changing God's, are experiments. It takes months before the cells get it right, and we'd only just started.

We stopped the rites. We stopped making love. The recruiters tested Trulia's urine. They waited a month, and she bled like any woman. Trulia never understood how barrenness could be beautiful and holy. But she knew that it was important, that strict rules had been laid down before my Lady would allow humans on her surface at all.

"The colony needs you," the recruiters said. "It's only a year."

I bit my tongue till it ached. I wanted her here, having our baby. But Trulia believed in rockets the way I believed in blood and privacy.

"They need me," she said. And I let her go.


I couldn't disturb the High Priestess in her Highest Days regalia. She must be utterly untouched in that diadem: even a tap on the shoulder could bring down my Lady's curse. I waited by the vestry until she had disrobed to a white linen shift.

"Trulia," I blurted, once it was safe to speak.

The High Priestess turned to me with tired eyes. "I don't know, Viola. The Lady of Blood and Stone didn't say."

"You didn't ask."

She snatched up the red silk cap she wears for everyday duties. "There were fifty thousand souls up there. Do you think I am one of the Un-God's sociopaths? Do you think I didn't ask?"

I took a deep breath in and hissed it out until I trusted myself to speak.

"I'm sorry," I said. "But you know what she is to me. Give me the afternoon off. I have money saved. I'll ask the Herdsman of the Dead—"

"No."

The answer was so sharp that it froze me.

"Our Lady has forbidden us to know. Whatever she is doing isn't finished. And if you pry, she'll curse you. You know our Lady needs privacy."

There were no tears. I was genuinely surprised when my voice cracked. "Then give me the afternoon off to grieve."

Her pity was a pool now, cold and dark. She had seen more bereavement than any of us. She knew its shape.

"Take it if you like," she said. "But I think it won't matter."


Trulia was a woman of numbers and careful measurement. She had the usual range of feelings—love, fear, rage, joy—but without numbers, she could not understand them.

"Look at that man," I said once, pointing to an image on our home video-screen. I was trying to teach her. "How is he feeling?"

Trulia squinted at the screen. "He looks tired."

It was a public health announcement, the Lady of Mercy and Discipline's propaganda. He was an actor playing a drug addict, wracked with regret and despair.

"Look at the quirk of his mouth. The way the corners turn down."

"What about them?"

"It means he's very sad, Trulia."

She sighed in disgust. "I don't even know how *I'm* feeling."

She never understood dreams, but she dreamed as everyone does. I built a tower of numbers in the dream world, every floor built from the angles of a single digit. More often than not, when we slept side by side, she found it. "Did you build this for me?" she said, and the familiar phrase shocked me lucid.

Sometimes she refused to believe she was dreaming. Sometimes all she wanted to do in a dream was make love, which is like making love in real life, only sometimes the bed turns into a giant piano when you aren't looking.

Other nights, a light went on in her head. "Let's go flying. I've always wanted to fly." Those were the good nights—hand in hand, soaring into the clouds.

Every morning, I asked what she had dreamed. She said, "I don't remember." Or sometimes, "I remember a cloud."

"We flew, Trulia. You met me in a tower of numbers. We flew over a city and into a cloud."

"That's what *you* dreamed. I just remember a cloud."

I tried to explain. "That must be it," she would say, humouring me. "That must be what we did." But she never really believed.

She promised to dream of me, but I knew it was hopeless. The tower of numbers stood empty.


Day turned to night, night to day, and the moon did not appear. My hands shook. I spilled wine and oil and had to start over. I bumped into walls and scarcely noticed. All I could think of was Trulia. Any second now, Friana might come running back in with news.

I knew my Lady would curse me for looking. I didn't care. I pulled books brazenly from the temple library, downloaded the colony's plans and schedules, searched for news with my phone. No one stopped me. I did my duties one-eyed, hunting vainly for clues.


Everyone had noticed the moon's absence by now. There were headlines, frantic arguments, tearful interviews with others who knew someone up there. Self-proclaimed scholars declared that this was nothing: it would blow over like all my Lady's moods, though perhaps not with all the human lives intact. I found nothing useful in the news, and turned to the oldest stories.

There were no stories of the moon disappearing, but there were some of the sun. The Lord of Fire and Sky, my Lady's father, sometimes tried to marry her to a god or a mortal hero. Enraged, she pushed him out of the sky.

The Un-God told us, later, that this was a lie, and that the sun's disappearance was astronomy and optics. But a story can be true and not true, just as my Lady is the moon and not the moon.

I thought about that, singing the Moon's Awakening over a moonless horizon. My Lady was the moon and not the moon. Could Trulia be alive and not alive?

One suitor, the Lord of Green and Crawling Things, was unusually persistent. He chased my Lady and sang songs of beautiful, many-limbed children. She cast him into darkness so complete that the other gods could not find him, but within the week, there he was, cavorting under a mossy rock.

"I plucked a leaf from my hair," he said, "and it found the ground. Leaves know how to fall." But he never chased my Lady again.

I could hardly even read. I would get through a page, or half a page, and Trulia's name would abduct me. Was she alive?

Once the Herdsman of the Dead sent a bleating messenger to ask my Lady a question. It found her asleep amid her stones, unclothed, with trickles of blood running down her divine limbs. It did not want to wake her. Bleating, trusting, too stupid to know better, it curled up against her thighs and joined her in sleep.

When my Lady woke up, panicked by the unfamiliar presence, she picked up the messenger and threw it off the moon, into a comet so cold that it broke and burned. Its bleats became screams, and it never stopped screaming.


I meditated every evening, willing myself to find Trulia somewhere in the twisted dream-world. It didn't seem to be working. Tonight I dreamed of a wailing darkness.

Cold, inexorable currents tugged at me. The gods can't enter dreams, but other dreamers can, and sometimes stranger beings. The current could have been theirs—or a part of my mind I didn't want to deal with. I thought of forcing myself awake. But what would I have then? An empty room and a head full of fear. So I let myself drift.

I washed ashore in a tower of numbers.

It was not quite like my tower. Mine was made of black numbers on a blue and salmon seashore, reaching the clouds. These were white numbers floating in the dark. Through their curving forms I could see stars.

I scrambled to my feet.

"Trulia!" The darkness swallowed my voice. I knew, deep in my gut, that she had made this place for me. "Trulia!"

No one and nothing answered me. I gathered my breath for a scream.

"Trulia!"

"I'm here."

She was suddenly behind me, buzzing softly with concern—and relief. I turned and crushed her in my arms. "You're alive."

"I missed you," she said. Her hair twirled around her face, longer than I remembered. Her belly was distended in a familiar way; we had often dreamed she was pregnant. Dreams can be like that: wish for something and it's so. She nuzzled me, warm and solid. I could smell her shampoo, feel her affection all around me. "It was a whole year."

"No it wasn't. Love, you're dreaming."

"I'm what?"

This is how it always went. She scowled at the dream-world as though it had lied to her.

"See? The tower of numbers. You're dreaming."

She took a deep breath, and her eyes grew a glint of mischief. She lunged and kissed me, covering me in the taste of her—the warm blush of desire inside her. "Well, if this is a dream, let's..."

Everything in me snapped to attention. I missed her so badly it hurt. But I couldn't. "Wait. I need to ask—"

She only kissed me more firmly. "Ssh. It's been a horrible month. Just let me touch you—"

"Trulia." I pulled away, held her at arm's length. "One of us might wake up. I need to know quickly. Where are you? What happened to the moon?"

"They're going to kill me. That's what happened." Her desire was ebbing into frustration, uncomfortable against my hands. "Why can't I touch you?"

I fought to keep my voice calm. "Who's going to kill you? Why?"

"I don't want to talk about it."

"I know about the moon. I can help you."

"No, you can't. You're just a dream. I'll forget you in the morning."

"*I* won't forget. Please just tell me—"

209

But then her phone's cheery ringtone blasted the air. A wake-up call. She startled, and in an instant, she was gone.

As the days crawled by I decided my Lady wasn't going to curse me. If she cared, she would have done it already. Her curses are swift and unsubtle. Even when there isn't screaming and sky-falling, there is always blood.

Once, on a slow afternoon, the High Priestess knelt beside me.

"What are you looking for?" she asked. "Even if you work out what happened, what makes you think you can do anything?"

I choked down a retort.

I really didn't know. I wasn't even sure, deep down, that the Trulia in my dream was Trulia. I had often woken up with memories she didn't recognize. Just because we *could* meet didn't mean we *had* met, and with me wanting her so badly, fearing for her so badly...

I had touched her, smelled her. But I was frightened enough to doubt my senses.

"I have to know," I said. "Even if that's all I can do."

That night I found the tower of numbers again, and Trulia was crying.

If she was Trulia. If she was real.

I put out my arms and embraced her. She buried her face in the crook of my neck. Her grief and fear felt real. Her body was as soft as ever, though her belly was too big, and her smell...

"Tell me what's wrong. Who's going to kill you?"

She sniffed. "All of them. It's the only way to bring the earth and the stars back. They didn't want to, but your Lady said they'd die if they didn't. So they're going to launch me in a ship and let me suffocate in the blackness."

Her fear cut worse than Friana's or the High Priestess's, worse than any fear I'd felt before. Maybe she was only dreaming that she'd die. But that would mean she'd dreamt it last time, too.

More likely, this was real, or at least a reflection of something real.

"A human sacrifice." We hadn't done that for centuries, not since the Lady of Mercy and Discipline threatened to stop healing the other gods' followers over it. Could they have regressed so far, so quickly? "What for? And why you?"

"Because it's my fault. I hurt her."

She clutched her belly, and I suddenly understood.

It was impossible, but there was a terrible warmth mixed with the fear. Mother love. Stronger than I'd ever felt it from her before. She wasn't dreaming of being pregnant. She was really...

Of course the Lady of Blood and Stone was having a fit. She was a goddess of chastity and solitude. Pregnant women weren't allowed in her temple. To let one walk on her very body—well, that was why they'd done the tests.

I opened my mouth to protest. It couldn't have happened. She would have to have slept with a man as soon as she left, and Trulia didn't even *like* men.

Unless...

"It can't be mine. They did the tests when we stopped trying. You weren't pregnant."

"Not then." She gave me a wobbly smile. "But it's the Changing God, and it always takes him months to work it out. Maybe he was working it out *inside* me. Maybe your cells were there all along, changing, and..."

She really believed that. I still half-thought this was my own mind, dreaming things up. But it was the truth to her. There hadn't been anyone else.

That only made everything hurt worse. If she'd stood her ground and said *no* to the recruiters, we'd be together now, having a baby, and we'd be so happy. Now they were both going to die.

"There has to be something we can do."

Trulia teared up again. Her despair was painful, and I had to concentrate to hear her words. "This is what she always does. You of all people should know. They won't see the earth again unless they put me on a ship and send me *nowhere*. Like the sheep in that story. Like the Lord of Green and Crawling Things."

I stared at her.

"The Lord of Green and Crawling Things survived. He had a leaf."

"He what?"

"He had a leaf. Leaves know how to fall."

"How the hell does that help me?"

I was babbling. I had no idea if this even worked for mortals, but it was the only thing I had. "Listen, Trulia. This is the most important thing I'll ever tell you. You're going to wake up, and you have to remember. Find leaves."

"What are you talking about?"

I squeezed her hands so hard that she winced. "As many leaves as you can. From the hydroponic gardens or wherever you can find them. Don't let anyone take them away. Hide them under your clothes if you have to. Then pray to the Lord of Green and Crawling Things."

She squirmed. "I hate bugs."

"It doesn't matter. Pray to him. I don't know that he can see you now, but the leaves will find him, sooner or later, on their way to the ground. Leaves and prayers, Trulia. Remember that. Leaves know how to fall. They'll guide you home."

She shook her head. "I won't remember. I never remember my dreams."

"You remember little things. Clouds. Do you remember dreaming of clouds?"

"Yes, but—"

"Then you can remember this. Find leaves. Leaves know how to fall. Remember."

Tears leaked from her eyes, but she nodded. "Find leaves. I can remember. Find leaves."

I held her as close as I could. We repeated it to each other, over and over, until the tower's every wall became a green, growing branch.


That day I walked around in a blur, not knowing if the dream had been real, if my words had saved her. The next night, I didn't dream, but I woke up aching. I rubbed my eyes, and my hand came back dripping red.

Blood. Pain. My Lady's curse.

But why curse me now? Why, when I'd been defying her for days?

I stumbled to the bathroom, peered blurrily into the mirror. My skin was a clotted mess. I showered and scrubbed myself spotless, but within the hour, the blood was oozing its way back.

I met the Acolytes of the Curse, outside my Lady's temple, with lowered eyes. They shook their heads. Everyone had seen this coming.

"You have to wear bandages," said the junior acolyte, as if I didn't know. "And never go in the temple of any god. You will be alone." She looked at me full of pity. She was even younger than Friana, and freckles dotted her nose. Her voice shrank to a whisper. "Was it worth it?"

By my Lady's rules, I couldn't answer. I wiped my bloody hands and shuffled away.


Here is the thing.

Some gods work slow. The Herdsman of the Dead's plans last lifetimes. The Changing God tries at random, for months, until he gets it right. But the Lady of Blood and Stone sees with terrible clarity. She acts in a moment.

Yet she didn't curse me when I looked in the books against her orders, when I sought Trulia in dreams, when I told her about the leaves. She didn't seem to care that I defied her. We both knew it was useless.

And this morning she cursed me anyway.

Something must have changed.

She wanted to punish Trulia. I think I must have stopped her. The moon hasn't risen yet; the sky is still black. But I won't doubt anymore. Why would she curse me now, unless Trulia found the leaves and slipped out of her grasp?

I don't know if the blood will drive her away, when she sees me again. It surprises me how little I care. It's enough to know that she's alive, that our baby is alive.

So I pace our apartment, washing as often as I can, scattering green leaves over the floor, so she'll fall here, and not some other place. I pray to the Lord of Green and Crawling things, though I'm not used to his liturgy, and even when the pain is at its worst, I am happy.

Trulia is alive, and she's coming home

# AUTHOR BIOGRAPHIES

**Claude Lalumière** is the author of two books from CZP—the collection Objects of Worship and the mosaic novella The Door to Lost Pages —and the Fantastic Fiction columnist for The Montreal Gazette. With Rupert Bottenberg, he's the co-creator of Lost Myths (lostmyths.net), which is an online archive of cryptomythology, a growing collection of pop artefacts, and multimedia live show. Claude has edited numerous anthologies in various genres, the most recent of which is Bibliotheca Fantastica, an autumn 2012 release. (lostmyths.net/claude)

**Marie Bilodeau** is an Ottawa-based science-fiction and fantasy author. Her space fantasy novel, Destiny's Blood, was a finalist in the Aurora Awards and won the Bronze Medal for Science-Fiction in the Foreword Book Awards. She is also the author of the Heirs of a Broken Land, a fantasy trilogy described as "fresh and exciting" by Robert J. Sawyer, Hugo award-winning author of WAKE. Her short stories have appeared in several magazines and anthologies, including the recent When the Hero Comes Home, edited by Ed Greenwood and Gabrielle Harbowy.

The native Montrealer is also a professional storyteller. Armed with a Bachelor's Degree in Religion and Culture with a minor in Archaeology from Wilfrid Laurier University, Marie mostly tells adaptations of fairy tales and myths, as well as original stories of her own creation. She's performed in multiple venues across Canada, including Ottawa's National Arts Centre. (MarieBilodeau.com)

**Kevin Cockle**—With an education in critical theory and literature, a professional background in finance, and a personal interest in the supernatural, Kevin's fiction frequently explores the occult possibilities lying beneath the ordered facade of the business world. Kevin has had a brief, but eclectic writing career to date, with credits including nearly twenty short stories; an idea credit on a screenplay; numerous boxing-related articles and interviews, and any number of writer-for-hire projects.

**Rebecca M. Senese**—Based in Toronto, Canada, Rebecca writes horror, mystery and science fiction, often all at once in the same story. She garnered an Honourable Mention in "The Year's Best Science Fiction" and has been nominated for numerous Aurora Awards. Her work has appeared in TransVersions, Future Syndicate, Deadbolt Magazine, On Spec, The Vampire's Crypt, Storyteller and Into the Darkness, amongst others. When not serving up tales of the macabre, mysterious or wondrous, she volunteers at haunted attractions in October to scare all the unsuspecting innocents. She also tends to her rabbits, Domino and Gunther, to stop them from embarking on their plans for world domination. (RebeccaSenese.com)

**C. A. Lang** is a product of Nelson, British Columbia, and it shows. While meandering through the natural health industry in everything from editing to personal training to sales, he frittered away nearly a decade writing widely, all the while nurturing an unhealthy affair with no less than six guitars. Growing up around Victorian architecture likely had something to do with his appreciation of steampunk, although we're not quite sure why he felt the need to ditch the steam engines and go all internal-combustion on the genre. He has settled in Kelowna, B.C., where sometimes he can be found abusing a gigantic jazz guitar in public, hanging around certain wineries, and running obscene distances just to atone for it all.

**A. Merc Rustad** lives and writes in Minnesota, USA, where she is well prepared for the zombie apocalypse (and other variations). She spends her spare time writing, reading, and creating multiple timelines and/or sliding into alternate universes. Her alternate spare time consists of watching far too much TV, movies, and reading comics or roleplaying. (Obligatory mention of pets: two ferrets and too many cats.) Merc's work has appeared in The Red Penny Papers, Daily Science Fiction, New Fables, and other fine venues. She enjoys hearing from people online, although she offers no guarantee you will meet the actual Merc from your universe. (mercwriter.livejournal.com)

**Krista D. Ball** was born and raised in Deer Lake, Newfoundland, where she learned how to use a chainsaw, chop wood,and make raspberry jam. After obtaining a B.A. in British History from Mount Allison University, Krista moved to Edmonton, AB where she currently lives. Somehow, she's picked up an engineer, two kids, seven cats, and a very understanding corgi off ebay. Her credit card has been since taken away.

Like any good writer, Krista has had an eclectic array of jobs throughout her life, including strawberry picker, pub bathroom cleaner, oil spill cleaner upper and soupkitchen coordinator. (KristaDBall.com)

**Theresa Crater** has published two contemporary fantasies, *Beneath the Hallowed Hill & Under the Stone Paw* and several short stories, most recently "White Moon" in *Ride the Moon* and "Bringing the Waters" in *The Aether Age: Helios*. She's also published poetry and a baker's dozen of literary criticism. Currently, she teaches writing and British lit in Denver. Born in North Carolina, she now lives in Colorado with her Egyptologist partner and their two cats. (TheresaCrater.com)

**David L. Craddock** lives with his wife, Amie, in a tiny apartment where multiple bookcases have forced all other furniture to huddle together and draw straws to determine which of them will be dismissed to make room for even more bookcases. A freelance writer and author, David happily devotes his days to personal and professional writing pursuits..... spanning a diverse array of topics and interests. (DavidLCraddock.com)

**Billie Milholland**—Born in Alberta, Canada. Spent time as a writer, a farmer, a weaver, a lamp installer, a tarot card reader, a writer, a visual artist, a gardener, a journalist, a photographer, a potter, a chef, an events coordinator, a wild crafter, a herbalist, a writer, a historian, a writer, an educational assistant, a student, a poet, a writer. Has some experience as a human bean. Recent published non-fiction includes articles for magazines and newspapers on the historic use of circumboreal plants for food and medicine. Recent published fiction includes a novella in the Aurora winning anthology, "Women of the Apocalypse" and a variety of stories, both short and long in the ongoing "10th Circle Project". (BillieMilholland.com)

**Isabella Drzemczewska Hodson**—Originally from Ottawa, Ontario, Isabella now calls western Canada home. She studied English, Theatre, and Creative Writing at the University of Ottawa and the University of Calgary, and has previously published in Ygdrasil, Liminalities, Making Tracks: A University of Ottawa Anthology, and Northern Flyer. She finds inspiration in legends and myths from around the world, fairy tales new and old, and the natural world around her. She has spent the last four years working as a seasonal Park Interpreter for Alberta Parks, and feels particularly at home in the Canadian Rocky Mountains and the foothills of Alberta. She loves travel, cycle touring, downhill skiing, and hiking, and delights in taking solo road trips across Alberta and British Columbia. She takes great pleasure in reading anything and everything, and particularly enjoys fiction by writers such as Neil Gaiman and A. S. Byatt, as well as non-fiction by Sid Marty, Robert Kroetsch, and Bill Bryson

**Tony Noland** is a writer, blogger and poet in the suburbs of Philadelphia. He takes his writing seriously, but has somehow gotten a reputation as a funny guy. He is working on his third novel.

An anthology of his short fiction, "Blood Picnic and other stories", is now available for Kindle, as is the collection "Poetry on the Fly". His works have been especially praised for his masterful use of language and keen ear for dialogue. His best known poem, "Ode to the Semicolon", has been featured on numerous grammar websites. Tony is a regular contributor of short fiction under the #FridayFlash hashtag on Twitter. His work has been featured in numerous e.zines, websites and anthologies.

Tony writes a monthly column of writing advice at Write Anything, and he is active on Twitter as @TonyNoland. (TonyNoland.com)

**Jay Raven** is a UK-based writer of horror, dark fantasy and twisted fairy tales—with the occasional chilling sci-fi tale thrown in. He specializes in unnerving stories with a historical theme, transporting readers back to an enchanted and violent age of monsters and muskets, highwaymen and harlots, gaslight and ghouls. His work has been widely published on both sides of the Atlantic.

Jay lives in Bristol, a brooding west country seaport with creepy alleyways, Gothic buildings, rain-soaked graveyards and a past littered with murderous deeds, ghosts, smugglers and dangerous secrets. (JayRaven.com)

**Lori Strongin**—Inspired by the likes of Joss Whedon and Piers Anthony, and fueled by the power of chai lattes, author Lori T. Strongin is a firm believer that "Normal is Overrated." She's an avid reader, a hard-core Taurus with a love for elves, zombie squirrels, and cannibalistic cotton balls, and can usually be found glued to her laptop, killing people.

Lori currently lives in theme park central—otherwise known as Central Florida—and is the author of more than a dozen creepy and twisted tales—most containing fairly high body counts.

Check out www.LoriStrongin.com for pictures, fan art, and the occasional murder spree.

**Shereen Vedam**—Though Shereen was born in Sri Lanka, her roots are firmly planted on Vancouver Island, BC, Canada. After thriving for five years in friendly Winnipeg with its -40ºC wind chill factor, she decided sandals and shorts for nine months of the year was infinitely preferable to six months of parkas, snow boots and frozen nose and headed west.

Vancouver Island's magical rain forest climate with its ancient red cedars, red-barked arbutus trees and giant weeping sequoias inspired Aloha Moon's west coast setting. (ShereenVedam.com)

**Amy Laurens** is an Australian author of fantasy fiction for both adults and young adults. She has lived in the same city all her life, which other people think is boring; she prefers to think of it as stable. At present, Amy lives with husband, brand new baby, and two yellow Labradors who think they are lapdogs. Surprisingly, the dogs are the most jealous of the time Amy spends on the laptop.

After a university education involving many twists and turns, Amy is a high school English teacher at an all-girls school by day. By night, she is a story-writing goddess; at least, that's what she tells herself to get the words done, and since it seems to work, let's not disillusion her. Her short fiction has appeared in magazines such as Allegory, Tower of Light Fantasy, and AlienSkin. ( ink-fever.blogspot.com)

**Chrystalla Thoma**—Greek Cypriot with a penchant for dark myths, good food, and a tendency to settle down anywhere but at home, Chrystalla likes to write about fantastical creatures, crazy adventures, and family bonds. After having lived in France, England, Germany and Costa Rica, she now lives in Cyprus with her husband Carlos and enjoys wandering the countryside sampling local food and wine. She writes mainly fantasy and science fiction, primarily for a young adult public. When not reading or writing, she works as a freelance translator and text editor. (ChrystallaThoma.wordpress.com)

**Edward Willett** is the award-winning author of more than 40 books of fiction and nonfiction for children, young adults and adults. He won the Regina Book Award at the 2002 Saskatchewan Book Awards for his YA fantasy *Spirit Singer*, and the 2009 Prix Aurora Award (Canada's top award for science fiction and fantasy writing) for Best Long-Form Work in English for his adult science fiction novel *Marseguro* (DAW Books); the sequel, *Terra Insegura*, was shortlisted for the 2010 Aurora. His nonfiction book *Historic Walks of Regina and Moose Jaw* (Red Deer Press) won the City of Regina Municipal Heritage Award. His latest novel is fantasy/steampunk epic *Magebane* (DAW Books), written as Lee Arthur Chane. A former newspaper reporter and editor, Ed writes a weekly science column for the Red Deer Advocate and online subscribers, and is also a professional actor and singer. He's married and has one daughter. (EdwardWillett.com)

**Ada Hoffmann** is twenty-four years old, and has been publishing speculative fiction short stories since 2010. She currently attends graduate school in Ontario, working towards a Master's degree in computer science. When the computers and short stories aren't eating her soul, she feeds the leftovers to online roleplaying games, church music, and her book collection. She enjoys blood and alone time, but would probably not kill people over them. Probably. Unless she was in a really bad mood that day.

Ada's previous short story sales include work in *Basement Stories* and *One Buck Horror*, as well as an upcoming tale in *Machine of Death 2*. (ada-hoffmann.livejournal.com)

CPSIA information can be obtained at www.ICGtesting.com
Printed in the USA
LVOW062300100212

268152LV00001B/4/P